KT-143-309

Timothy Mo, the son of an English mother and a Cantonese father, was born in Hong Kong and educated both there and in England. On leaving Oxford, where he read history, he worked for the *Times Educational Supplement*, the *New Statesman* and *Boxing News*.

The Monkey King was his first novel and won the Geoffrey Faber Memorial Prize in 1979. His second novel, *Sour Sweet* was shortlisted both for the Booker Prize and the Whitbread Prize in 1982, and received the 1982 Hawthornden Prize.

'Absolutely charming' *Sunday Times*

'A brilliant novel' *Scotsman*

'The domestic guerrilla warfare is very funny, though the novelist preserves a correctly inscrutable face and moves without a twitch of the stylistic eyebrow from rich farce through scenes that are by turn nasty, exciting, and touching' *Guardian*

Also by Timothy Mo in Abacus:

SOUR SWEET

Timothy Mo

THE MONKEY KING

AN ABACUS BOOK

First published in Great Britain by André Deutsch Ltd 1978
Published in Abacus by Sphere Books Ltd 1984
Reprinted 1984, 1985, 1986, 1987, 1988, 1990

Copyright © Timothy Mo 1978

All rights reserved.
No part of this publication may be reproduced,
stored in a retrieval system, or transmitted, in any
form or by any means without the prior
permission in writing of the publisher, nor be
otherwise circulated in any form of binding or
cover other than that in which it is published and
without a similar condition including this
condition being imposed on the subsequent
purchaser.

Printed and bound in Great Britain by
Richard Clay Ltd, Bungay, Suffolk

ISBN 0 349 12393 4

Sphere Books Ltd
A Division of
Macdonald & Co. (Publishers) Ltd
27 Wrights Lane, London W8 5TZ
A member of Maxwell Pergamon Publishing Corporation plc

The people and incidents of this novel are imaginary and do not intentionally resemble any actual persons or government departments of Hong Kong. I have also changed geography and the dates of historical events where it suited me. At the same time I have tried to keep the colonial background as accurate as possible. In doing this I supplemented personal knowledge with sociological and anthropological studies, particularly of the rural areas of the mainland. H. D. R. Baker's *A Chinese Lineage Village* and James L. Watson's *Emigration and the Chinese Lineage* were especially useful. The communities studied in these books are not, of course, the invented one of this book.

Part One

1

On the whole Wallace avoided intimate dealings with the Chinese. Despite a childhood spent cheek by jaundiced jowl with the Cantonese in Macau, he still found the race arrogant and devious. Worse, they revelled in the confusion of the foreigner: turning blank faces to the barbarian and sneering behind his back. Like his fellow Portuguese, Wallace made the best of the situation. In fanciful moments he saw the Chinese and himself as prisoners together in a long chain-gang, the descendants of the original convicts.

There was a kind of tenuous, mutually patronising relationship between the Portuguese and the Chinese. Wallace recognised this. That did not mean he had to like them all the time. He possessed the impeccable Cantonese of most of his compatriots but affected not to understand that vulgar, braying dialect.

While he was alive Wallace's schoolmaster father, Mr Nolasco senior, a widower and an Anglophile, sighed over his son's idiosyncrasies. He told Wallace: 'Understand the English and you will understand the Chinese, too.' Wallace did not dispute the analogy. The English were a nation of crafty hypocrites as well. Their cousins, the Americans, were more straightforward and might be given the benefit of the doubt for the time being.

When Wallace was instructed to marry May Ling, he found it no stranger than being required to ally, say, with a White Russian or an Indian. In many respects it was easier to marry a Chinese, although (he had to admit) the Poons would not have been his own ideal choice. What the Poons – more accurately Mr Poon – had, though, was money. Plenty of it, according to the rumours; which was not the situation of the Nolascos.

The Nolascos called themselves Portuguese, a courtesy title, and thanks to the unremitting clannishness of the Chinese were so known. But, physically, it would have been difficult to tell them apart from their Chinese neighbours. Centuries of mixed marriages with the Cantonese had obliterated whatever had been distinctive about their shadowy buccaneer ancestors since they had built their flat hill-top fort over the Pearl estuary four hundred years ago.

Here and there amongst the Portuguese of Macau – the Mecanese, as they liked to call themselves – an atavistically flared nose or a rounded eye hinted at the past and the possessors of those distinguishing features wore their names like badges: Da Souza, Da Silva, Oliveira, Remedios.

In Wallace's case the legacy of his progenitors was a blueness around the jowls, still ineradicable after even the closest shave, and a certain squareness in the jaw. He was proud of the dimpled cleft in his chin, having a habit of thrusting his neck forward in conversation, especially when challenged. For the rest, he was small and had the blue-black hair and flattened nose of any Cantonese.

After his enforced return from engineering college in Foochow, shortly before the Reds won the Civil War, he had joined several Portuguese clubs. In his first year at home he had been a regular visitor to them all. But their attractions had palled. He enjoyed watching matches at the hockey club but resented having to rub shoulders with the Goan Indians, hairy, dextrous men. Keen on demarcation, he cut the neighbours at every opportunity. 'Damn Choges,' he would mutter as the stink of the bean-curds they broiled in garlic wafted into his room from the warren of kitchens across the road. Pyjamas were symbolic of all that Wallace detested. They were decadent, sloppy, sleazily suggestive and, in the last analysis, part of the accoutrements of Chinkiness. In Foochow and now more brazenly in Macau, the Chinese would appear on their balconies in singlets after the sun had gone down, rubber sandals shoved onto their bare feet, their baggy, inadequately corded pyjama trousers gaping to reveal an unwholesome, sere acreage of ancient underwear. At such moments Wallace would retire to his bedroom and return to his balcony dressed in a tie. He courted the hoots and abuse of the younger Chinese as affirmations of his own superiority.

The elder Mr Nolasco's separatism took a different form from that of his son. Next to Wallace's school diploma, which hung prominently in the study at his father's own school, there was a celebrated Victorian photograph of British officers with pirates they had just captured. It was taken in a field, obviously behind some wild bay in the New Territories. The Englishmen were not in uniform. They wore their boots and jodhpurs with flair. On their heads were sun-helmets. The heads of the pirates had been severed, with remarkably low flow of blood, from their trunks which were piled untidily in the foreground, lending an impromptu touch to the picture; they dangled from oily pig-tails, clenched like coconuts in the fists of moustachioed representatives of the master race. One pirate head had been placed neatly on the soil. It leered out of the photograph, the teeth square, strong and regular. High, arched eyebrows, slant eyes, and elevated cheek-bones made it a caricature of the Oriental.

Wallace remembered what the Japanese had done to the British during the Occupation but refrained from taunting his father with unedifying memories. The Cantonese had assisted as spectators at atrocities which the Japanese had visited impartially upon them and their colonial masters, assembling in droves with the same eager curiosity which they now reserved for victims of road accidents.

The Poons lived in one of the oldest parts of Hong Kong island, on a steep hill above the bustling Western District. They occupied the top two floors of a four-storey mansion built in the latter part of the 1880s. The lower floors were sub-divided and inhabited by numerous families who paid rent to Mr Poon; they were mostly Shanghainese, refugees of the revolution, reputed to have fled in possession of large amounts of precious metals and stones. Government census takers had been baffled as to the exact population of the mansion's lower regions.

Over the cobbled road was a malodorous, uncovered nullah, about thirty feet deep and twenty wide. When Wallace arrived at the beginning of the dry season it was choked with festering rubbish: rinds, cat-corpses, coils of excrement, and – occasionally – the body of an abandoned infant. Beyond the nullah was a children's playground, screened by tall trees.

Having lived in the house at Robinson Path for twenty years as a tenant, Mr Poon had bought in the freehold just after the war. Rumour had it that he had made the money by supplying rice to the Japanese internment camps but his enemies could not prove this. As far as appearances went, the Poons were conspicuously down at heel. The rooms were furnished in a mixture of two basic styles: classical Chinese and government surplus. The bulk of the former was heirlooms from Mrs Poon's father, the latter had been acquired down the years by Mr Poon in job lots at Indian auctions held annually in a large godown on the mainland side of the harbour, in Kowloon. Brass cuspidors, strategically disposed throughout the house, also came from this source.

In the reception room a tinted photograph of Mrs Poon's father, the

5

patron of Mr Poon, imposing in the cap and robes of a junior Manchu mandarin, frowned down on the angular black furniture, aromatic teak chests and cabinets that had been his in life. The cramped bedrooms were identically equipped with a pair of ambiguously stained camp beds (bloodstains from Japanese tortures, it was opined out of Mr Poon's hearing) and a large porcelain chamberpot that it was, in fact, forbidden to use.

In the long, strangely wide corridor that ran through the lower floor, pinned to the parquet by one leg of Mr Poon's desk, just before the spiral iron staircase to the top floor, was the pelt of a scruffy, astounded polar bear.

The wooden floor terminated abruptly at the kitchen, which was surfaced in jagged concrete, dyed red by the servants with a wax polish. The amahs inhabited the kitchen by day, retiring at night to a screened room, structurally an extension of the kitchen, where they slept on a wooden bed, undisturbed by the endless drip of a single, incontinent tap into the enormous concrete trough that doubled as bath and sink.

The exterior of the mansion was more uniform, a monolith of dirt and neglect. Tatters of congealed filth hung from the stone balustrades of a balcony that opened off the reception room. Paint fell off the front door in scabs and strips whenever a stranger inadvertently knocked instead of calling up. Tradesmen and hawkers never entered: the rickety wooden staircase had taken its toll of broken crowns and limbs. Instead, a basket was lowered from the balcony by a thin rope and purchases or messages hauled up in this way. Once, at the lunar New Year, someone, no one had seen whom, had called, had the basket lowered and deposited a fizzing fire-cracker. It had exploded just as Mr Poon was hauling it over the balcony. Naturally no one was fooled by anything so superficial as appearances and as the house deteriorated so Mr Poon's stock in the Chinese business community had risen.

May Ling, 'Beauteous and Sweet', was not a proper Poon. Her mother was Mr Poon's second concubine. The first concubine was accommodated, with her children, in a tenement in Kowloon. (Concubinage as an institution lacked glamour.)

May Ling and her family had originally been housed in Canton, where Mr Poon had extensive business interests. After the Japanese had begun their drive south in 1937 he had moved them down-river to

Macau. Wallace remembered May Ling, dimly, as a small child in plaits and a flowered pyjama-suit at his father's school.

Shortly before December 1941, Mr Poon paid a visit to May Ling's mother and took her youngest daughter back with him on the paddle-steamer, forty miles across the shallow South China Sea, to Hong Kong.

Because May Ling's mother was an inferior concubine he was able to do this without arousing protest from Mrs Poon. May Ling's mother posed no threat to her. Indeed, in pre-war days, Mrs Poon had regularly sent presents of preserved sour fruits and the outgrown clothes of her own children along the rambling railway to Canton.

Three weeks later the Japanese had annexed the colony. In the early years of the Occupation Mr Poon found himself unable to support May Ling's mother any more and communication lapsed.

Then in the summer of 1945, just before the Japanese surrender, the sisters, Mrs Poon's own daughters, were molested by a group of Japanese non-commissioned officers. The same soldiers had earlier bayoneted the caretaker of the Baptist Chapel further down the hill, for failing to salute as they passed.

The girls had eluded their would-be ravishers, who were too drunk to be capable of serious pursuit and were returning to barracks after a satisfactory visit to the troop's official brothel, or Field Consolation Unit. Throughout the Occupation. Mrs Poon had enforced the wearing of two pairs of drawers on all females in the household. Though this expedient had not actually been put to the test, she ascribed the sisters' escape to her own foresight. Unfortunately there were to be serious repercussions to the incident.

After the war it had proved impossible to obtain husbands for the sisters. Despite the fact that neither had actually been violated by the Japanese, a stigma still attached to them. The substantial dowries Mr Poon was known to have laid on both had not proved sufficient inducement. Now just into their thirties, old maids by the unforgiving standards of the colony, both were completely unmarriageable.

May Ling could consider herself fortunate to get the match with Wallace; indeed she was lucky not to have been sold into a brothel in the first place. At some point during the war, her family in Macau had disintegrated. Her mother had died of small-pox. Her brothers had simply vanished. A baby nephew survived. Neighbours brought the child to Hong Kong, where it was handed over to the care of the servants. May Ling ignored it.

She was a scrawny, sallow girl, just twenty at the time the marriage negotiations started. Near the end of these, Mr Nolasco senior succumbed to the chronic tuberculosis which had dramatically worsened during the war years. The basic contract had, however, already been hammered out in studiedly elliptical meetings between himself and Mr Poon. Wallace, out of necessity as well as filial respect, simply followed the matter through, on slightly less advantageous terms. Mr Poon, however, did pay for the simple funeral.

His motives for marrying May Ling to Wallace were complex. Classically, daughters of a certain age became liabilities to be jettisoned as rapidly as possible. In May Ling's case this was not the issue.

What Mr Poon wanted was posterity, the more the better. He had two grandsons at the present and no immediate prospect of more. Even a concubine's grandchildren could venerate an ancestor. On the debit side, betrothed to a Chinese, May Ling would have found a new household; married to Wallace, the pair would have to co-habit at Robinson Path. The family would acquire an additional member, with consequent expense. But to have married May Ling, the daughter of a second concubine, into a respectable Cantonese family would have been an impossibility. Alternatively, setting her sights lower within the Chinese community would have been a major loss of face. Under the circumstances, a poor Portuguese was a creative solution. It would be possible to economise on the initial capital outlay of the dowry to balance out defrayments on an additional mouth. Wallace might also have his uses in certain business projects Mr Poon had in mind. And while not a celestial, Wallace was not a real *faan gwai lo*, a foreign devil. Compromise was at the centre of Mr Poon's political system, and in securing Wallace he had achieved such a balance.

After making his last arrangements in Macau (the school passed into the headship of the deputy principal, a lean Parsee) Wallace came to Hong Kong. He stayed in a small hotel off Nathan Road, on the mainland side, near the quarter of Indian leather-workers, before the marriage ceremony and his formal induction into the household at Robinson Path.

2

Wallace and May Ling were the second married couple in the house, apart from Mr and Mrs Poon. Ah Lung, Mr Poon's eldest son, lived on the top floor with his wife Fong and their two sons. The sisters and Mr and Mrs Poon were on the lower floor. The newly marrieds' quarters were also here: Mr Poon had evicted the amahs from their room and they now spread their sleeping mats on the kitchen floor. May Ling's nephew was left in the bedroom.

Mr Poon had been aggressively benevolent towards his son-in-law. 'Anything you would want, you would just ask for it, hah?' He waved a plump hand, smothered in liver spots, smaller and more regular than the patches of pigmentation on his bald head. His thin limbs, bizarre, youthful adjuncts to his pot belly, gave him the look of a potato man. He was motivated by the desire to defuse in advance any obstreperousness about the dowry.

Wallace had remained unappreciative. 'I would hope he didn't think I intend marry you for fun,' he told May Ling. 'No one go and pull wool over my eye that easy.' May Ling giggled placatorily.

A few days after, Mr Poon took him aside.

'Son, there was something our family want to give you.'

He put his arm around Wallace and led him into the unlit corridor where, walled in at his desk by stacks of old newspapers, he had been sitting in rubber sandals and pyjamas, doing his accounts.

'There is this gift we want to give you. Here.' The old man fumbled and patted his chest. 'Ah, in the drawer.' He produced a gold fob watch with a conjurer's flourish, its chain and seals rattling as he swung it mesmerically.

Wallace said: 'Wah! A fine one.'

Mr Poon chuckled. 'I hide it all through the Occupation. Those Jap never dream I had it. They could knock out all my gold teeths. Tcha! They were beating me on foot but I didn't mind so long as they never found this. It was my father and his father before him watch.'

Tears flooded Wallace's eyes. He weighed the watch, heavy in his palm, while the old man scratched at one of the links. He pulled it out of Wallace's hand.

'Now I keep this for you, safe and sound in my drawer. These day very unsafe to carry this sort of thing around. These fellow robbing you with big knifes.'

'At the bank...' began Wallace.

'And you know, the home really the safe place of all. Some of these fellow all in big suit and tie in bank were the biggest rascal of them all. You never could trust anybody, Wallace. I would hope you didn't forget that advice. Still, you could always be proud of the watch.'

He turned the key in the drawer and adroitly hid it beneath an abacus. 'Any times you want to show it off to friend you could ask me to show it to them.'

Ah Lung was in the kitchen when Wallace went through to lie down in his room. He cackled when he saw Wallace's face. 'The old man been showing you watch, hah? Hee, hee. He show that damn watch it must be fifty time now.' His thin titters pursued Wallace into the bedroom.

He heard the clink of crockery as Ah Lung ladled himself a bowl of bean-curds in syrup.

Ah Lung brushed aside the bead curtain and shuffled in to the room. In his early thirties, he was some five or six years older than Wallace. He was afflicted with a muscular twitch in his right cheek and this flicked now, exposing his blackened teeth. He wore a singlet tucked into a pair of underpants that rose well above his navel.

'Hey, the old man sure looking after you.' He jangled the wire coat-hangers on their string across the two walls of a corner. He kicked off a sandal and rubbed his thin calf with a bare foot. 'Bee bee, bee bee.' He tried to wake the sleeping child.

'What the hell you were doing?' Wallace lay on his stomach on the camp bed. In the orange-box that served it as a cradle the child stirred. It began to cry.

'Is that how you were talking to your new brother?' Ah Lung pronounced it 'brudder'. 'I come here to make friend with you and all you could do was give me bad word.' He drank noisily from his bowl. 'My friend all calling me "Jack" by the way. You could call me that, too.'

Wallace rolled onto his back.

'I could be a great help to you here,' Ah Lung confided to Wallace who showed not a flicker of interest. 'Don't worry I would stop you getting rich out of the old man. There plenty for two.'

Wallace yawned and sat up. He started to rub the dead skin away from between his toes.

'OK, Nolasco. That the way you want it, that the way you damn well go and get it.' Ah Lung stormed through the beads, jostling May Ling who was bringing a glass of tea for her husband.

She looked fearfully at Wallace. 'Eiyah! What you said to Ah Lung?' Wallace burnt his mouth on the tea and swore.

He had already made enemies of the amahs. Eviction from their room had not endeared Wallace to them. In any case they were unhappy about having a Portuguese in the household. The two old women conspired to make life difficult for him. They returned his shirts grubby at the collar; they smeared polish on the inside of his shoes; gave him a dirty bowl at meals and, he suspected, adulterated his tea which arrived cold in the reception room on the same tray as May Ling's steaming glass.

At first he tried to ignore the provocations, resorting to bluster as the war intensified. 'Damn nubian,' he cursed them, referring to the nature of the two spinsters' friendship. In the end he learnt to endure their ministrations in silence.

In general, the servants held the household to ransom. They had been with the family before Ah Lung had been born. They freely ignored or insulted sons- or daughters-in-law, to which dismissive category they relegated May Ling as well as Wallace. But on Ah Lung, 'Jack', they doted. He had the run of the kitchen, otherwise jealously guarded against interlopers. Sweet bean-curds, the favourite confection of his childhood, were always available in a wooden bucket, covered in muslin. It was watched as if it contained a religious relic from the church in Macau. By special dispensation, Ah Lung's sons, Kwok Kei and Kwok Chung, were also periodically allowed a bowl of curds.

The amahs ignored May Ling's nephew except at its feeding times. Although still without a name, the child was already over four years old. At the time of Wallace's arrival it could neither walk nor talk but lay in its orange-box. The servants had been instructed to feed it and keep it more or less clean. They discharged this obligation conscientiously.

Wallace had just been listening to the Rediffusion English language news service on the latest developments in Korea, when he saw the child fed for the first time. According to the newscaster, large detachments of Red Chinese troops were massing in Manchuria, preparatory to invading Seoul. It was, apparently, the first step in a plan of concerted communist aggression throughout Asia. The newscaster managed both to panic the listener and at the same time to reassure – something in the modulation of the voice. It appeared the Reds had also been sterilising recalcitrant Tibetans. Wallace went through the kitchen to horrify May Ling.

The amahs, Ah Doh and Ah King, were dropping morsels into the child's mouth from their chopsticks. They first took a tit-bit from the dish and put in their own mouths, masticating slowly and thoroughly. Then the mashed nourishment would be shaped into a ball by rolling it with the tip of the tongue against the barrier of the front teeth. The amahs forced the food out through pursed lips, gathered it in their plastic pincers and transferred the pre-masticated pellet into the child's mouth.

He almost forgot what he had come to tell May Ling.

Mrs Poon daily served one official meal to the adults in the household. Her grandsons ate at school and had a bowl of rice and vegetables when they came home. Food was not otherwise provided after dark. Mr Poon returned to the house at midday to have the main meal of the day but, in the evenings, tended to entertain clients in restaurants. The family were not in a position to help themselves to his bounty while he was absent.

Ah Lung was in the habit of slipping out early in the evening to return sometime after Wallace had retired; he assumed Ah Lung must eat outside.

In the mornings the servants heated rice congee and oily dough sticks to dip in the grey gruel. Wallace sat in the reception room while the early risers in the kitchen sucked up nourishment, the ebony of the formal furniture chilling his buttocks through his trousers.

He read Mr Poon's Chinese newspaper furtively: a front page of scandal about delinquent starlets of the Mandarin cinema or the high incomes enjoyed by Communist businessmen ('Fat Cats', as they were popularly known), a back page of world affairs, and an intervening morass of stock-market quotations. After slowly re-reading the back page, Wallace went to perform his ablutions with the aid of a bald toothbrush and an enamel mug.

Earlier, he would have woken to Eldest Sister's gargling, a fierce pitch-switching roar, culminating through several distinct changes of gear in harsh retching and the discharge of large volumes of water from a great height. Hearing this for the first time, half-asleep, through the cardboard partition between his bedroom and the washroom, Wallace had dimly dreamt of a medium sized animal lying at bay in great pain. After a pause ('and she really need that,' he remarked to May Ling in the sporting commentaries he took to giving) she would continue her toilet. At crucial moments the wall continued to manifest all the insulating properties of a sieve. 'My Gods, the wall shake like anything,' Wallace sniggered.

One day in his first month in the household, he heard the door of the washroom open and, eager to be seen awake, intercepted Eldest Sister in the passageway. She smiled demurely at him and tripped away, singing, on tiny slippered feet. 'Eiyah! The thing I find in there!' Wallace told May Ling on his return. The description lost nothing in the telling.

Following her dawn performance, Eldest Sister went back to sleep until the middle of the morning. As was their privilege, both sisters rose late. To a lesser extent, it was also a persisting habit of May Ling's which duly exasperated Wallace. After a perfunctory wash she joined the sisters for a glass of tea, then retired with them to their bedroom for a hair-braiding session.

Hair lengthened with seniority. May Ling wore hers bobbed around the ears, as did the amahs and Ah Lung's wife, Fong. Second Sister's brushed the nape of her neck. Eldest Sister's attained mid-spine, a thick, solid brush of living jet, which she sometimes gathered with red rubber bands in two heavy coils, thumping against her back. Mrs Poon's, though thinning, was also long but as befitted a matron in her position she wore it in a bun.

The midday meal was served every day of the week at precisely five minutes past twelve and consumed to the strains of the Rediffusion Chinese language service, relayed at full blast on the household's ancient wireless. Wallace, watchless, knew when to anticipate food because the servants switched on the set to warm it up exactly three minutes before they served the dishes, the period, as he discovered by experiment, that he could go without breathing. By the time his face had mottled, he knew it was time to go in. Dizziness did not seem to impair his appetite and certainly, as he found out early on, it was fatal to be late.

The quantities of food served would have been sufficient for three hungry adults. Eight, and in the school vacations the adolescent grandsons as well, sat down to the round wooden table, loosely shrouded in its plastic cover.

First came soup, steaming inside a hollowed marrow with three or four pieces of water chestnut bobbing on the surface. Those currently in favour with Mr Poon, and that included Wallace in his first weeks in the household, could also hope for a sliver of marrow shaved off the sides with the soup ladle. At a signal from Mr Poon the servants, who had flanked him while he was chewing, removed the flaccid marrow shell and replaced it with three fried eggs, skimming around an enamel dish on a thin film of grease.

By contrast with the ordered distribution of the soup, the eggs constituted an anarchic free-for-all, due respect paid to Mr Poon's precedence. Apart from this consideration, the only factors regulating the disappearance of the eggs were the reach of the participants and their facility with their chopsticks. At his first meal, the day after the wedding (celebrated at an ice-cream parlour after the Baptist service) Wallace was too slow to play a useful part in the fray: the chopsticks rattled on the enamel like arrows on a breastplate; within a minute even the spilled yolks had been mopped up.

Next, the amahs brought on a dish of fried cabbage and another of salt fish or grilled soya bricks. Rice was then served from the tureen. At the time of his war with the amahs Wallace would find his portion consisted of burnt rice, welded together into balls, from the bottom of the tureen. In the end he even acquired a taste for it.

Mr Poon would always be the first to pull his chair back, belching contentedly ('He could do so all right,' Wallace thought bitterly) and then start mining his teeth with his gold pick. The room emptied, its occupants slid off their chairs with a sense of anti-climax and walked somewhat unsteadily to the door, leaving Wallace staring wistfully at the gleaming plates. Then he joined May Ling for siesta.

The child slept with them. Or rather it did not sleep. The orange-box was no longer an adequate repository for it. Its limbs now stuck awkwardly over the sides, offending Mr Poon's sense of meticulousness. He would stuff them back in, only to have the members on the opposite side sprawl over. These were the only attentions Mr Poon bestowed on it; his altruism began and ended with May Ling.

A month after Wallace's arrival, the child began its crying. It had not cried, very much, during its teething stage a few years earlier. Now its wails carried through the house. They were not those of a baby but a strong, hopeless child's bawling, mechanical and impersonal, a metaphor of misery. It cried when it was hungry. It cried after feeding ('wind,' Eldest Sister diagnosed sagely). Especially it cried at night, and Wallace ground his teeth for sheer rage.

Under that monotonous affliction they all tossed, reliving childish horrors in their sleep.

Directly above Wallace, in Ah Lung's room, there would be creakings, then heavy footsteps, crossing repeatedly from one side of the room to the other.

After the first week it was not possible to sleep, even fitfully. The child was moved from the newly marrieds' quarters to the kitchen but that did no good. In turn the amahs pushed the child into the corridor.

Now that even siesta was impossible, Wallace caught up on what sleep he could outside the house. He used to sit on a bench in the playground on the other side of the nullah, watching the children at their games, or he would stroll down the hill to the Botanical Gardens and perch himself perilously on the edge of the large ornamental fountain. He munched sugared olives to appease his hunger after the day's meal. Several times his head drooped onto his chest and he almost toppled in onto the giant water lily leaves. He was not alone in his trials. Heavy bags under Ah Lung's eyes showed that, while seemingly immune to the effects of his alleged late night debaucheries, the child was wearing him down. He looked increasingly haggard.

May Ling disclaimed any responsibility for her nephew. Her memories of her mother's family were hazy. 'I think the boy sick,' Wallace remarked to her after food one day. She shrugged, continuing to rub Tiger Balm into her temples, filling the room with the odour of camphor.

Wallace had reached the stage where he would jerk sharply awake from any sleep he might find. His abrupt, random returns to consciousness were unsynchronised with any external disturbances; they generally occurred in interludes of quiet. Nights were colder now and he explained these aberrations by the sharp drop in temperature. After some argument, he prevailed on Mrs Poon to give him extra quilts. He wound the coverings around himself in a cocoon to prevent them from slipping off the camp bed. By pulling the quilts over his ears he could also, partially, cut himself off from the cries of the corridor.

Proof of their effectiveness came when he enjoyed several nights of sound sleep. However, his measures soon became redundant. The child died in the night a week later. He had been bragging to May Ling in the morning as they listened to Eldest Sister's toiling salute to the day.

'Only I heard Ah Lung make noise upstair and wake up. But I didn't hear crying myself and I was more near.'

May Ling said 'Wah,' dutifully.

He was encouraged to give her a demonstration of what he meant. He could hear Eldest Sister quite clearly through the mufflers. He stuck his head out. 'You get some quilt for your ear, too, May.'

Wallace did not find out about the child until the evening. He had missed its ritual feeding by the amahs. The family were curiously evasive, embarrassed. He bearded Mr Poon at his accounts. Via circumlocution and euphemism, he ascertained the facts, such as they were. He enquired about funeral arrangements.

Mr Poon was evasive. 'No, no. We already do funeral. Not making trouble. Family things, ah?'

'Bury already?'

'Already bury.'

'Ah.'

Wallace retired, leaving his father-in-law to his accounts. He was still puzzled. He could have understood the rapidity of the process had it been high summer. He saw the child's box by the door to the reception room. The pillow was missing. He found May Ling staring out of the balcony windows as the sun set across the harbour and its vessels: junks, rusty merchantmen, and grey warships. From the rooftops of the slum tenements in Happy Valley delicate paper kites were flying, their thick strings invisible in the fading light. They reached extraordinary heights, some higher than the mansion, climbing jerkily until brought up at the end of their tether. They did not float; there seemed to be a tension, as if at any moment one might snap its cord and go even higher. It was not unknown for this to happen. The tattered, splintered wrecks were a familiar sight on the telegraph poles of the mid-levels.

There was one in the nullah. The remnants of its broken string had snagged on tins at the edge of the sluggish trickle of water. Rubbish floated by, including a bloated dog, its belly so distended its legs seemed like the teats of a monstrous udder. The carcass circled in a murky whirlpool, then spun off at a tangent towards a mud bank in the centre of the nullah. At the last moment it was swept off into one of the forks of deeper water on each side and disappeared into the tunnel under the road and, eventually, the harbour.

3

Wallace's honeymoon with Mr Poon did not last. Two offences committed before the lunar New Year, the first an accident, the second a wilful act of rebellion, put him out of the household circle. At the time it seemed almost beyond redemption.

Towards Christmas the cold weather sharpened. It was not feasible for Wallace to spend the afternoon outside nor, in the fresher weather, did he feel the need for a post-prandial nap. He would pace about the reception room, looking at the bare trees outside. May Ling sat before the empty fireplace, swathed in quilts, contriving to doze after the morning's excitement of braiding the sisters' hair and finally finding a dreadful, earnest somnolence in a miasma of moth-balls.

Wallace had tried to have the fire lighted before, without success. The amahs ignored him. Mr Poon had been shifty. Wallace considered taking the amahs' meat-chopper to the orange-box, now reposing in the kitchen, but feared that the noise would give him away before he could present the household with the accomplished fact.

Instead he left the house, creaking stealthily down the stairs, proceeding downhill to the labyrinth of market streets above the main Chinese commercial quarter. At a small emporium, he bought bundles of faggots and a brown paper sack of coals. As an afterthought, he stopped at the streaky glass jars of sweet-meats by the exit and bought a bag of plums, preserved in aniseed and liquorice.

In his absence May Ling had draped the plastic table-cloth over her quilts. She stifled a sneeze when she saw him. He dropped the bag of plums into her lap. 'We go and get ourself warm at last, ah?' Emboldened now, he went into the kitchen and returned with the chopper, box, and several newspapers purloined from the stacks around Mr Poon's bureau.

'Eiyah, Wallace!'

He began to split the wood, inexpertly. At length he scattered the blood-stained splinters in the grate and screwed the newspapers into balls.

Smoke began to spiral off the little heap of combustibles in sulky curls.

'Never mind, Wallace. I never remember fire here. Maybe chimney all block up.'

Behind them, hovering in the doorway, it could have been for minutes or seconds, Ah King hawked throatily and spat into the brass pot by the door.

Wallace hitched up his trousers. He swept past the amah, returning with an earthenware bottle of rice wine. He showed May Ling the label, written in English. 'Fragrantly delicious,' she spelled out laboriously. 'Good for starting Fires.'

Wallace sprinkled the wood in a priestly manner. 'And all we needed now was the one little match.'

The fire took immediately.

Wallace pulled the coverings off his wife. 'Meet the world champion fire-lighter, May.'

By the time Mr Poon returned the blaze was drawing well. May Ling huddled into a corner when she saw her father. Unabashed, Wallace gestured at the grate. 'Look, see the thing I do. I was making all the house warm for you.'

Mr Poon picked up the cuspidor in a surprisingly swift movement and advanced on them.

Wallace took a step backwards. 'Now look, Uncle...'

Mr Poon dashed past him and hurled the contents of the spittoon onto the fire. The brown water described a neat arc and sizzled on the flames. Mr Poon scrabbled in the chimney, swearing as he scorched his hands on the hot bricks.

May Ling coughed tearfully as the room filled with smoke.

Two black bricks tumbled with a clang into the grate to be followed by another and another.

'Wah, only the little fire,' Wallace breathed.

Mr Poon produced a nail file from his shirt pocket and ran it over the surface of a brick, scoring thin, shiny tracks in the soot, holding up one brick after the other, like trophies, to the light.

Later, Wallace was not contrite. At table the next day, he contrived to be rather more adept with his chopsticks than usual, to the scandal of the sisters and despite the reproachful looks May Ling gave him. Ah Lung snickered, while Mr Poon subjected his son-in-law to an elaborate ostracism.

'Huh,' Wallace told May Ling in their bedroom. 'All big fuss for nothings. Any fool would tell you gold not melting till about eight hundred degree. It serve him right for not trusting anyone and keep it up chimney. The Jap gone six year already, if you didn't know that. I tell you, God looking at him and punish him for being an old miser.'

Later that night, when the house was quiet, Mr Poon removed the ingots one by one from the chimney and wrapped them in a tarpaulin. He lowered this carefully into the wide cess-pipe behind the amahs' quarters. The parcel was heavy and he was sweating and breathing hard by the time he had finished.

The major treason was foisted on Wallace by Ah Lung. It was an act of impulse but nothing could convince Mr Poon that it had not been long premeditated, seeking only an outlet.

Relatively late in his marriage, Ah Lung had become addicted to beating his wife. This departure from the previous norm of neglect worried no one. What did disturb Mr Poon was his son's mania for gambling, a passion that made itself concurrently felt. He would beat Fong, then go out to gamble, using funds wheedled from Mrs Poon or, occasionally, the amahs. Mr Poon was himself a gambler, a daring entrepreneur, but he was a successful one. Ah Lung lost heavily. And Ah Lung's bad luck could only be seen as confirmation of moral turpitude; good luck sanctioned all. Several times he had remonstrated angrily with his son.

Wallace was teaching May Ling how to play Chinese checkers, with dice, in the reception room when Ah Lung joined them. He was dressed in an olive tweed suit; on his feet he wore pointed suede shoes with brilliants on the buckles.

Fong could be heard whimpering in the kitchen.

Ah Lung stood close to the seated couple, trawling a comb through his quiff, using his reflection in an antique cabinet. He pinched his nostrils between forefinger and thumb, blew his nose, wound a strand of mucus elegantly round his fingers and flicked the parcel accurately into the cuspidor. Involuntarily, May Ling flinched. Ah Lung laughed.

'Once you were reaching my side, you could crown your checker and make him king.' Wallace competed with Ah Lung for her attention. May Ling's eyes flickered uneasily from side to side. Her husband's last remark gained her attention.

'Why not queen?' she demurred. 'It should be queen if I was woman.'

'That was just the way it was. You want to learn this game or what?'

19

'So the two love-bird quarreling already,' Ah Lung broke in mockingly. 'He go and beat the hell out of you later, May Ling. You better had watch out.'

'Don't notice him, May. Stick and stone could be breaking my bone but word never could harm me.'

'That was what you thought, Nolasco.' Ah Lung went into the corridor where they could hear him rummaging among the piled newspapers by Mr Poon's desk. He continued round to his mother's room.

'Now, May, you didn't pay attentions. I tell you that if you were forgetting to take my piece then I could huff you. Look, huff, huff, huff.' Wallace threw the wooden pieces back into their box.

May Ling swept the remaining pieces off the board. 'Silly games. You tell me all the wrong thing, so you could win. It not fair.'

Wallace sucked his teeth in exasperation. 'OK, we start again and this time I would give you a start of three king. How about that, hah?'

May Ling pouted. 'How about you gave me four king?'

The staccato exchanges of an argument in Cantonese had been registering as a peripheral distraction while Wallace administered the *coup de grâce* to his wife. The high voices grew clearer. There was the crash of a heavy weight falling, the impact causing the glass in the cabinet to vibrate sympathetically. Ah Lung burst in with his newly greased hair now sticking up in spikes and tufts. He was hobbling on one shoe, pursued by Mr Poon who was brandishing a golf club which he swung in wide arcs at Ah Lung's legs, striking with the wood end.

'Eiyah! Eiyah! He go and kill me, Wallace! Save life! Save life!' Ah Lung fell on his knees, supplicating his father with clasped hands.

Mr Poon reversed his grip on the club and rained blows on his son's shoulders, carefully avoiding his head and landing with the handle.

Ah Lung wept, making no attempt to avoid the heavy strokes. 'Give face. Give face.'

Wallace pulled the club out of Mr Poon's grasp.

The old man flailed at Ah Lung with his stick arms. 'I go kill you all right after the moneys you take.'

Wallace dragged him away. 'What madness is this. You beat him? He was grow-up man, older than me. Ah Lung, why you let him do this thing to you?'

Mr Poon was too surprised to be angry with Wallace. 'He do wrong. I punish him. It in the bible. It was our old Chinese custom.'

Wallace tried to snap the club over his knee but failed. He rounded on Mr Poon. 'You couldn't behave like this in the modern ages. You thought you was the God of us all or something?' He strode over to the balcony and with the strength of rage projected the club – he was lucid enough to wonder where it had come from – as if it were a javelin, into the nullah.

'You would never oppress anybodys with that again.' He stormed out to his bedroom. Silence followed his departure. Ah Lung remained on his knees. At length May Ling broke the silence with a heartfelt 'Eiyah!', speaking for all of them.

As the long, endless days became short, flashing weeks, the short weeks interminable months, Wallace's isolation came home to him. Even the servants abandoned their japes, letting his shoes lie outside the door, collecting dust, too indifferent to bother about soiling them. Latterly, Ah Lung slunk rather than swaggered out of Robinson Path in the early evening, groomed for revelry with something less than his old panache. Since Wallace had rescued him, he had stopped his baiting. This Wallace regretted: it was another relationship ended. He craved stimulation, some identity in the eyes of the others, even if it was only the recognition of feud. But, in the higher echelons of the household, with Mr Poon and the sisters, disapproval took a submerged, sneering course. Rancour, even when it had assumed the proportions of a collective hostility, was not to be given the outlet of words but was expressed as a form of loss in empty faces, a denial of his existence. And this posture fed rather than relieved the original resentment, swelling feeling long after his original misdemeanours had been forgotten and compounded by others. Only Mrs Poon remained neutral and this was for May Ling's sake.

4

The New Year arrived. Not the new year of the government calendar. Not Hogmanay: that day when the sober, hard-bargaining Presbyterian factors of Mr Poon's acquaintance, husbands and fathers, men of substance, dressed themselves in kilts, to the imperfectly concealed derision of Mr Poon: a day when the Poon girls were placed in protective custody and drunken members of the garrison roamed the streets. Not that festival but the lunar New Year, Chinese New Year, as Mr Poon called it with proprietorial emphasis.

The Poons observed the anniversaries of the Occidental calendar with varying degrees of intensity. Christmas, for instance, was too near the lunar New Year – a matter of six weeks at its furthest remove – to be celebrated with single-minded enthusiasm. Still, as a member of the Baptist congregation, Mr Poon had his obligations. At the end of November, Wallace had noticed the appearance of a mutilated stump in the corridor. This was the Poons' Christmas tree. Down the years a series of accidental amputations had given it the appearance of a weather-beaten totem pole. Despite its bedraggled condition, it exerted a powerful hold over the imaginations of the amahs and the youngest, most suggestible members of the household. Ah Lung's sons did not care to be alone with it in the dark corridor.

For their part, the amahs worshipped the Christmas tree as a potent phallic symbol. The colony's major fertility cult centred around a large, thrusting rock, high on a bald hillside overlooking the harbour, but access to this involved a long, penitential climb. The amahs were in the habit of making a pilgrimage to it twice a year. They welcomed the opportunity to venerate the tree, which apart from advantages of proximity and convenience, was also more likely to expedite personalised requests. They burnt joss sticks in cigarette tins before the stubby talisman, bidding for a generation of worshipping descendants through their brothers' families.

Mr Poon indulged them in the hope. In his own room a sadistically technical crucifixion reclined across the belly of a chubby bronze Buddha. In an enterprising moment the sisters had streaked the gaunt Christ's pallid ivory body with red paint. 'You could be better safe than sorry,' was Mr Poon's stock reply when interrogated by pedants.

No such embarrassments vitiated the New Year which exemplified tradition in its purest form and was, moreover, a holiday recognised by the colonial government. And, as Mr Poon was fond of pointing out, even over the Border, they – the Reds – secretly liked to celebrate the festival, which made it a people's holiday as well and not just a fragment of ancient superstition.

For days the women prepared. It was one of the few days in the year when the family fed well, and then they ate prodigiously, encouraged by Mr Poon who – as if to recover at a single sitting the ground lost in a year – pressed food on his grandsons until their taut stomachs touched the table.

May Ling was entrusted with a minor part in the manufacture of the glutinous puddings of the season. She was helped in this by Fong. Together they ground the rice flour. In time the natural revolution of marriage and death would see them move up the chain. Then Fong would have the mortar and pestle to herself. At the summit of the hierarchy, Mrs Poon stood in the middle of the kitchen, directing operations, while the sisters giggled companionably over the block of pudding they were moulding out of the ground rice. Tolerant of the invasion, the amahs chopped meat and vegetables and stirred arcane, steam-shrouded recipes in a shallow pan.

Sitting on his camp bed, Wallace heard the excited voices in the kitchen and worried about losing face. He had left himself without the means to give lucky money on New Year's Day. The tiny inheritance he had brought with him from Macau was almost exhausted and buying plums for May Ling, as well as fuel for the fire, had been recklessly improvident.

At that time of year it was the custom for those who were married to present others with cash in red envelopes, this being the colour of luck. Single persons could not confer lucky money, although they might receive it. Claimants offered compliments, demanded money, and appended thanks in one breath. It was a characteristically blunt Cantonese procedure.

Wallace did not resent the obligation to give. In the hands of an adept, what appeared to be an onerous duty converted into a subtle social weapon – a chance to remind the unmarried of their supernumerary status in the household. Specifically, Wallace looked forward to avenging numerous slights and insults from the sisters. He was determined to extort utmost value for his money.

He had considered other methods of fund-raising but always returned to the stratagem of pawning the watch which Mr Poon had presented to him. Of course, this would have to be done discreetly. Not that what he intended could be construed as in any way reprehensible. He snorted at the conceit of stealing one's own property. But Chinese susceptibilities could be delicate. 'I didn't want to hurt Uncle feeling,' he rationalised to himself.

To have asked for immediate payment of the dowry would have been out of the question; it would have been an irretrievable tactical blunder. Sensing desperation, Mr Poon would ruthlessly have beaten him down. He would have become a client fixture in the household, in name as well as fact. Once the dowry became a point of necessity he was degraded.

All he needed for the New Year was a loan. The in-coming flow of cash would balance the out-going, maybe even (he tantalised himself) show a modest profit. For he, in turn, could expect money from the married. Mr Poon's and Ah Lung's packets would negate his own gifts to them. Perhaps, befitting the head of the household, Mr Poon's gift would be enough in itself. Then, following the festival, he could redeem his pledge.

He settled on this course of action, fixing night as the best time to repossess his wedding gift. He decided to keep his plans a secret from May Ling.

It was all easier than he had dared to hope. The house lay silent as he located the key, marked its position, opened the drawer, and replaced it under the third bead of the fourth rung of the abacus. He was glad the child was no longer around.

Early next morning he set out for North Point, where – Ah Lung had once mentioned – the best pawn shops were found. The establishments, with their Sikh guards and high, grilled counters, were unmistakable. The area with a floating population of immigrant mainlanders, had the advantage of being on the other side of the island from Robinson Path. As an added precaution, Wallace changed trams three times on his return journey.

That evening he spread on the discoloured canvas of his bed five of the most expensive brand of red envelope, with an ornate message of luck embossed on them in gold leaf. Beside them was the money they were to contain: a prodigal heap, an autumn-leaf drift of green ten dollar bills, brown five dollar notes, and a single red hundred dollar bill. They were stiff and new from the press. Wallace sniffed the hundred dollar bill and it was fragrant. He threw the others in the air and they floated to the floor. On reflection he decided to keep the large bill; ostentation would attract unwelcome attention. As he folded the other bills with razor creases, he chuckled in anticipation of the sisters' faces.

The family rose in a group, somewhat earlier than normal for the sisters, on New Year's Day. This was a gesture of solidarity that also spared Wallace Eldest Sister's usual agonised performance in the bathroom. The normal routines of the day were abridged. No one washed. The women dressed themselves in their finest clothes and made their way to the kitchen where they ate a monster breakfast.

Wallace sent May Ling ahead while he rubbed Vaseline into his hair and raked it into a glossy skull-cap. Then he wiped his fingers on his trousers and brushed through the bead curtain into the kitchen. He was last. Mrs Poon presided over a steaming pot of congee. The sisters were in long, glowing cheongsams, daringly slashed to the knee at the sides. Eldest Sister's was orange, Second Sister's primrose. Their necks looked unnaturally elongated in the stiff, orthopaedic-style stock collars. Despite their brocade jackets, they shivered guardedly, rippling the clinging silk of the dresses. The hems of the cheongsams rose, revealing the toes of frayed slippers. May Ling was wearing an obsolescent, now matt, version of the sisters' costumes, a hand-down from their wardrobes. The sisters themselves were thin but the dress hung on May Ling. Fong wore a still shabbier cheongsam. She watched the amahs hand steaming bowls to her sons.

Wallace honked with satisfaction over the congee which had been specially enriched with meat. He helped himself to another dough-stick. Ah King scowled. This was the first breakfast Wallace had ever taken in the kitchen. He grabbed another stick and ate them together from his fist.

The family had been seceding into the reception room. Only Fong and Wallace were left. He smacked his lips provocatively at the amahs and followed the others. Fong trailed after him.

Blossom plants had been planted in tubs around the room and they had perfumed it overnight, laying down scent in heavy coils in the centre, leaving subtler eddies to permeate to the corners. The fragrance was strongest by Mr Poon's ceremonial chair which was framed by a pair of the largest pots. Pink and yellow petals had fallen onto the severe ebony. Mr Poon placed his hands over the roaring lions' heads carved at the ends of the arm-rests. His shod feet dangled a few inches clear of the floor. Mrs Poon stood next to him. On a footstool in front of her was a pile of red envelopes. Wallace joined the rest of the family who had formed a queue by the windows. There was a strong draught.

Ah Lung advanced. He clasped his hands, interlocking the fingers, and bowed. He muttered the terse formula of congratulations and request.

Mr Poon's face resembled an unbaked clay mask from a Chinese opera. Mrs Poon switched on the lamp above his chair, turning Mr Poon with his egg-dome and drooping eye-lids into Buddha.

Ah Lung withdrew to the side. His sons came forward. Mrs Poon beamed encouragement at them. She handed two packets to Mr Poon who shook his head. She gave him smaller envelopes, without ornamentation. The boys joined their father. The sisters were next. They swelled the little group on the sidelines.

Kwok Kei, Ah Lung's eldest son, held his packet up to the lamp-light in an attempt to compute the sum inside. Second Sister slapped his hand down. Ah Lung took advantage of the distraction to snatch the envelope from his grasp but his youngest son was too quick for him. He dodged behind the sisters. Ah Lung shook a finger at him and put his hands behind his back in a pompous, nautical pose. From his place by the window, Wallace could see him surreptitiously kneading the envelope.

Wallace and May Ling went up to receive largesse together, after Fong and before the amahs. Mrs Poon had a personal gift for May Ling, which she produced from a capacious hand-bag. The envelope had birds and flowers as well as a written message on it.

Ah Lung sidled crab-wise up to the beneficiary. He whispered in her ear. May Ling shook her head vigorously and put her hand through her husband's arm.

The amahs now uncovered lacquer dishes of salted melon seeds and sugared fruit in unexpected parts of the room. Ah Lung's youngest son poured tea into delicate thimble cups from an antique pot.

The sisters saw Wallace coming and retreated into the narrow space between a corner and the cabinet. He swaggered, hand in the inside pocket of his jacket. They were trapped. He felt like Humphrey

Bogart. He waited, ready to draw. They ignored him. He coughed. Louder.

'Hah?'

'Hah?' he mimicked. 'What day it was today, I was wondering?'

They shot him glares of equal malevolence. Slowly, he pulled his two packets from his jacket, holding them up by the corners at eye-level. The sisters reeled. The scenario altered. He might have been offering garlic to a pair of vampires. Helpless against the huge tug of convention, Eldest Sister pulled herself together and bowed. She muttered the words. Second Sister kowtowed robotically and followed suit.

'Maybe next year I got something from you, hah?' Wallace left them staring at what they held. He was now accosted by Ah Lung's sons. 'Congratulation, Uncle Wallace. Wah, thank you, thank you.' They caught their father's eye and circled evasively around the edge of the room.

Ah Lung had already made his presentation, to May Ling; he dawdled in her vicinity, waiting for Wallace. 'Gung Hei, Nolasco. Wah, thank, thank.' He put his arm round Wallace's shoulders as they followed the others back to Mr Poon's lion throne to drink tea.

The amahs removed the cups. Mr Poon rose. His court dissolved around him. Ah Lung led the boys downstairs to let fire-crackers off in the street.

As was her custom on this day, Mrs Poon regaled a little group of women with lurid accounts of foot-binding, an ordeal from which Sun Yat Sen's revolution had delivered her in the nick of time. One of the prime benefits conferred by that movement, her manner implied. The amahs particularly relished her description of how the family retainers had whipped her elder sisters around the courtyards to maintain the circulation to their bandaged stumps. Walking on the swaddled extremities was so excruciatingly painful that even flogging was often ineffective. Modern girls, the sisters shuddered deliciously and twitched in their slippers.

From the street a string of sharp cracks signalled the handiwork of Ah Lung and his sons. A muffled boom succeeded the previous crisp reports. A moment later a shining, rotating object shot past the balcony, hung level a moment, then fell with a clatter the two storeys to the ground. Ah Lung was blowing up tins which the boys had found in the nullah.

Mr Poon strode onto the balcony. Since the incident of the booby-trapped basket he had been sensitive about fire-crackers. He called angrily down. His last words were obliterated by another, louder explosion which had been set in train just before his appearance. The battered tin sailed up on its second flight, making Mr Poon duck; it fell through the window into the room. The sisters put their hands over their ears as Mr Poon flung a volley of oaths and imprecations into the street.

The front door slammed. Mr Poon re-seated himself on his throne, drumming agitatedly on the lions' heads with his fingers. There was a tense silence during which the family listened to the squeaking of the stair-joists. The delinquents were taking their time. The inside door clicked almost imperceptibly; footsteps went down the corridor to the kitchen.

The family relaxed. Mrs Poon resumed her narrative at the point where her seventh sister's foot had turned gangrenous.

Ah Lung and his sons skulked in the kitchen until the serving of the midday meal. This was a gesture of contrition which appeased Mr Poon and was in no way to their disadvantage since it gave them first pick at the dishes of fried pudding that left the kitchen for the reception room at regular intervals throughout the morning. Wallace suspected as much from the ragged constellations of sweetmeats on the dishes.

Food came slightly earlier than usual as Mr Poon wished to finish eating before his poor relations and tenants arrived to pay their annual homage. The meal was an earnest affair, partaken in dead silence, punctuated only by the click of chopsticks and the snuffling of food from bowls. In his haste Wallace inhaled rice and blew it in grainy spurts through his nose. Most of this exhalation arrived on Eldest Sister's arm but she ate on without wiping off the debris.

Of recent years Mr Poon's dependents had taken to arriving increasingly early. Mr Poon dated this kind of behaviour to the war. But, as if to compensate for the increased time he had to play host, every year death in the forms of typhoid and tuberculosis slashed the ranks of the importunate; he was obliged to less for longer: a fair exchange.

Mr Poon did not openly attribute this accounting to the workings of a benign and arithmetically minded providence, busy rescuing the philanthropic from the consequences of their own excesses, but he implied it in the grim tally he told with his forefinger as his indigent kinsmen filed before him.

Between two and three o'clock they arrived in scrubbed, expectant groups. The tenants came a little later. They stood quietly apart but Mr Poon's relatives were unable to maintain their initial solemnity for long. Soon their natural garrulousness took over. There was laughter. Mr Poon scowled. He hated them for their cheerfulness. In their circumstances he equated it with moral obtuseness.

Meanwhile, in the plenitude of a good meal, the family quarried their teeth. Mrs Poon fanned a discreet hand over her nimble pick. She belched comfortably. The sisters sucked oranges and sipped tea. They stared scornfully at the visitors who had not been offered seats. They grinned foolishly at the family. A milky-eyed old woman with cataracts kept nodding at Wallace. He acknowledged feebly but she kept jerking her head.

Mr Poon signalled for refreshment to be brought. The amahs served the guests superciliously, holding their trays at arm's length.

'Fifteen only this year,' Ah Lung hissed in Wallace's ear, leaving him to plug at the moist aftermath with his index finger. 'You know, soon the old man not have to spend any money at all on the New Year Day.'

In past years Mr Poon's donations to the various client groups around him had taken the form of flat-rate cash payments, low but nonetheless certain. This year he was departing from his previous practice. He had decided to institute a lottery. The idea appealed to him. It combined elements of suspense and genuine drama (for the beneficiaries) with, on his own part, a pleasurable sense of power and possibilities of overall control of distribution.

Now he raised his hand for silence. The buzzing of the guests diminished to an expectant twitter. In the valley fire-crackers popped faintly. The silence intensified. Mr Poon snapped his fingers to the amahs who wheeled in a small oil-drum on a swivel. The cash prizes were placed in their envelopes on the footstool. Mr Poon gave the drum a vigorous swing. The whole contraption juddered perilously. The amahs circulated with folded scraps of paper. Wallace's bore the number 5.

At length the drum came to a halt. Mr Poon unscrewed the cap and pulled out a painted ping-pong ball. It was a 7. Second Sister semaphored back to her father with a twist of paper. Family and guests applauded.

The next ball was a 3. Ah Lung waved urgently. This stroke of good fortune was greeted with immoderate enthusiasm by the rest of the family. Now Mr Poon held up a 2. It was Eldest Sister's. The guests muttered amongst themselves. A fourth ball was claimed by Ah Lung's eldest son.

Mr Poon read out the number on the next ball, a 13. There was some delay. Wallace shrugged at May Ling. Mr Poon frowned significantly at Fong. Ah Lung prised her limp hand open.

Both sisters clapped jubilantly over the punctured sigh from the guests.

The fifth ball was a 5. Despite himself, Wallace experienced a feeling of genuine gratification.

Mrs Poon moved among her guests but was unable to quell their murmurings. The next prize went to a tenant, the subsequent and last to Mr Poon's third cousin from Wanchai. If anything, their good fortune added fuel to the flames.

Mr Poon waved his hand to indicate that the audience was over. He was immediately assailed by his relatives, as the tenants quietly slipped away. They thrust infants at him, clawed his clothes, implored. For a moment it seemed they were lynching their patron. The sisters panicked. The Eldest clutched Ah Lung's sleeve. 'Eiyah! They go kill Ah Dairdee!'

'You think they would?'

Mr Poon's bald head bobbled briefly out of the ruck, like an egg in a pan of seething water. He struck viciously at the bawling child a young mother held out to him.

Mrs Poon watched impassively. Behind her spectacles Wallace imagined, then lost, a hard glint of satisfaction. Second Sister shook him. 'You had to do something.' Mr Poon had, however, already forced his way out of the scrimmage.

They heard him dialling three digits at the telephone on his desk. The floor-boards protested their recent abuse.

Mr Poon re-seated himself on his lion throne. He sipped tea reflectively with hooded eyes, watched by his cowed dependents. He looked carelessly at his wrist-watch and held up five fingers.

In the valley a siren could be heard.

Mr Poon pulled back his cuff and stared intently at the dial of the watch. His lips moved soundlessly, as if he might be counting. The guests stirred uneasily. Arms akimbo, the sisters smiled smug smiles of satisfaction. A bell rang urgently above the whine of the siren. It grew louder with every second.

One of the kinsmen, an old man, made for the door. The others paused, then followed in a body, overwhelming the amahs outside the door. The stairs thundered.

The family flocked to the balcony. The first of the fugitives were already rounding the corner at the bottom of the hill. As the last of the stragglers turned the bend, a large red fire-engine materialised in the narrow, rutted road cut into the hillside behind the house and, as if a bullet discharged along rifling, was gone.

The noise died away.

Mr Poon gazed thoughtfully after the cloud of dust raised by the vehicle. He shook his head. 'Too many accident were happening on this day. The firecracker all so dangerous.' He swung the basket on its thin rope.

Mrs Poon had not gone to the balcony. The rest of the family found her prodding chestnuts in a brazier she had caused the servants to bring from the kitchen. The acrid charcoal fumes mixed with the sweetness from the roasting chestnuts. Mrs Poon's face was flushed from the heat.

She motioned her son-in-law over. 'War-less, Ah War-less.' It was the extent of her English. He was given a chestnut, too hot to handle, which he juggled from hand to hand; it was crisp-skinned, slightly charred at top and bottom, with yellow meat bursting through the fluffy seams.

Mr Poon snatched himself a shrivelled treat from the brazier with spit-moistened fingers. It looked like a cinder. Steam seeped ominously out of the cracks. Mrs Poon put on a fresh load for the rest of the family.

Wallace licked the last grains of chestnut from his fingers and poured himself tea. There was a stifled bang which caused him to jump and pour tea over his shoes. Someone had lobbed a firecracker into the room. That was his immediate assumption. He clapped his forearm over his eyes against the eventuality of a second missile. He retrospectively analysed the bang as more of a loud pop, with an echo to it, unlike the flatter detonations of the morning. He removed his shield and looked for fragments of red cardboard on the floor from the shattered firecracker but could find none.

'It go bomb up,' Mr Poon spluttered. Light broke in on Wallace. Mr Poon spat blood and shell into the gilded tea-pot.

He allowed the sisters to escort him to the washroom, whence drifted sounds of gargling and exhortation.

Wallace caught Ah Lung's eye and sniggered but was snubbed with a cold stare.

The day appeared to have found a premature ending. One by one, the family left the room. Apart from Mrs Poon, Wallace was the last to retire. He left her seated on the lion throne, where she remained long after it had grown dark. As the dusk was descending, the mountains of the mainland glowed purple in the last of the daylight. In the following darkness they were a sombre, half-suggested mass. Memory prompted their outline, which was almost obliterated by the glare of the neon lights on the water-front, bounced off the polluted waters of the harbour.

In privacy, Wallace counted his takings. He knew, somehow, he would not be seeing his lottery prize. Still, after he had added May Ling's gleanings, the red envelopes made an impressive pile.

He snapped his fingers all the same. 'There was more, girl.'

She was all wide eyes.

He reached over to give her pockets a cursory pat.

May Ling tried to look offended. 'So, you thought I was stealing you, hah?'

'You never could trust anyone. You live here so long, I would have thought you know that.'

He opened one of the envelopes.

A button fell out.

Wallace stared at it as if to misdoubt the evidence of his own eyes. It was definitely a button. A brown button with four holes.

He poked it with his draughtsman's pen.

'It probably was his fly-button, too. The bastard, when I give him ten dollar.'

'Who?'

'Ah Lung, of course. Who else go and do thing like that? He go and lose all the money when he gamble.'

May Ling crackled the next packet by her ear. 'This one make noise like paper money, Wallace.' He snatched it from her. The note he pulled out was a one cent bill, denomination used only in accounting transactions, so useless it was printed by the Waterworks Company.

In all the packets contained twenty dollars. Fifteen of these were in the envelope presented by Mrs Poon.

Wallace said 'Shee!' as the last packet was opened and a few coins rolled out, his voice shrill and breaking. His sight blurred and he had to rub his eyes. He rolled on his stomach. May Ling found his reactions rather excessive. She had learned to moderate her own expectations where the Poons were concerned. She heard him mutter: 'It serve him right he never seeing it again.'

'Hah?'

He did not answer her.

A few days later Wallace was reading in the bedroom when Fong entered with a summons to assembly in the front room. The others were waiting for him. At last Mr Poon entered with Mrs Poon, serious-faced, behind him. He launched straight into a harangue in clipped, energetic Cantonese.

The flow stopped. Mr Poon began again in English. He stared at Wallace throughout. 'A viper in our bosoms,' he concluded, pronouncing it 'wiper'. 'Now we would make search.'

Ah Lung was genuinely mystified. 'What the hell was going on, Nolasco, hah?'

Wallace protruded his lower lip. 'You could search me.'

Mr Poon clapped his hands. 'There would be silence.'

They returned to their rooms in Indian file.

Mr Poon had already worked his way, rather cursorily, through the other rooms in the house when he came through to the kitchen. He stepped through the bead-curtain silently, startling Wallace. He and May Ling received Mr Poon at attention in front of their beds; it was the first visit he had paid them since the marriage. The metal hangers jangled on their string as Mr Poon went through the pockets of Wallace's two jackets.

Beneath Wallace's pillow were his sleeping underpants, which Mr Poon unfolded and looked inside. He gyrated in baffled circles. Without prompting, Wallace turned out the pockets of the jacket he was wearing. Mr Poon pointed at his shoes, and he stepped out of them.

There were no other hiding places in the room. The naked light bulb picked out every pock and pimple of May Ling's flawed complexion, finding a pale reflection of itself in the patina of secretions on Mr Poon's scalp. His right eye twitched in a spasm reminiscent of Ah Lung's affliction. He stamped along a crack in the stone floor as if the fissure would open into a robber's cavern. He followed it through into the kitchen. They heard him turning over the pots and pans.

The servants, exempt from the suspicion with which Mr Poon regarded the rest of the household, were making their evening meal.

They ate on incuriously with their backs turned.

Mr Poon's disembodied head pierced the beads and spoke. 'There was a lot of funny thing happen here which never happen before.'

Wallace kept his face expressionless.

That night he removed the screwed-up hundred dollar note from an empty, thumb-nail size tin of Tiger Balm and burnt the pawn ticket in the washroom. He held it with his nail scissors until it crumbled into the stained pan. Then he flushed away the evidence.

5

In making a stand against the Poons, Wallace incidentally lost the dowry. He had reasoned that acceptance of the cash inducement would prevent him from using May Ling as a weapon in the domestic battle.

Mr Poon had, in fact, intended to pay the dowry – in his own way. He had banked on a campaign of attrition: fair words and – their effectiveness expiring – the introduction of delaying tactics of another variety, with broken deadlines, stagey ultimatums from Wallace met with bland deferrals by himself. He would appear to ignore the whole problem. Finally, when resignation had succeeded to hysteria, he would give Wallace half the original sum contracted. He would present it to him in crisp, small denomination bills. Thus the presentation would smack of the bestowal of a free gift; he would not be acting as a man under pressures that were vulgarly immediate, and he would have exercised both his firmness and magnanimity on his son-in-law.

When Wallace stopped mentioning the dowry, he felt almost cheated.

Wallace drew closer to May Ling instead. This new intimacy was a form of revenge. If the Poons snubbed him, he would spite them by consorting with his wife! He would detach her from them. But this meant pushing the marriage beyond its original mercenary limitations. Otherwise his action would appear a reflex born of desperation, a drowning man clutching at his straw. He had to set an enhanced assessment on May Ling, make her literally priceless, turn her into the companion of his leisure hours, not a liability he had been paid to remove. 'No reason why we couldn't be friend, hah?' he justified himself to her.

The significance of his actions was not immediately apparent to the household at large, still less to May Ling, but he was patient to wait.

In the bedroom Wallace extracted companionship from his wife. He stood in front of their cracked mirror and preened in his jockey shorts.

'Look, girl,' he boasted, 'look at my Roman leg.' He adopted the pose of a discus-thrower, found it fore-shortening, and turned to a profile position.

Behind him May Ling pulled faces at the alien pages of an American magazine he had given her with the admonishment: 'I would not want the typical know-nothing, say-nothing, play-girl Hong Kong wife.'

He looked over his shoulder. The soles of her feet were presented to him for inspection; the toes were infuriatingly complacent little bulbs of flesh.

He slapped one of the offending members.

'Ow, Wallace.'

He glared at her. Breathing heavily, he went behind his jackets to change into his sleeping pants.

Although putting on a front of sullen unconcern, May Ling trembled before Wallace's latest attentions. She was made nervous by his constant proximity to her, even in the public rooms of the house. She wished he would leave her alone, as in his first months at Robinson Path, but he towered over her now like some monstrous, chivvying pedagogue. This was not a question of learning a few pointless, if convoluted, parlour games, humiliating though that ordeal had been. Or flicking desultorily through page after half-comprehended page of the *Reader's Digest*. (May Ling had baulked at the condensed books Wallace had brought with him from his father's library and which he swore by: 'What the point of reading all the long boring stuffs, hah? When you got all the nugget of it just took out for you?')

This was more; it amounted to a systematic attempt to destroy her points of reference and stability, leaving her at the mercy of the prevailing current of barbarian culture, in the sure knowledge that if it did not sweep her into her husband's arms, fright would.

The family resisted it as such. Any change Wallace brought about in May Ling would impinge directly on them; it would affect them more than May Ling. She had never existed as more than the aggregate of their joint expectations. To change one aspect of her personality was to destroy one of her functions in the household. And their very menialness made their loss the more acute.

When Wallace made her rise early to cook a separate breakfast for him, that was not an isolated action inconveniencing only the sleepy-eyed May Ling, it was a wilful disruption of the entire household's diurnal rhythm. The amahs were furious about the intrusion into the kitchen. May Ling's presence at that hour also cramped Eldest Sister's washroom rituals: she did not like another woman about her. Later, when May Ling was required to braid and heap hair and was too tired to ply with the expected nimbleness, each hair scragged in the rubber bands, each millimetre the crooked partings deviated from the true, the sisters blamed on Wallace; although this did not stop them reserving their pinches and scoldings for May Ling. Even Mrs Poon missed her foster-daughter's services as mascot at her marathon mah jong parties – the only formal entertainment permitted in the house by Mr Poon. At these functions May Ling had been required to stand immobile behind Mrs Poon's chair for hours at a time, keeping her glass filled with tea and generally giving her luck. Now, with May Ling monopolised by Wallace, Mrs Poon began to lose.

The reports came in to Mr Poon, each more disturbing than the last. Wallace was making May Ling brush her teeth three times a day; drink milk with her tea; he was buying her cosmetics. This last was a calumny concocted by Eldest Sister, herself chastised some years ago when a tube of lipstick had been unearthed in her room.

Matters came to a head when Wallace refused to release May Ling to massage Ah Lung's youngest son's neck after school, on the grounds that May Ling was herself studying.

'Studying what thing, hah?' demanded Second Sister indignantly. She was loitering in the kitchen with Eldest Sister, her hands on her thin hips; her pelvis resembled a pair of empty parentheses. They were talking to each other in English in loud voices instead of their usual Cantonese, obviously for Wallace's benefit. She smoothed the thin cloth of her cheongsam over her flat belly. 'That Wallace-husband of hers make her do bad thing. I tell you it so dangerous for Kwok Chung to come home from school with all the idea bubble over in his head and not have massage. It could give him...' she faltered.

'Brainstorm,' suggested Eldest Sister as Wallace emerged.

'Yes. The brainstorm.' She rounded triumphantly on Wallace. 'Murderer,' she spat at him. 'You kill Ah Chung, hah?'

Wallace was thrown off-balance by her virulence. 'You had gone crazy or something?'

'Huh,' she shrilled her disdain. 'Ah Dairdee knew what to do with you.' They marched off down the corridor in deputation. 'Bandit,' was her parting shot from the corner.

For once Mr Poon was at a loss. So prolific in his expedients, so subtle a negotiator, the famous fashioner of loaded compromises was faced with a novel crisis. With simple delinquency he could cope: Ah Lung was no problem. A straightforward beating, a carefully modulated tantrum, these sufficed. The other types of mutiny, mostly female in origin, were not so much rebellions as communications, part of the machinery of consensus: such as the mass deputation sent at the time he had pared the ration of salt fish. In the last resort he controlled even the amahs.

But Wallace! Wallace's actions did not fall into a category, and what he could not name disturbed Mr Poon. The damage Wallace did was not personal but delegated; he merely put May Ling up to the mischief. It was insidious, subversive. He could not be directly reprimanded. On the surface his behaviour was profoundly unselfish, even altruistic. But the old man suspected that some grotesque, disguised egotism lay at its heart. He could only hope that Wallace's actions would rebound on him.

As it stood, he had to make do with vague intimations of his displeasure. After the mollified sisters had left, he sat in his chair, absent-mindedly flicking the beads of his abacus. At length he sent Fong to summon Wallace.

He heard Wallace come whistling down the corridor; he trod in shoes, unlike the others who shuffled in slippers.

'You sent for me, Uncle, hah?' He was poker-faced with insolence. 'Please sit, please sit.' Mr Poon used the polite Cantonese formula, sending tremors of unease through Wallace, who perched on the desk, swinging his legs.

Mr Poon reverted to English. 'What was all this I hear about May Ling? Her sister say she got so cheeky?'

'Not with me, I was happy to say.'

'Ah,' Mr Poon frowned. Wallace's answer had not been the one he wished to hear: Wallace spurned his cues, taking his questions at face value instead of responding to the query's concealed point. This was a deliberate, aggravating obtuseness, masquerading under the guise of manly, Westernised directness. What was at issue was not May Ling but Wallace.

'Would that be all, Uncle?'

'All, all.'

'OK, glad I could be of a help.' Wallace headed down-corridor. Just before he turned the corner, Mr Poon called to him; if he behaved like a barbarian, he would be treated like one.

'Yes, Uncle?'

'What you really were doing?'

'Doing, Uncle? I do nothings except I walk down corridor.' He laughed.

'Well, whatever you were doing,' Mr Poon snapped, 'I didn't like it.

You be careful.' He bent over his accounts again. After a long moment Wallace left.

He made automatically for the kitchen before remembering with dread May Ling's blank, pasty face. It would have been too daunting after Mr Poon. He stealthily retraced his steps and mounted the iron staircase to Ah Lung's room.

Fong was polishing her husband's shoes, kneeling at his feet, rubbing an old sock across the leather. Ah Lung sent his eyebrows into his hair in mock surprise.

'Well, well. Look who was coming on the visit. Mr Bigshot himself. I don't suppose you got any room in your class for one more, hah? Fong like to learn how to smoke cigarette and all that big stuff, too, I expect. Hah, Fong?' He kicked her between her small breasts and Wallace heard the breath leave her body but she steadied herself on one knee and resumed her task without looking up.

Ah Lung grinned; like a wolf, his gums were red and wet. 'I got her well-train, hah?' He gave his high, out of control laugh.

Wallace chuckled ingratiatingly. 'You sure could say that.' In a gesture of complicity he experimentally prodded Fong with his foot. Ah Lung's eyebrows closed together into a scowl. 'OK, Nolasco, that was enough of that. She couldn't hit you back, you know.'

'Sorry. I was sorry, Ah Lung.' Wallace withdrew his foot foolishly then drew circles on the floor with the toe of his shoe. He started to whistle.

'You come in to give concert, hah?'

'Ah,' Wallace cleared his throat. He looked from side to side, up at the cracked ceiling, down at the floor, but found inspiration nowhere.

'Well, I would say goodbye, Ah Lung.'

Ah Lung stared mockingly at him. He looked triumphant before shrugging his shoulders dismissively. Wallace's anticipation of Ah Lung's cackle, catching him with his neck half-retracted as he went down the staircase, did nothing to assuage his mortification.

When May Ling saw his face she shrank. He crashed his fist into his palm. 'That bastard always laughing at me. I would really make him say "Wah!" one of these days.'

May Ling stood up. 'Drinking tea, Wallace?'

He nodded abstractedly and she handed him a full glass.

'I get all of this in my neck just for you.' He drank, adding with sudden violence: 'You ought to be more grateful.'

May Ling lowered her head and said nothing.

6

It became obvious to Wallace that what he needed in the struggle for May Ling was an ally. Futile to take on the Poons single-handed. He needed someone outside the household but who was at the same time familiar with the situation at Robinson Path. Someone imbued with proper values, not too modern, not too servile. Someone for May Ling to copy: a woman, preferably.

His thoughts turned to Pippy Da Silva and Mabel Yip. They were an excellent combination. What qualities one did not have, the other supplied. In fact, being honest with himself, Wallace doubted whether any one person could have fulfilled his high but vague expectations.

He would anyway have had to get in touch with Pippy in due course. She was younger than himself, a distant cousin on his dead mother's side. Pippy's own mother had re-married an Englishman after the death of Pippy's father, Stanley. Pippy lived now in her step-father's house in Kowloon Tong. They had a walled residence with a garden and gardener, and were somewhat better off than they had been while Stanley Da Silva had been alive.

Mabel was married, at least that was the consensus of opinion, to Yip, Mr Poon's sleeping business partner. Through Pippy's family Mr Nolasco senior had met Mabel and through Mabel he had been introduced to Mr Poon in pre-war days.

Mabel had instantly impressed Wallace as a woman of character and influence, even originality. She was the ugliest woman he had ever met, so ugly people turned their heads in the streets to stare. Her ugliness was a kind of distinction. It was not a mere plainness, the absence of symmetry or a single flawed feature, but a fierce, positive rejection of any kind of comeliness or softness. It seemed almost an act of choice: a mutilation. 'Really Mabel look rather fine when you stop to think about it,' her friends agreed, and those who called themselves the friends of Mabel Yip were many.

She pulled her hair tightly back from her broad forehead, gathering it into a bun at the back, in the manner of any Chinese matron. Her skull narrowed from its extreme width across the temple to a long jaw, above which was set a small imperious mouth. Her nose was not large but it was high-bridged and broken and, situated in the middle of scarred, Mongol cheekbones, gave her the appearance of an owl. Her eyes were deep slits.

Mabel made no concessions. She dressed in the latest, most expensive fashions available in the colony and some that were not; she put her outfits together with flair and ingenuity. Her collection of jewellery was legendary. At any one time she might be laden with a good third of it: jade rings of the darkest and most even hue – more precious than diamonds – on every finger and each of her long thumbs. pendulous ear-rings, gold brooches hammered and spun into butterflies, turtles and mermaids, ropes of pearls, layers of bracelets. She clanked as she walked in a cloud of French perfume.

People, both friends and enemies, were unsure of Mabel's age. According to mood, she varied it but she was never reluctant to volunteer some kind of figure, generally in the deadlands between the middle thirties and early forties. Her friends appreciated this openness.

They all agreed that Mabel had been born in Shanghai. Mabel herself liked to tell her friends that her mother had been a White Russian princess, reduced to penury in China, magically rescued from prostitution by her father, a wealthy Shanghai businessman who was later shot by the Reds while in Siberia buying lumber. Of all the versions of her origins, this was the one Mabel preferred, as it had the effect of making her no older than thirty-five. Other stories, while potentially as glamorous, necessarily made her slightly older: such as the one involving flight in a gun-boat down the Yangtse, accompanied only by her Belgian nanny, at the time of the Boxer rebellion. This latter story had gradually been phased out of the mythology surrounding Mabel.

Unkind gossip had it that she was the illegitimate daughter of a brothel-owner (Shanghainese, it was true) and the youngest daughter of a Sikh nightwatchman in one of the foreign concessions.

Privately, Mabel thought this was harsh. Her parents might not have been formally married but her father had disposed of controlling interests in business other than his chain of brothels. Opium, for instance.

What had made one generation preserved the next. Mabel kept herself in a style to which she had been totally unaccustomed through the judicious regulation of the supplies of opium reaching her husband, a helpless, wizened addict. Her dealings with Yip had been shrewd.

Fifteen years ago at the establishment she had inherited in Macau, a combined massage and opium parlour, she had rapidly ascertained the measure of Yip's possibilities as something more permanent than a client and had made unsubtle overtures to the invalid. The elderly addict needed little persuading; he was more in need of a nurse than a wife, and Mabel had moved to Hong Kong.

Not even Pippy was acquainted with this most recent chapter of Mabel's history. Although Mabel had never shared the same room as her husband, nor had her conjugal duties ever gone beyond inserting the pellets into Yip's pipes, she was more than a plunderer, conscientiously fulfilling her marital duties by mixing powdered rhinoceros horn with her husband's tea. She was a formidable figure, respected by even her few daring, open enemies.

Pippy was, in Wallace's eyes, altogether less worthy of veneration, a mere girl barely out of her minority. Still, because of her proximity to Mabel she had to be cultivated; besides she was nearer May Ling's age.

Mabel was devoted to Pippy, whose mother she had first met through Indo-Chinese friends at the *Alliance Française* when Pippy was just starting at the King George V school. The older woman had taken the young girl under her wing during her adolescence. Over teas at the Peninsula Hotel she closely vetted Pippy's numerous unnerved boy-friends, finding eventual fault in all of them whereupon they were discarded by Pippy. Wallace, a cousin, though male, she had decided to patronise and advance, if insinuating him into Robinson Path could be so described. In public an aggressive anti-colonialist, Mabel was secretly proud of Pippy's blue eyes, raven hair, and sharp Iberian features. She felt they complemented her own beauty.

Wallace spoke to Pippy the next day. His heart beat rapidly as he dialled from Mr Poon's desk. There was a fixed quarterly charge for the telephone which did not vary, irrespective of the use made of it – as if to cater to the loquacity of the Cantonese – but Mr Poon still restricted the use of the instrument. Speaking in a low tone, and somewhat irritated by Pippy's bright voice which he feared would carry through the house, Wallace arranged to meet Mabel and Pippy over tea at the beach. He replaced the receiver undetected.

7

The cavernous, shadowy ballroom of the Repulse Bay Hotel throbbed with music and a great roar of small-talk, counterpointed by the clink and rattle of the hotel's expensive, imported crockery and the insistent rapping of teaspoons. Some freak in the hall's acoustics carried small sounds more clearly than large, a fact of professional life with which the resident Filipino band had learned to live. Their leader, a fat, thick-lipped giant of a fiddler, beamed and waved his tiny bow at the band to stop – to the diminutive and struggling cellist's obvious relief. The band's bizarre allocation of personnel to equipment had much, Wallace felt, to do with their obvious popularity.

As the last bar of the tango died, Mabel Yip, who had seen a thousand tea dances at the Repulse Bay, enquired in the pause before the applause: 'You would have the milk or the lemon, Wallace?'

'The milk, I would think, Mabel.'

She flared her nostrils. 'Pippy?'

'Lemon with two sugars, thanks.'

'Yes, so much more refine, I think.'

'You really ought to remember by now, Mabel. Goodness knows how many cups of tea you must have poured for me.'

Mabel smiled tolerantly. 'You young girls always were changing your mind. All your dietings and the rest of it.' She stirred the tea for Pippy.

'And you, May Ling, how you drank your teas?'

'What was the good way, then, Mabel?'

'I suggest you try with the lemon and the little bits of sugars.'

'Ah. Yes, it taste real good, Mabel.'

Wallace sat back in the cushions of his wicker-work armchair and drank his muddy brew. They were sitting near a French window, opening onto a flowered verandah which ran the whole length of the ballroom. They were sitting squarely in the middle of a path of sunshine which extended through the darkness of the hall on each side – a spotlight almost – to fall on the band. The light picked out gold threads in Pippy's dark hair.

He was confused. So, in proper circles, milk was not taken with tea.

All the years he had studiously clouded the amber beverage. And all the time the Chinese way had been half of the right way. He shook his head.

'Do you feel unwell, Wallace?'

'No, Pippy, I was OK. Just thinking, you know.' He changed the subject. 'What you did today?'

'Oh, just the usual stuff. Got up late, too late for breakfast or anything. Crossed the harbour and had an early tiffin with Daddy, just the two of us. And then Mabel came along and we took the taxi here. Did you drive?'

'Taking bus,' May Ling broke in.

Wallace glared at her.

'More tea, May Ling?' Pippy, a good-natured girl, enquired hurriedly.

Mabel now spoke languidly, waving her lacquered cigarette-holder at the flower-smothered verandah: 'Life change so quick, you know.'

The others turned to her expectantly. Mabel stared out over the balcony to the sea and the islands that studded it up to the horizon. She was silent. Smoke coiled around her crudely planed features like joss around an idol. Uncomfortable in such an extended pause, Wallace was about to speak when Pippy, who was innured to Mabel's more disconcerting habits, elbowed him.

The oracle spoke. 'Yes, it change so quick.'

'Wah,' said May Ling.

Mabel gracefully acknowledged this spontaneous tribute with a sad half-smile. The cigarette-holder drooped wearily.

Wallace chipped in helpfully. 'In the *Reader's Digest* they got one nugget saying those New Zealand Red Indian, what they were calling them, Pippy?'

'Maoris?'

'Ah, that was right. Those Maori, they thought the time wasn't going back or forward in one line but you was rowing around on this big lake, hah? Then you went round anyway you like on it.'

He leaned back after his explanation but was disappointed by the reception of his 'nugget'.

Mabel resumed, a little frostily. 'That thought just coming to me when I was looking at this beautiful verandah. When I think back only a few year. All those brave boy who dying here.' Tears came to her eyes now, Wallace's interpolation forgotten. 'They was the real hero. See this verandah we sitting on now: the Jap rushing at them and they were rolling the grenade down it like they were playing bowl or something in the alley. Bang! Bang! And the toilet all over-flow after they were here for one day. Stinky like anything. And I help bandage them all in the hall here. And it was the same place and I was the same person. Only time changing.'

Wallace could not help himself interrupting: 'But, Mabel, I thought you was in Yennan then. You once told me you was with the guerilla in the cave there.'

She crushed him with a look, her eyes flashing.

Pippy rushed to Mabel's support. 'Yes, don't be so glib, Wallace.' Routed, he drank a mouthful of cold tea.

Mabel turned a smile of great charm on May Ling, revealing her discoloured teeth. She offered her a cigarette from an ivory box. May Ling simpered. 'Oo, Oo. You would turn me into real play-girl.' She choked on the mauve tube but persisted as Wallace looked on approvingly. He lit a Lucky Strike for himself. Pippy drew negligently on her cigarette, bound in pink paper.

'Well, well,' Wallace chuckled. 'The two play-girl and the one play-boy all having the good time.'

They finished smoking, then Mabel snapped her fingers to the 'boy' for their bill.

After a fortnight's silence, Pippy rang with instructions from Mabel. They were to meet 'in town' for some shopping.

Shopping! Wallace had been as unnerved as May Ling by the first outing. In fact more so, since May Ling appeared to have acquitted herself rather better, actually receiving a peck on the cheek from Pippy and a gruff handshake from Mabel as Wallace shuffled in the background. But with a trick of phrasing his social ambitions revived.

It was a word to conjure with – shopping – with its connotations of wealth, leisure, and taste. It was a pre-war, fundamentally Imperial recreation. What the 'Missies' did: an expeditionary descent from the mist-wrapped seclusion of the Victoria Peak. No cash ever soiled the hands of shoppers. The quick, arrogant flourish of a signature – 'Boy! Mark it up!' – and the transaction was complete. Nor did shoppers ever burden themselves with their purchases: the grinning cook-boy was an escort without a function, just for show. The fruits of shopping had to be delivered, materialise, a feat of commercial magic.

Wallace succeeded in making May Ling as nervous as himself. They had been due to meet for coffee in Whiteaway's but arrived early and to kill time and escape from the month's growing heat strolled through the Gloucester Arcade, a favourite promenade of Wallace's.

It was May Ling who spotted Pippy and Mabel. They were in the cloth shop, talking to its proprietor, a big Sikh. Bolts of unfurled silks and brocades covered the entire length of the wide counter and Mabel was ordering the proprietor to bring down more.

Wallace rapped on the window.

Pippy nudged Mabel who raised an eyebrow at Wallace before gesturing to the Sikh to show her the material from the topmost shelf. He swarmed up his ladder with undiminished alacrity.

Outside Wallace grinned foolishly. Pippy waved him in. He entered abandoning May Ling.

'These cloth so rubbishy,' Mabel was saying to the panting Sikh. She cut short his protests with an imperious hand. 'Not so good as last year. Really you were cutting your own throat and didn't know it. I would tell my friend to go to Mishra's from now on.'

'Oh, Madam,' the Sikh remonstrated, 'that I could not coun- tenance. I could not be happy in my mind that they were going to such a place. There they would be cheated right, left, and in the centre.' His eyes implored Pippy, who remained a smiling neutral.

'Sir, I ask you. Look at these fine cloths.'

Wallace assumed a mask of judicious severity. He pinched a gorgeous roll of brocade between indifferent fingers.

'This cloth OK,' he admitted.

'OK?' The Sikh made as if to tear his beard out by the roots. 'It is the very best, from Thailand. I am the only outlet.' Reverently, he rolled it up again.

Mabel deigned to notice Wallace. 'For a man you not so stupid, really,' she complimented him.

She turned to the Sikh. 'My friend here the big *tai pan*, you know. He knew all about the business and cloths. You couldn't fool him.'

The Sikh looked Wallace over sceptically. He started to house his wares.

'But I would make you a final offer of ten dollar.'

The Sikh considered.

'And I could recommend my friend to buy from you and not Mishra.'

The Sikh pursed his lips. 'Even ten dollars would be ruinous.'

'Eleven,' Mabel interposed swiftly.

'Only because you are an old customer and for the good will.' The Sikh counted the notes carefully.

'Don't forget to tell your friends,' he called as they left.

On the marble floor of the arcade, Mabel thrust the parcel into Wallace's arms. 'You could make yourself useful anyway,' she snapped. She slipped an arm through Pippy's and walked ahead.

Pippy called to May Ling: 'Come on, silly.'

May Ling looked doubtfully at her husband before joining them. She walked awkwardly, her stiff arm seeming to trap Pippy's friendly hand. She looked back at Wallace with every other step.

At the taxi-rank Mabel allowed Wallace to jump ahead and open the door. May Ling mechanically followed Mabel into the little red car.

Pippy broke the coffee engagement gracefully, adducing 'Mabel's migraine'. Wallace speculated what this might be but fell in with Pippy's almost conspiratorial tone. 'OK, OK, Pippy. Not far to come. I would take May Ling to watch the people getting off the Star Ferry now.'

Mabel took the parcel through the rear window. 'Pippy going to the beach with me next Sunday,' she informed Wallace. 'She like to swim,' she explained indulgently, 'and it was the first time you could really go this year. You could bring your wife and join us at South Bay.'

The taxi moved off enveloping Wallace in its exhaust but he waved back to Pippy who smiled at him through the rear window. A hundred yards further on the taxi stopped and disgorged May Ling.

Ah Lung had been a silent, sardonic witness of these manoeuvres. Although Wallace regarded the connection with Pippy and Mabel as in the nature of a deadly secret, he was unable to restrict access to his wife altogether. He did his best to keep May Ling incommunicado by arranging protracted reading sessions for her during the hours of mass circulation at Robinson Path. And at meals he monitored her every word. Ah Lung, however, had pumped May Ling assiduously in the brief moments he had managed to get her to himself, most frequently while Wallace was taking his constitutional in the Botanical Gardens.

A few days after the abortive shopping expedition, Wallace found the Gardens closed for the day and returned early to Robinson Path. He found Ah Lung closeted with May Ling.

He spat as Wallace entered, startled but seemingly without guilt. 'Whee-oo!' he whistled, a fashionable American sibilance. 'Look who here now.' This appeared to be the limit of his synthetic social repertoire. He hawked but caught Wallace's eye and swallowed what he had in his mouth.

'What you doing here, nosey-parker, hah?' Wallace's voice shook with rage.

'I just return the compliment of your visit, Mr Big-Shot.'

'May, what you have told him?'

May Ling was suddenly interested in the *Reader's Digest*.

'She told me enough, Nolasco. All this tea-dance and stuff. I wonder what my father say if he knew?'

Wallace paraded a bravado he did not feel. 'How he would find out then? And even he did, you think I would care?'

Ah Lung smiled at him.

Goaded, Wallace assumed a falsetto to mimic the sisters. 'I tell Ah Dairdee, Ah Dairdee know what to do with you.'

Ah Lung looked serious. 'So you gone and turn to make the insult about my family? We were not good enough for you, I suppose, that you got to go to the beach with your girl-friends.'

Wallace reflected. 'What you would be doing Sunday, Ah Lung?'

'Me?' Ah Lung said with exaggerated surprise. 'Nothings I would think.'

'Well, why you didn't come to the beach with us?'

'Wah, that so nice of you. I look forward so much to it.' He brushed the bead curtain aside. In the confines of the kitchen his burst of laughter had an almost concussive force.

Ah Lung knew Mabel from the days when she had accompanied the invalid Yip to Robinson Path. Nowadays Yip was too debilitated even to stir from his reeking bedroom and Mabel dealt with Mr Poon herself, by telephone. Ah Lung remembered Mabel had completely ignored him on her business trips. Pippy he knew of allusively and now he had blackmailed his way into seeing her.

For Wallace Ah Lung was merely another problem, of many. He looked forward to the excursion with a combination of eagerness and dread, the latter presentiment generally dominant in his outlook. He was, for a start, uncertain what time to arrive. Mabel had even omitted to specify a rendezvous, although Wallace consoled himself with the thought that South Bay was only a small beach. He decided that the best thing was to arrive as early as possible, then pretend they had only just come when Pippy and Mabel turned up. Better than arriving to find their hosts had already decamped.

He was fierce as he impressed the need for co-operation on May Ling. 'First of all you would have to get up when normal people does. Otherwise it would all be dark and empty by the time we were getting there. And another thing: don't tell everyone how poor your father was keeping us all this time, OK?'

'OK.'

But she wore that blank expression he knew so well.

All that could reasonably be done to avert disaster, he performed. He bought May Ling her first swimming-costume, new trunks for himself, creams, floppy white hats to protect against sun-stroke; excavated his toe-nails, cautioned a deprecating Ah Lung.

On the night before, he put May Ling to bed immediately before her evening tea, at a time when the children were still shrieking in the playground. He joined her soon after.

That night he hardly slept. In the morning she woke him, wordlessly, with a glass of tea. She had already packed.

He went to the washroom in shirt, shoes, and socks, pre-empting Eldest Sister. Ah Lung was already in the kitchen, fully-dressed, gobbling curds, an apparition in an orange safari suit. Under his arm was a rolled towel. Wallace retreated to the bedroom.

As before they went by bus, an unprestigious mode of transport, second only in ignominy to the tram. Wallace could never understand how, in the public view, Mrs Poon embarked and disembarked from the great green cans with such composure. On this occasion he remembered to swear May Ling, and Ah Lung, to secrecy.

Ah Lung readily fell in with the plan. 'We could say we come in big pink car,' he suggested helpfully, 'with fin at back.'

'And our chauffeur took it away,' May Ling chipped in, anxious to demonstrate loyalty.

Wallace shook his head regretfully. 'No, it had better be taxi.'

The bus journey was uneventful. After disembarking, it was a little time before they could locate the steep steps leading down to the cove.

May Ling staggered under the weight of their rattan suitcase. Once she slipped and grazed her knee but the men did not turn around. At last they were at the bottom of the cliff. They walked through a grove of stubby palms, the earth surrendered to white sand, they stood on a deserted beach.

'Nine o'clock only,' Ah Lung announced, stunned at the enormity of being abroad at such an hour. 'I tell you it was too early.'

'Coo-ee!'

They jumped but recovered with the first echo.

'Wah, it was Ah Pippy.'

'OK, May Ling, but where the hell she was?'

Ah Lung spoke. 'By the house, there was someone.'

On the other horn of the beach stood some flat-roofed houses, made of concrete blocks and daubed in pastel colours, not unlike the style in Macau. Standing on a deck-chair, waving, in front of the smallest and farthest of these was Pippy.

'We here already, Pippy,' Wallace called back superfluously. They started to plough across the sand.

'What took you so long? I've been here ages.'

'The taxi-driver go and lose his way,' Wallace lied. 'Mabel was swimming already?'

'I should say not.' Pippy jumped lightly to the sand. 'She won't be here till later but that needn't stop us having fun.'

'This May Ling brother, Ah Lung. You could call him Jack, you wanted to.'

She shook his hand. 'Nice to meet you, Mr Poon.'

Ah Lung whinnied. 'I could see you was a real polite girl straightaway. No one ever call me that before.' His shoulders heaved alarmingly in his orange jacket.

Pippy turned to May Ling. 'Just drop that there. Poor May Ling! A fine pair of Hong Kong gentlemen you two are.'

The two men shuffled in pleasurable embarrassment.

'Well, come on in. You can get changed. I've got my costume on underneath my frock.'

Ah Lung stared hard at that garment.

'Boys in the first room, girls in the second.'

Ah Lung whispered to Wallace with excitement as they went in: 'Then there would be other girl coming, Wallace? You never tell me.'

It transpired that Ah Lung intended to swim in his underpants.

Wallace exploded. 'You mean you telling me you go and buy all this big suits and you couldn't even buy a pair of swimming-trunk?'

'Well, it woulda cost a lot of money, Wallace. You would never know the difference I was once in the water.'

When they emerged May Ling had already changed into her costume.

Ah Lung tugged his arm. 'She so skinny she like the pluck chicken in the cook-shop, hah?'

Pippy looked coldly at him. 'Such a nice costume, May Ling. I love the little pleats. And is that a little bow tied over the bust?'

May Ling tittered. 'No, I was too skinny to wear it really.'

'You should thank your lucky stars. I know I could never get away with it.' Pippy ran her hands disparagingly down her rounded breasts and flat stomach, tautly defined beneath her plain black costume. 'At least you've got a costume,' she added pointedly.

Taking May Ling's hand, Pippy led the way down the beach. Ah Lung walked by himself, twitching and muttering.

The sea – the calm, cold water of morning – was perfectly transparent. Not a ripple disfigured its surface. Wallace stepped doubtfully out to his knees and was immediately besieged by a school of tiny fish; they swarmed and nipped with surprising aggression. He leapt out in mock alarm.

Pippy laughed. 'Tickle, don't they?'

'Wah, like anything.' His arms and chest had come out in goose-pimples.

'Come on, May Ling,' Pippy exhorted, 'you've got to jump in all in one go. It's easier that way.'

Over their heads a large stone thumped into the water, scattering the fish in panic flight.

'You go to the other side of the beach if you want to play the giddy goat, Ah Lung.' Pippy glared at Ah Lung, who looked around in offended innocence. He spread his arms wide as if to indicate that some mischievous, but invisible, fifth party had launched the projectile. He sat on the sand, like a protesting Indian in the Pathé newsreels of a few years ago, Wallace thought.

By this time the beach was inhabited by a small, commercial population. The ice-cream men had pedalled out from the Dairy Farm depot on their bicycles. These were unwieldy vehicles with large ice-boxes slung from the handle-bars. They were parked at the top of the beach.

Further down, an entire family, down to the smallest, totally naked children, were erecting a row of striped, square tents to hire out to bashful changers. Clients had yet to appear.

'Whee! It's wonderful!' Pippy had dived into the shallows in a flat, athletic arc. She sleeked her wet hair back.

Reluctantly, May Ling pulled her tight bathing-cap, festooned with rubber roses, over her head.

'Come on, you lot.'

Wallace wavered, then lowered himself in, bottom first, lips compressed. His baggy trunks ballooned around his hips. A large, vulgar bubble welled to the surface and popped. Wallace snickered. He swam a few strokes and got out. 'I would wait till later, Pippy,' he said apologetically.

He ran back to the villa to fetch his towel.

Mabel had arrived. She brushed aside his greeting. 'I saw you bring that good-for-nothing Poon Lung with you. No, don't say anythings. We just would see.' She threw him a towel, larger and softer than his own.

'Hello, May Ling. I saw you was sensible at least and didn't go in yet. Your husband dead of the double pneumonias before twelve o'clock.'

'Wah.'

'Pippy swimming, hah?' Mabel enquired.

'That girl was crazy like anything,' Wallace offered.

Mabel nodded. 'Ever since she was a little girl she always was the same. The real tomboy. She would be coming up from the water soon.' Mabel poured tea from a thermos.

Wallace noticed that she was wearing even more jewellery than the last time he had seen her at the Gloucester Arcade.

'You was satisfy with the cloth you buy?' Mabel looked puzzled. 'From the Arcade,' Wallace prompted her.

'Ah, yes, it was for Pippy ball-gown when she went to the Garrison ball. But these Indian were such crook.' She paused for effect before adding with sudden vulgarity: 'You know they was wiping themself with their bare hand?'

Gratified with their reaction, she continued in a lowered voice: 'And I saw one old Indian fellow do it in the street. Yes, just like that. It was outside that temple they got in Stubbs Road. So you could see what sort of businessmen they made. At least we Chinese was the cleanest people of the world.' It was a habit of Mabel's to preface her odder pronouncements with the phrase 'We Chinese'. It enabled her to get away with many things.

Now she passed around the glasses of orange, milky tea.

Wallace looked at his in puzzlement.

'It was different for drinking tea on the beach,' Mabel informed him crisply. 'Only with lemon for the tea-dancing. Now I wonder where Pippy get to? Sometime she climb up hill after swimming.'

She went out. 'Yes, there she was, just like a black dot. It took quite long time. I suggest you rest.'

Wallace fell asleep in a deck-chair. He awoke with a heated face, the consequence of exposure to the torrid spring sun. His cheeks and the gullies of his nose prickled. May Ling snored gently in the other deck-chair. Pippy was buttering bread, chatting to Mabel who fanned herself gracefully.

'Hallo, sleepy-head.'

'Where Ah Lung disappear to, then?'

Pippy laughed enigmatically. 'Oh well, he should be here before dark.'

They spread tinned pilchards on the bread Pippy had buttered. It was traditional beach-fare for young Chinese picnickers. They ate eagerly. Wallace dropped a fragment of fish into his navel and scooped it out with a curved finger. 'It sure is true what they say about the open air make you hungry.'

Mabel, her mouth full, made affirmative gestures, staring down the mother of an English family that had encamped nearby.

They were no longer alone. The beach pululated. The invasion had come in two waves: Europeans in the mid-morning, Chinese in the early afternoon. The first pioneering detachments of the afternoon had filtered down to the water's edge where they congregated in irresolute clusters, watching the *gwai los* in the water.

On Pippy's suggestion she and Wallace left to buy popsicles from the ice-cream men.

The sand was now baked to a super-intensity; it shimmered, distorting the air above in curves and bends. Through eyes screwed into slits, Wallace saw that Pippy's legs ended at the knee, with her shins and feet jutting out at right angles from the joint. Like one of the tormented, he danced and gibbered on an enormous, fiery plate.

They arrived on the cooler concrete.

Pippy grinned. 'Pretty fierce, isn't it?'

The ice-cream men chortled. They had stripped off their monogrammed company shirts and sat in shorts, exposing their mahogany torsos. With their ferocious, uniform hair-cuts they looked like a gathering of convicts in an interlude during hard labour. Their bulging calves, developed through pedalling heavy loads uphill, appeared lashed to the leg by crinkled, hosepipe veins. The muscles belonged to men stones heavier. They were incongruous above the men's feet. It was the foot, not the leg, which appeared deformed.

'Four red-bean popsicles and one Vitasoy,' Pippy requested of the nearest. 'The soya milk's for Ah Lung,' she explained. 'I'm told he likes it. No, don't worry, I can manage them.'

They sprinted back over the hot sand to find Ah Lung returned. He accepted his bottle sulkily. The others bolted their ices before they could melt. Pippy collected the sticks and put them in her BOAC bag (to Wallace's certain knowledge she had never been on an aeroplane in her life).

'Righto, time for a dip.'

No one moved.

Pippy appealed to Wallace. 'Come on, Wallace, it'll cool you off.'

He levered himself up. 'OK, May. Pippy would teach you how to swim.'

'Oh, I'd love to. Let's get a ring.'

Mabel remained in the shade of the villa while the others trooped down to the water. Pippy stopped at the tents and hired a black rubber ring for May Ling. This was not a plastic toy but a monster, the inflated inner tube of an aeroplane wheel. Ah Lung and Wallace were as wet as swimmers when, working under Pippy's directions, they hurled it into the sea.

This was not the sea of the morning. It had become an opaque sheet, the colour of liver, flecked by a line of spume, darkened elsewhere by clouds of sand churned from the bottom by children gambolling in the shallows. The white belt, too thick for salt foam, was spit, a perimeter of phlegm, randomly deposited by the afternoon's swimmers and swirled into a pattern by wind and current.

Ah Lung added his contribution.

Within this boundary a gang of Chinese fathers were cheerfully ducking their screaming sons. They appeared convinced that the successful inculcation of aquatic technique began with total immersion. They seemed to be competing to see which child could hold his breath the longest. The boys bobbed up in succession, choking and gasping, leaving the winning father to clap his spluttering champion on the head and send him to recuperate on shore.

'Straight to the raft,' Pippy suggested.

Threading the ring over May Ling's head, they negotiated the crowded shallows, using the tyre as a ram to breast the barrier of saliva. Just before they reached the raft, Pippy duck-dived and surfaced with a shell.

May Ling clapped her hands. 'Beautiful! Beautiful!'

Pippy placed it for her on the side of the tyre.

They clambered onto the raft, dragging the tyre up with them.

Ah Lung's wet underpants clung to the contours of his loins, the colour of his flesh apparent through the soaked, transparent cloth. Pippy and May Ling were careful not to look at him but reclined against the tyre. It formed the hub of a wheel, of which their legs were the spokes. May Ling placed her hands over her face.

Wallace came from the edge of the raft, where he had been rehearsing a dive, and kicked her amiably. 'Why you did that?'

'I wouldn't get so my face was burn. Only the low-class peoples was looking brown.'

Pippy smiled. 'What a funny idea.'

'You should tell May Ling about how to look smart. She need a woman advice about the make-up and other thing.'

'I'll teach her how to swim first. That'll be enough on my plate.'

She eased herself into the water having firmly parted May Ling from the tyre. 'Hold on to the ladder. That's right.'

May Ling's spine was rigid with tension.

'Relax. Just let your legs float up behind you. Right, now kick.'

May Ling churned the sea behind her in frantic, scrabbling strokes, devoid of rhythm. The spray drenched the raft.

Wallace called out. 'Hey, May, you make the lovely rainbow behind.' May Ling turned her head and immediately sank. Pippy pulled her up by the biggest rose on her bathing cap. 'Whatever you do, keep your hands on the ladder.'

May Ling's eyes were red with salt. 'Pippy, I was tire now.'

Wallace sat on the ladder, barring access to safety. He pushed May Ling down with his feet. 'You must go on.'

The desperate thrashings resumed.

Meanwhile, two swimmers, Europeans to judge by the energetic crawl they employed, had been approaching. They trod water and shook the hair back from their eyes. They called in unison through cupped hands.

Pippy waved back vigorously. 'John! Roderick!'

'Your friend, hah?'

'They're army officers,' Pippy explained. 'From the border. Roderick just got promoted last month. It was in the gazette. I'll be back in a jiffy. You keep plugging, May Ling.' Pippy's eyes had a new sparkle. She joined the swimmers, floating in between them, then they struck out for the line of buoys beyond the raft.

May Ling took advantage of the diversion to gain the platform, toppling onto the rough matting at the other end from the men. Her chest heaved.

Pippy had reached the buoys behind her companions and was

pulling herself along the line to the other horn of the beach.

The breeze freshened, clouds passed over the sun, and the raft rocked on wavelets.

'Better go back, hah?' Wallace rolled the tyre to the edge. He helped May Ling into its centre and pushed off. She clutched her shell.

As the sun reappeared, Ah Lung leapt into the sea in a tight bundle, narrowly missing the tyre.

May Ling lost the shell which spiralled into the depths. She looked appealingly at her husband. He shook his head, considered, then submerged. He felt his eyes start out of his head with strain. Seemingly a long way below, the shell still fell. He drove harder; it neared. Now he was falling with it. He missed and caught it with his return stroke. Awkwardly, he somersaulted for the surface. Ah Lung and May Ling had advanced a surprising distance to the shore. He called. He blew water out of his ears and was still deaf. Pippy, he noticed, was still on the buoys. He was impeded by the shell. He dropped it and continued to the beach.

While they had been gone, some children had built a complex series of fortifications near the water's edge. They had cast towers of sand, using buckets as moulds, and scraped a moat for the sea to fill. Wallace gave the edifice a respectful berth as he caught up with Ah Lung and May Ling at a run. They walked to the villa together and changed quickly.

Mabel had joined a group of acquaintances at a villa further down. Wallace decided to take advantage of her absence to steal to the bus-stop undetected. The day was beginning to pall. He made them take the first bus that came and they walked home from the nearest stop.

They limped, the trapped sand grating with every step.

8

Embroilment with Mabel had kept Wallace from getting into mischief at Robinson Path. But the association proved a temporary diversion rather than a genuine escape. The phone stopped ringing with Pippy's calls and Wallace again found himself confronted with the silent disapproval of the Poons.

The state of the marriage was giving concern. So far May Ling showed no indications by thickening, vomiting, or bizarre cravings, of contributing imminently to the next generation of Poons. In fact, she was looking thinner than ever. And Mr Poon brooded on her disrespect. May Ling was failing in her primary duty to him, which was the production of descendants. He regarded her less as an individual than a potential vehicle of his own immortality.

There had been false alarms, of course. May Ling had drooped after the escapades with Pippy and Mabel. She was bored in the house now. Wallace had destroyed the framework of her old day with its little privileges and stolen pleasures, as well as its chores, and had substituted nothing permanent in its place. May Ling spent an increasing amount of her time in bed, remaining there while the sisters put up each other's hair. She had always quite enjoyed discharging this particular task but Wallace had spoiled it for her. Detached from her familiar supports, she floundered and sank.

Mrs Poon drew her own conclusions, mistaking this listlessness for the prelude to fruition rather than the battening disease it was. She grilled May Ling on details of the marriage, eliciting giggles and drawing a blush to her foster-daughter's sallow cheeks. But successive disappointments gradually dampened even Mrs Poon's enthusiasm; she abandoned her enquiries. She felt a totally unmerited sympathy for Wallace, confusing her desires with his. For he was as backward here as in his other obligations.

In the first months he had kept a furled newspaper under his pillow. He would shake it open with much deliberation while May Ling undressed. He had read every page of the paper; many of the stories he knew by heart and he returned to them as if to old friends, mouthing the words as the print swam up almost meaninglessly at him.

May Ling removed her first layers of clothes slowly. Then, incited by the cold, divested herself with growing recklessness, the untidy heap on the floor rising as her coverings shrank. As she stabbed her legs under the tight sheath of quilts on her bed, Wallace would snap his paper shut. Three long strides, in his underpants, would take him to the light-cord and he would carry back an image of exploding suns, imprinted on the retina, as he retraced his steps in the dark. He would listen to the church clock striking the quarter hours and the scurrying of the disturbed geekos as they ran over the cracked ceiling. At last he would fall asleep.

He felt no desire for May Ling. And there were positive reasons to abstain. Mr Poon had not exactly welched on his contractual obligations but Wallace had voluntarily turned his back on the dowry; he would not give something for nothing. Mr Poon could expect no grandsons from him in the immediate future.

Once, motivated by lectures from her foster-mother, May Ling had inched her trestle-bed nearer her husband's in graduated phases during the night. Growing impatient, she had knocked the pillow off her bed. Recently Wallace had been reading in the *Reader's Digest* about the Indian cult of *thugi*. He awoke to find May Ling standing over him with her pillow in her hands. He jerked upright with clenched fists.

'My God, May, what the hell you thought you were doing?'

She clutched the white cushion to her chest.

'You go back to your bed. And move it away where it was before.'

She obeyed.

'Crazy. Crazy. The whole family crazy like anything.'

After this she left him alone.

Meanwhile, unknown to Wallace, others were labouring on the family behalf. At least three of the joss-sticks that had smouldered before the tree at Christmas had been spontaneous intercessions for May Ling by the amahs. Subsequently, Mrs Poon had also bribed the servants into making the pilgrimage to the phallic rock and leaving food before that suggestive spur of granite. It had been a long walk for the old women. In fact, repenting of her access of good will, Ah Doh snapped one of the brittle yellow sticks of incense they had planted in a cave underneath the rock – a fell stroke that drew a feeling wince from Ah King.

If Wallace had felt a twinge, he had not shown it, and the marriage continued to provide food for malicious speculation in the servants' quarters and amongst the tenants.

Unlike Wallace, Fong had never been a parasite on the body of the family. Apart from distinguishing herself by producing sons and no daughters, she had – fifteen years ago – brought a sizeable dowry with her to Robinson Path. This had been invested for Ah Lung by Mr Poon. He had never seen the interest.

Having paid a somewhat excessive sum to be rid of a daughter, Fong's father – a prosperous ship's-chandler – had washed his hands of her. The new family might do with her as they wished. All that remained of Fong's old life, mementoes of those who had abandoned her – photographs, ribbons, certificates, a plait of hair – she kept in a flat tin that had once contained chocolates. Who had given Fong chocolates, no one knew. After beatings from Ah Lung she would lie on her bed, clutching this box.

Fong's given name was 'Doh Tai': 'Bring more Brothers'. The Poons had, however, always referred to her by her family name. The familiar 'Ah' had been gradually dropped from addresses to her and she became known simply as Fong. Fong she remained.

This abrupt vocative mirrored her status in the household. Traditionally, the existence of a daughter-in-law was a minor hell on earth; as an unpaid drudge her condition was worse than that of most servants; although she might console herself with the anticipation of the indirect revenge she would take on recruits to her husband's family when she was a mother-in-law in her own right.

At first, Fong was fortunate. Mrs Poon had always been kind to her. The transferred glamour of her father's money had also purchased the respect of Mr Poon, who found no grounds for complaint about Fong's part in extending the male line. But with the sisters it was a different story. They loved to torment Fong, and had not missed an opportunity to do so since her first days at Robinson Path, to which she had come, as a frightened child-bride, with considerably more ceremony than would greet Wallace in his turn after the war.

The pattern of the sisters' behaviour had been set as they joined the rest of the household in pelting Fong with blossom as the door clicked behind her. The sisters had flung handfuls of petals at the new arrival's eyes, advancing through a scented blizzard to thrust their fists down the back of her dress.

From bursts of menacing giggling when alone with Fong, the sisters had progressed to pulling faces behind her back, later to her face, to prevaricating tale-bearing and – on one unforgettable night – to an outright assault in the corridor when they kicked Fong to the ground: scratching, pulling, gouging, biting with the ferocity of a duo of young sharks. Fong had been heavily pregnant then with Kwok Kei, a circumstance which had saved her from further punishment, for the sisters had known what to expect if damage was done to Mr Poon's embryonic grandson. (There had not been a moment's doubt that it would be a boy.) The sisters' native caution had quickly reasserted itself and they had pulled off, panting, into a corner as Fong dragged herself up the wall.

That had been the climax of the sisters' first campaign. It had not been an exercise in gratuitous sadism. Fong was a walking affront to them: an interloper, with child.

Then, at a critical juncture, May Ling had arrived, diverting their attention from Fong. Since May Ling was a blood relation, they had to be more circumspect about persecuting her. They contented themselves with turning her into a hanger-on. Then the marriage to Wallace had inflamed them to vengeance. In their eyes, this had been a major piece of treachery. It being unthinkable to blame their father, they had made a scape-goat of May Ling. Their revenge was to be exquisite and prolonged. But their plans had been frustrated by Wallace's eccentric interest in his wife. Against the cunning and ruthless adversary he had shown himself to be, they had no choice but to retreat.

Ah Lung took no sides in these cat-fights. He stood by while the sisters goaded Fong but (as Wallace had discovered to his chagrin) he would not brook interference with her from another male in the household. As there was a strict division of labour at Robinson Path, so there was also a strict demarcation of conflict. The chief aggressors were the sisters and the amahs, in that order of bellicosity as far as feuding against Wallace was concerned. Their vendettas, at first sight no-quarter affairs, were conducted according to an understood set of rules. The situation resembled a board game where certain pieces could not take others, or the Chinese hand game of stone, paper, scissors. This system of checks and balances prevented a collapse into complete chaos, with quarrels spilling over beyond the original protagonists and finally drawing the whole household into a vortex of dissension.

According to this system, Ah Lung behaved correctly, while Wallace cheated; he abetted May Ling in what was fundamentally a woman's quarrel. Denied its proper outlet, the sisters' redoubled rage and frustration rebounded once more on the innocent Fong with an intensity that would not have been possible if the system had been allowed to regulate itself without interference. In this sense, the repercussions were Wallace's direct responsibility.

The weather was increasingly oppressive. The temperature had not risen by more than a few degrees since Wallace had led the excursion to the beach but, more than the heat, the soaring humidity sapped everybody's strength. The exception was Mrs Poon. She bustled efficiently through the house, opening windows and closing shutters. For all her exertions, the heat, competing with the dank air, poured wetly through. Their discomfort increased hour by hour without hope of relief.

Wallace had been amusing himself by poking a spoon through the slats of an old electric fan and interrupting its feebly rotating blades, much to the annoyance of the sisters who were wafting tepid air over themselves in wristy strokes with a set of their mother's antique court fans. Tiring of his game, Wallace peeled himself off his chair with the sound of toffee being unwrapped. He went to the balcony, leaving a ring of sticky perspiration where his back had been resting. He saw Fong at the nullah. She had a box of ashes which she threw down into the water-course. The grey flakes fluttered into the air. She crossed the road with the box, which Wallace could now see was a blackened and buckled tin, and put it in one of the empty dustbins by the door. She did not go up the spiral stairs to her bedroom on the top floor but went instead to the washroom. The door closed gently behind her. A little later the amahs raised the alarm.

Fong's attempt at suicide disturbed the house very little: far less than Wallace's clumsy efforts to tamper with its arrangements. Her action even met with modified approval, for instance from the amahs, as an honourable revival of a defunct custom. Such had been the conventional revenge of harassed daughters-in-law in olden China: an act of retaliation that put the culprit beyond punishment.

The question of how serious Fong's attempt at self-extinction had been was not raised. She had slashed her neck and wrists quite deeply with Mr Poon's razor. The amahs had noticed blood trickling through the gap between the lumpy blue mosaic floor of the bathroom and the bottom of the door. There was, of course, no latch in that public household and this had saved Fong from gradual exsanguination.

Mr Poon arranged for Fong to go to a convent hospital. Fees were high but the sanatorium was more discreet than one of the government establishments. The shrewd commercial practices of the sisters enhanced rather than lowered Mr Poon's estimate of Catholicism and for a while he gave Christ pride of place over Buddha, nailing the crucifix high on his bedroom wall.

The family visited once before Fong came home. The lacerations on her neck and wrists had been quick to heal but the fractured ribs and concussion she had sustained when the ambulancemen dropped her on the staircase were more serious.

As far as the hospital was concerned, Fong had been in an accident with a mangle, although the house was actually innocent of such an appliance, the amahs wringing the washing with more or less enthusiasm, depending on the standing of the wearer.

'So you think the good sister would believe she go and stick her neck through the rolling bar?' Wallace asked Ah Lung scornfully. 'You would have to do better than that.'

Nevertheless, this was the fiction they were instructed to concert, and maintained, on their visit, just as all the young Portuguese girls confined to the hospital's leafy grounds for the duration of their pregnancies were apparently war-widows bereaved in Korea.

It was Ah Lung's turn to be scathing, as he and Wallace strolled in the hospital gardens. He snorted: 'A funny thing, hah? The Red kill so many soldier they should win the war already. Anyway, I didn't know you Portuguese fellow was fighting there.'

Wallace replied defensively, but without heat: 'We did our part. Just because a country was small didn't mean it couldn't help.'

Ah Lung nodded absent-mindedly. He had not been listening. 'One thing about your Portuguese girl. They all had nice eye.' He winked roguishly at one. 'It always make me happy to see woman big like that.'

They retraced their steps to the convalescent's room. The family were sitting around Fong's bed in silence. Mr Poon was staring ruminatively out of the window at the bursar's office.

A cigarette hanging rakishly out of the side of his mouth, Ah Lung unwrapped a crackling bottle of Lucozade. He poured two glasses for his sons, who drank eagerly, watching their mother over the rims of their blue plastic beakers.

Ah Lung patted Fong's legs under the bed-clothes. 'OK, Fong, hah? You soon would be out and well.' She gazed vacantly out of the window into the tree tops. She did not seem to hear their noisy farewells.

9

Fong was discharged in time to sweep the ancestral graves at the Ching Ming festival, that annual obeisance the quick paid the dead in the season of renewal. Mr Poon conspired to surround her return with the trappings of normality. May Ling was sent to the hospital and brought Fong home on the tram. Ah Lung and the sisters had been sent out on some specious errand but the amahs relieved May Ling of Fong's roped cardboard box of effects at the bottom of the hill. Mr Poon put his daughter-in-law at her ease when she came in: 'Tcha, Fong where have you been?' And the incident was relegated to history.

The Ching Ming rites were hard work at the best of times; in the unprecedentedly hot spring weather they would be a physical ordeal. Wallace doubted the wisdom of having Fong accompany the family to the graves while she was still recovering but kept his misgivings to himself.

The cemetery was on the other side of the small mountain ridge that formed the spine of the island, on the Pacific Coast, near the fishing village where the first British naval landings had taken place. The graves were cut into the hillside in steeply ascending terraces, platforms so narrow that unsubstantiated rumour had it that coffins had to be slotted into the cheaper plots in an upright position.

The morning buses were crowded, and Mr Poon let several pass before supervising a mass embarkation. Soft drinks stalls and flower stands were already doing a roaring trade at the cemetery's imposing porcelain gates when the Poons arrived. The family waited while Mr Poon bargained unsuccessfully for a small wreath; the boys stared at a row of frosted bottles, licking beads of perspiration from the soft black down on their upper lips.

At length Mr Poon retired, empty-handed, from his negotiations. He waved the family on. Following him down a steep flight of steps, they had to run the gauntlet of yapping dogs that, day or night, were to be found by the gates. Wallace found their well-fed appearance sinister.

The full extent of the day's demands broke in on him as he came out of the shade of an avenue of trees and saw the graveyard in the midday sun. The architecture of the cemetery was itself a cogent reminder of the continuing power of the dead over the living. Mr Poon's ancestors were dotted in random, disobliging clumps over the entire hillside, thus attesting to Wallace that key characteristics of that irksome family were transmitted beyond death itself. Or, at the least, the Poons died in character.

For the next four hours the family descended, back-tracked, and circled in the hottest part of the day. Trips to the different burials could not be scheduled according to any logical plan, so far as considerations of time and effort were concerned, but had to be made in strict order of familial precedence. The men's shirts stuck to their backs in transparent patches. Mr Poon set a gruelling pace, never turning to look behind himself. His black trousers, stretched taut across the rump, were speckled with silver friction marks. They glinted like a mirage before the family, always at the same distance. Even had he wished to do so, Wallace would have been unable to overtake the old gentleman. Mr Poon still prided himself on his agility but, more than this, he drew strength from the discomfiture of the others.

May Ling and Fong brought up the rear a little distance behind the sisters, as Mr Poon arrived at the first tombs. He had economised on tips to the groundsmen the year before with the consequence that the Poon plots were now heavily overgrown with weeds. Ah Lung's sons, in their school uniforms of blue canvas trousers and white shirts, produced trowels from their satchels. There were not enough of these tools for the entire party but numbers were made up with the distribution of European-style cutlery. Wallace found a fork more efficient than a spoon or knife.

At a major grave such as this, the tomb of Mr Poon's grandfather, thick stacks of counterfeit money would be sacrificed, while the family bowed their heads in contemplation. The money burnt fiercely but inconspicuously in the bright sunshine, crumbling into flakes which were carried upwards on shimmering waves of heat. It was almost as if the stack was being destroyed by the concentrated energy of prayer. Then a single pale finger of flame would point skywards and the pile collapsed upon itself.

Before departing, Mr Poon appropriated a wreath from a nearby plot, which looked recently swept, and placed it on the grave of his ancestor.

A little later, they stopped for a meal, spreading a white cloth over a grave and using it as a picnicking table. As customary, Mr Poon had bought a whole suckling pig. The family ate with relish.

The important graves had all been tended before the meal. Afterwards the sweeping became increasingly perfunctory. The newer plots had an odour of decay about them that was absent in the old sites, a smell compounded of fresh earth and corrupting vegetation. A jacket of grey plaster covered the hillside behind one of the most modern interments. The plaster had cracked and buckled under stress in the rains. Scabs had broken off, exposing the red clay and raw sandstone beneath like inflamed sores.

Fong slipped with the now empty picnic basket as she came up the steps to join the others on the small platform.

Ah Lung nudged Wallace. 'If she would have try harder maybe we all had worship her today, hah? Instead she got to do walking, walking all the way round.' He laughed unpleasantly.

The rest of the family were at work weeding. Wallace noticed a grave at the far end of the plot, newer than the others, but still too old and far too big to be that of May Ling's nephew. He tugged Ah Lung's sleeve: 'I didn't see the baby grave.' Ah Lung took a trowel from his youngest son and bent for the first time that day.

After a brief respite, ostensibly for meditation, they began a long, shallow diagonal ascent that would take them most of the way across the mountain. At one point they came within twenty yards of the gate again, only to be curved once more into the descent by Mr Poon. The family were well strung out by now, the sisters having fallen behind May Ling and Fong. The stragglers were joyfully harried by the cemetery dogs. The sisters' shrieks had the effect of inciting a pair of the larger animals in the pack to leap up and snap at them.

At the last grave, inconveniently at the bottom of the hill, Mr Poon circulated a flask of 4711 cologne which the women dabbed onto their wrists and temples. The men dipped twists of their handkerchiefs into the bottle and wiped their faces. Thus refreshed, they sat in the shade of a large tree: Mr and Mrs Poon on a single bench, the others on the tree's thick, writhing roots. As far as a tall man could reach, carvings embossed its trunk: the usual crop of initialled hearts pierced by tufted arrows, a stick man (the creation of a macabre mind) gagging on his gallows, names single and linked.

'One of those tall Northener must have come and carve his name on our Cantonese tree,' Ah Lung deduced. He strained to find a virgin patch higher on the trunk. His sons crowded him as they watched him carve their names into the trunk in English. Ah Lung stood back and critically appraised his handiwork; it passed muster. 'Clarence Poon, Hogan Poon. Your names would sure stand out, boys.'

His sons smirked uneasily, caught between the obvious pride of their father and their grandfather's patent disapproval. The sisters swooped to confiscate the knife from Ah Lung.

'You got the bothersome Auntie, boys.' Ah Lung shook his finger half-heartedly at the sisters.

Hawkers had now spotted the family and came up to offer wares from pannier baskets slung on yokes across their shoulders. Wallace bought some dried sour plums, mistaking the wrappers for a gelatinous coconut confection to which he was partial. He was left behind by the rest of the family as he paid the vendor. As he scrambled up the terraces, rising in daunting tiers before him, he sucked the plums. The sour little rocks puckered the lining of his mouth, leaving him in even greater need of refreshment than before.

10

Ah Lung's sons got on well with Wallace. He saw hope in the new generation. They were quiet, diligent boys, just into their teens: quite the opposite of what their father had been as a youth when he was already cutting swathes through the brothels and dancing halls of Wanchai.

'Clarence' and 'Hogan' – Wallace had never suspected them of being the bearers of such enviable sobriquets (Ah Lung had so named them in reaction against the drabber Occidental alias bestowed on him by his own father) – were undergoing classical education at a notably old-fashioned Chinese Middle School.

In accordance with the regulations of this academy, they wore their hair cropped close to the scalp after the style of the Whampoa Cadets before the Soviet instructors withdrew and the institution went soft under Chiang Kai Shek. This distinctive cut gave the boys the look of bonzes. Hygiene and convenience should have been its compensations but, in summer, their lack of hair merely made them more vulnerable to mosquito bites. The boys' heads would swell in lumps and angry blotches, aggravated by sweat, and their scalps would have to be painted with gentian violet. The antiseptic dye ran erratically and, together with the slightly uneven shave their aunts gave them – stubble at the sides, with the hair bristling on the crown – they resembled the savage Mohicans whom Wallace had seen in a film dramatisation of James Fenimore Cooper's novel. He was too tactful to mention this to the boys who lacked their father's sporadic sense of humour.

Wallace wondered whether the boys might have warmed to 'Uncle' after the lavish tip he had given them at the lunar New Year but put the thought away as unworthy.

He encouraged them in their studies; having been unable to complete his own, he set a higher value on theirs. 'One thing about Chinese peoples,' he admonished them, 'they all were revering the scholarship.' The boys lapped up his praise; they got none from their father.

Ah Lung belittled their efforts. His attitude implied that success in the scholastic sphere was too facile a challenge for the superior man.

Whereas open derision would have been a cultural enormity, this tactic kept him on the frontiers of orthodoxy. When the boys presented him with their termly marks a few weeks after the ancestor festival, he was at first grudgingly appreciative. 'Ninety per cent average, hah? And Ah Lung get ninety-five on sums. The old man be please with you. His blood in your vein. Eiyah! What was this? Hey, Nolasco, Hogan get ninety-nine per cent on Nature Study. Show to Uncle Wallace. You could go the safari, boy. A lot of money in that sort of thing.'

Wallace said warily: 'They were good boy you got, Ah Lung. You could be proud of them.'

The boys surrendered their examination papers to their father. 'Hah? But what was this?' The boys crowded him anxiously, one on each side, their three heads colliding, purple and black, like some man-eating plant, over the printed sheet of questions Ah Lung held. These were from the only curriculum the school did in common with the government schools, a course in English history set from London.

'You got thirty question here, I was right, hah?'

The boys nodded.

'History essay. Number one: "Was Alfred's Navy the major factor in his success against the Danes?" (Who the hell this Alfred was anyway? We maybe had a Alfred here for a governor one time, Nolasco?) Number two: "Did the Conquest alter the character of English life?" Number three...' He broke off incredulously, with stagey amazement. The boys looked at him with hurt, reproachful expressions. The youngest spoke: 'Father, why were you laughing?'

'Why I was laughing?' Ah Lung's helpless knee-slapping ended with suspicious alacrity. 'You telling me you got, what it was?' He referred to the rubric at the top of the paper. 'Three hour, three whole hour just so you could write yes or no about all this stuffs, hah? I could get fifty per cent if I just was guessing them. Yes, No. No. Yes.' His finger stabbed the page.

'No,' his eldest son broke in. 'It was like this. You got only four questions to answer but...'

'Four?' Ah Lung's voice broke in the upper octaves. 'Four! My Gods! It taking you three whole hour just to make up your mind to say yes or no about four question?' He threw his hands up in the air in mock defeat. 'So that was what you did in the school in these modern day. Well, boys, I was only glad it wasn't my money you were throwing down the drains there. Four question!' He rose with a triumphant grin. He was followed to the door by his youngest son, still protesting and waving the examination paper. Ah Lung sang snatches of nonsense in Cantonese to drown him out. The door of the washroom clicked behind him.

Kwok Chung, 'Hogan', came in with his head lowered. His eyes were bright with tears. Wallace reminded the boys gently: 'Time you two were doing your homeworks. Your holiday not very long. I thought I hear the midday gun fire already this morning.'

The boys took their books and pencil boxes from their satchels and spread them on the table. Wallace had seen the boys at homework before. They spent most of their time at brush-stroke exercises, copying out classical poetry, extolling the virtues of life in the countryside. But, apparently, this was term-time work. They would be engaged mathematically for the duration of the vacation. Wallace saw they had their compasses and pencil-boxes out. There was a coloured transfer of Sun Wu Kung, legendary king of the monkeys, on Kwok Chung's box. He was dressed in a black tunic suit and cloth boots, whirling his traditional staff, tail jauntily in the air.

Wallace scratched at the flaking colours with his finger nail. 'That monkey was really clever,' he lectured the boys. 'He could even make himself invisible if he had to. He was so brave but sometimes he got up to bad mischiefs, so his master, the priest, made an iron band to go round his head to control him. But monkey always manage to get himself out of the trouble he got into in the end.'

The boys shuffled their feet.

Wallace picked up an exercise book with the school's crest stamped on the front and flicked through its pages. He nodded approvingly at what he saw. 'You got a lot of tick and star there,' he praised. 'When I was a boy in Macau I never got so many. Wah! And here was a "Excellent" the teacher write in English.'

The boys did not respond. Wallace persisted. 'I bet you both would be getting more prize-book in the summer. With your name stick inside, hah? Then you would have a whole shelf of them.' He sharpened the youngest boy's pencil for him, twirling delicate shavings out of the slot of the sharpener. He handed the furbished instrument back.

'We use the pencil specially to do the sum,' the boy volunteered. 'Ink was in the other book.'

Wallace nodded. 'Just like when I was a boy in Macau. I suppose it was so you could always rub out your mistake.'

The eldest boy chipped in: 'No, we had to leave our mistake for teacher to see and then do correction in margin.'

Wallace's eyebrows met. He placed a heavy hand on the table and leaned over the boys, then abandoned this pedagogic pose as the joints creaked ominously. 'I tell you what, if I could, Clarence and Hogan.' He savoured this, the first appellation. Those names!

The boys craned their necks, dropping their pencils.

'You Chinese boy had only one fault. You were all so hard-working but you never had any imagination. You never ask the reason for doing anything, like we Portuguese boy did. You just did it because it was always done that way. You know, I bet all your teacher would be so please if you ask why sometime. Like why you wrote in pencil and not ink. No, no, you better do in pencil still this time.'

He halted at the door. 'One other thing I always thought was funny. Why the hell we always did our sum with pound, shilling, and pence when everyone knew we had dollar in Hong Kong? And same with Macau money?'

The boys nodded. It was a conundrum that had perplexed more than one generation of schoolboys.

'Well, you two could ask your teacher when school began again. That was what they were calling initiatives. Maybe he would give you another star. I would take you to the cinema if you gave me the answer.'

The teacher's answer, a fortnight later, was pragmatic but swift and, when Wallace thought about it, entirely consistent. Despite himself, he rather admired the classic simplicity of the stranger's response, this man he had never seen but the imprint of whose work and character had lain before him on the open page.

The reply was not without its metaphorical overtones, the traffic in symbol and gift between anthropologist and savage, exchanged mutually unseen in some neutral glade: the propitiatory gift spurned and hideously defiled, awaiting the explorer's return on the morrow.

Murdering time in the interval between completing his ablutions and the serving of the midday meal, Wallace read from his volume of condensed books. He prepared himself to surrender credit gracefully to the boys.

The amahs snapped on the wireless in the echo of the noonday gun; it warmed to a crescendo; still there was no sign of the boys. Perhaps they were having stars stuck in their books; maybe an interview with the headmaster: a handshake and a personal commendation. 'And my respects to Uncle.' Wallace shifted in an ecstasy of self-deprecation as he rehearsed the imaginary dialogue to his satisfaction.

The stairs creaked.

He addressed himself to the 'nuggets' of literature, so skilfully refined by the abridger.

The boys usually called to the amahs as they slung their satchels on the pegs behind the door. Today they were silent, although they made no attempt to move quietly.

Kwok Chung, 'Hogan', came in first. Wallace folded the page of his book in half and closed it. The welcoming smile congealed on his face.

'Eiyah! What gone and happened to you two boys?'

They responded with muffled abdominal gruntings: the kind Eldest Sister made in the morning. They did not have much choice. Their lips were sealed with sticking plaster. Whoever had performed the operation had not been a subscriber to half-measures: their mouths were criss-crossed with several strips, the last layer of plaster ending just below the ear.

Hogan squirmed away when Wallace tried to remove his plasters. He had a note in his hand, which he now showed to Wallace without releasing it. Wallace recognised the ideograms as classical. They informed him that Poon Kwok Kei and Poon Kwok Chung had that morning manifested a trouble-making spirit, disturbing both their teachers and their classmates and were undergoing merited punishment. Let the family cooperate: by leaving the plasters in place, by removing them only when afternoon school was over and by feeding both offenders white rice in the evening without soya sauce.

Wallace was speechless.

But Mr Poon received the message calmly. 'Sung dynasty,' he remarked eruditely. Wallace did not understand. Mr Poon explained, as if to a cretin. 'The writing was very old in its calligraphy. Calligraphy mean hand-writing.'

'I knew what calligraphy mean. But what about Clarence and Hogan?'

'Hah?'

'Kwok Kei and Kwok Chung. They got to eat, too.'

'No. They would only feed in the evening. The school say so.'

Wallace's blood boiled. 'They were the victim of stupidity. They only show a little intelligence and look what happen.'

'So, Nolasco, I thought you was somewhere involve.' Ah Lung entered the exchange.

Wallace retreated. 'If only that damn teacher wasn't so blind . . .'

Mr Poon showed the note to Mrs Poon. 'Sung,' he said with undiminished pleasure. Mrs Poon showed approval in the way she adjusted her spectacles; although her examination was not more than perfunctory. She nodded. It was things like this that justified the high fees charged by the school.

Second Sister now jumped on the band-waggon. She shook her finger at the gagged boys: 'Sung,' she admonished them. With his own chop-sticks Mr Poon pincered a tit-bit from the soup and deposited it on the rice in his youngest daughter's bowl. The boys watched hungrily. A look of intense virtue suffused Second Sister's otherwise unremarkable features, filling Wallace with the desire to thrust a chop-stick from one of her shell ears through to the other.

It was one of the most concerted meals since the war. In the generous heat of the moment, the amahs actually served the sisters. By the end of the sitting they were waiting on Fong and May Ling in an orgy of abasement.

In the circumstances Wallace could not but carry out his promise to take Clarence and Hogan to the cinema. They were not spiteful boys and did not harbour a grudge against him. Together they leafed through the entertainments pages of Mr Poon's newspaper.

'The Roxy was always good, boys. We could go there.'

'What was on, Uncle Wallace?'

'Something good, anyway. If you chose the cinema well, you could alway leave the film to itself. Just like the old-fashion way: if the family was good, so was your wife. What did I tell you? They alway got the best cowboy film on at the Roxy. Like now they got one with Cisco Kid.'

'It got the Red Indian in it too, Uncle Wallace, hah? I only like the one with Indian in it too. The cowboy all was boring by themself just drinking and punching. I like it when the US Cavs come at the end.'

Wallace looked doubtful. 'Hm. I knew what you meant, Hogan.'

'I was Clarence, Uncle Wallace.'

'Well, you still were right. That Cisco and Pancho were never fighting with Red Indian in all the film of theirs I ever saw. You know, those Spanish fellow always got on better with the Indian than the American did. It was like the Portuguese people and the Chinese in Macau when you thought about it. Actually those Red Indian didn't

72

fight each other either. In the *Reader Digest* it say they play a game with ball and a net on a stick and the winner got all the land. Maybe one or two brave die but not a lot. The game call Lacrosse – you hear of it you two?'

Clarence shook his head.

'There was gangster film at Sheraton,' Hogan suggested, changing the subject.

'No, no. Not suitable, Ah Chung.' Wallace had not heard of the film but the Sheraton had an unsavoury reputation, being frequented by sailors of the American Seventh Fleet when they were in harbour.

'Ah, now this looked fun. They had comedy on at the New York with cartoon show too. You would like that you two, hah?'

The boys looked at each other uneasily; they nodded without enthusiasm.

Wallace relented. 'Well, maybe the gangster one was OK.' The boys brightened. 'Perhaps the cinema change hand recently. It usually only was those French film there.'

The film, about protection rackets in Chicago, was a success. Even Wallace's enjoyment had only been slightly marred when a large negro rating in the seat behind had threatened him, following a series of loud questions (from the boys) and hissed answers (from Wallace). The boys had been confused by what, in the context of a film about the American underworld, 'insurance' meant.

Afterwards, Wallace took the boys to the same ice-cream parlour where they had celebrated his marriage. The boys walked behind him in the choked gutter, holding hands. Over their complimentary soda-waters Wallace reminisced about his schooldays. 'But figures was alway my strong point. I was going to finish the college at Foochow to be a engineer if the Red didn't get in when they did. Still, we had our fun, too. And I alway was the leader of that.'

'What sort of funs, Uncle Wallace?'

'Ah, we was the real little devils. Like putting a pin on teacher's chair and he would jump and say "Ouch".'

The boys' eyes widened.

Wallace continued airily. 'And there was lots of other mischiefs. Some were much worse. Once we had one of those cushion that made rude noise. Hah?' Wallace blew a raspberry.

The boys looked aghast at him but with the glimmerings of a new respect. 'Wah, Uncle Wallace, we never would be daring enough to do a thing like that.'

Wallace shrugged modestly, hinting at further delinquencies he might reveal if he chose.

'Well, we were a special gang in those times. There was no one like us nowaday. We wasn't frighten of the rule. If we didn't like them we made our own. But we knew when to help the others. Like in the Occupation we used to run message and gun. I carry a stick of TNT's to blow myself up and take a few Jap with me if I ever was caught.'

'Eiyah! You had a gun, too, Uncle Wallace?'

'Colt .55.'

'Wah!'

'In shoulder-holster. Now finish your drink. Everyone knew it was rude to leave food that was free. Captain! I would have the bill.'

On the bus he basked in their open admiration. And at their homework on Monday they consulted him with their problems. But he would not be drawn in front of Ah Lung. 'Ask your father, he would know.' And he retired to May Ling's company.

11

Mr Poon had plans for Wallace. And the moment had come to introduce his son-in-law into the design. Wallace had not worked out quite as he had expected but he was used to making the best of imperfect material; it was the story of his business success. Moreover, time (usually a great ally of Mr Poon's) did not seem to be on his side in this instance. He did not see Wallace's behaviour improving; indeed, in the long term, he saw it deteriorating. He might have felt more comfortable if his son-in-law had taken the dowry or some portion of it. However, he was determined not to offer money unless actually asked: he placed economic priorities higher than political.

Although a wealthy man, Mr Poon was dissatisfied. Using the dowry Mrs Poon had brought him, he had by craft, thrift, and daring accumulated a substantial fortune. His thriving network of businesses and investments was sufficiently diversified for him to be unconcerned about fluctuations in a particular commodity or service. Above all, the war in Korea had brought unexampled prosperity. But for some time now he had wished to establish the foundations of this wealth on a sounder dynastic basis.

He was unillusioned about Ah Lung. He had long abandoned the idea of his son as a business successor. He disciplined Ah Lung for appearances' sake. The little demonstration with the golf club at New Year, sabotaged by Wallace, had been so intended. The issue which really exercised Mr Poon was how to proof his estate for survival, more or less intact, until his grandsons came of age. None of the males in his family for the past five generations had lived beyond their middle sixties, and he was nearing that dangerous age.

The commercial empire he administered could be controlled only by himself; only he understood its complex interrelations and dependencies. With his own death it would break up under the kinds of strains and pressures only he had been able to moderate. He was looking now to simplicity and security rather than the speed and size of returns. This was a complete contradiction of all his practice to date. The major portion of Mr Poon's capital had come from playing the stock market with a gambler's intuition and disdain for risks. He now wished to leave some tangible memorial behind himself. Some artefact. It would not matter that his name might not actually be linked with anything he built. It would be in the nature of a tribute to an unknown soldier.

After long thought he had decided to enter the construction industry: specifically the building of highways, jetties, roads, tunnels, and bridges. He saw opportunities here, especially in the rural hinterland of the New Territories. There was a certain logic to the growth of communications. One began at a point and measurably worked to another. It was discernible. He would begin a road. His grandsons would finish it. And if he entered the field quickly enough he would be able to capture enough to be consolidated after his death.

But how to get into the industry? It was not technicalities that worried Mr Poon. He could employ others to master these. He would be the financier, the one occupied with the grand view, while others were bogged down in the petty details. It was *getting* the work that was difficult. And it was here, in the area of contracts, that Wallace could be useful.

Mr Poon found Wallace and flung an expansive arm around his narrow shoulders. Wallace started. He had been comfortably digesting his ration of morning congee. Now he felt it curdle in his stomach.

'Just borrowing your newspapers for a while, Uncle.'

'Any time OK, son. What was mine was also yours.'

Suspicion displaced apprehension in Wallace's mind.

'Come to my office for a while. More private. I got some good news for you.' Wallace understood Mr Poon to mean his desk in the corridor.

'It was a bit early in the day for good news to arrive already?'

'Sit, sit.' Mr Poon beamed. His manner was reminiscent of the days before the marriage when he used to visit the Nolascos in Macau. 'Now, Wallace, I could see you were getting unhappy just lying about with nothings to do. It was demoralising for the young fellow like you.'

'Demoralising?'

'Yes, demoralising mean . . .'

'OK, OK.'

Mr Poon's smile lost none of its blandness. 'The sweet, Wallace?' They were sour plums. 'Put some in your pocket. I knew you like them.' He chuckled indulgently, then with unexpected bluntness said: 'I got a job for you.'

Wallace dropped the preserve he had been holding. He regarded Mr Poon with deep suspicion.

'Please or not please, Wallace?' Mr Poon left Wallace in no doubt which answer was expected of him.

'You would have to tell me more about it first.'

Mr Poon ostentatiously hid his wounded feelings. He gave vent to a sigh, which suddenly turned into a belch. 'That congee always gave me hiccup.'

'No, that was burping you did.'

Mr Poon frowned. 'I didn't like how that word sound. We Chinese, as you knew, have no word like that. Our culture was too refine.'

The sisters arrived with glasses of steaming tea, quartered oranges, and perfumed flannels.

Wallace sensed he was in a position to barter something, what he was not exactly sure, but he was correspondingly emboldened. 'Where was this job?'

'Government job. You work in department for building and that kind of thing.'

'PWD, hah?' Wallace looked forward to the challenge of employing some of his engineer's training.

'No. Not the same as PWD but doing same sort of things. It was good job. Your pay not too much but you could help your friend and family to make money, then you all got rich together.'

Wallace grasped the general idea. 'But that was corruption!'

'Wallace! Wallace!' Mr Poon raised his hands in horror. 'You didn't understand.'

'I sure did. You want me going to Stanley Prison? Anyway it was bad thing to do.'

Mr Poon wiped his lips with a fragrant blue flannel. 'Wallace, Wallace. This was the Chinese way. It was our custom, it go on thousand and thousand of year. You help your friend, you help your family. What was so bad about that, hah?' He wheedled, his voice soft and silky. He filled Wallace's tea-cup. 'You got a chance to make new friend for yourself, too. Beside, when you staying here a little longer, you found everyone knew everyone else here. It was small place. So how you stop from giving your friend business, hah? And I tell you something else. It was so expensive for the English to make a government here. It cost money to pay for these civil servant in their suit and tie. When they got a commission it was just like a tax so they could keep going.'

Wallace fiddled with his orange segments.

Mr Poon tried another tack. 'You know, Chinese people *like* to be doing their business this way. You didn't ask for tip: they *wanted* to give it to you. It wasn't like you were in the police or something, Wallace. It wasn't like going round showing your gun and asking for tea-money from street-hawker.'

Wallace could not disagree with this. He peeled the ends of the rind away from his piece of orange.

Mr Poon pursued his advantage with a pragmatic argument. 'How you thought everyone here getting so rich? How you thought we all got the work done quick-quick, not like in England, hah? I tell you why: you gave commission, it made more work and it got it done fast. No one going to help you for nothing, Wallace.'

'You know, Uncle, I never thought of it like that before.'

Mr Poon shrugged his shoulders modestly.

'And I got some tip out of it, hah? Like you said, no one did nothing for nothing.'

'Of course son, of course. You wouldn't have to do anything wrong. Just helping with some entertainment.'

'And it help our family, Uncle?'

'It helping us. Also helping Mabel. You like that, hah?'

This was a pleasant surprise to Wallace. It confirmed his decision. He fitted the quartered orange to his teeth and stripped it efficiently from the peel, sending the juice trickling out of the corners of his full mouth. Mr Poon passed a flannel to him.

'Good, son, I knew I could depend on you.'

The office was situated a little distance away from the government's main administrative complex, which was located off Garden Road, and was a few hundred yards from offices of the rival Public Works Department near Cotton Tree Drive. It faced a dock where submarines re-fitted; immediately behind it was a barracks, dating from the early Victorian period, which had been used as a torture chamber during the Occupation and was said to be haunted. The Department premises themselves were comfortable, almost residential-looking, in a low building with a large verandah. The heads of sub-sections, Englishmen, were accustomed to smoke cigars in its shade after tiffin at the Hong Kong Club.

The walls of the big room in which the clerks worked were lined with expensive teak panels. They gave the chamber the atmosphere of a smoking-room. Four surprisingly powerful fans rotating on the ceiling, their blades painted a regulation cream, were the only bureaucratic touch. In the centre of the room there was a railed compound entered through a saloon-type swing door, hinged to open at waist-level. The chief clerk, a stocky Hakka, sat in here at an enormous roll-top bureau. New employees also sat in here with him for a short probationary period.

After a fortnight, Wallace was released to sit in an outer orbit.

Along with another new clerk, he had been given a formal welcome by Mr Allardyce, head of their sub-section. Allardyce, a bachelor in his early fifties, liked to think of himself as an Old China Hand. He had come to the colony fifteen years previously, having left the Indian Army with the rank of Captain. He had spent the war in internment. While a prisoner, he had become seriously ill with beri-beri and dysentery. He owed his life to a certain masseuse who at considerable risk to herself had smuggled food and medicine in to him. After the war he had toyed with the idea of going to India or Kenya but had chosen to remain in Hong Kong. Subsequent developments on the sub-continent and elsewhere had not given him cause to regret his decision.

The chief clerk had ushered the recruits into Allardyce's tiny, frosted glass cubicle of an office in one corner of the big room. He remained there during his superior's address. Mr Allardyce gave the same pep talk to all new government servants. It emphasised team-spirit and the subordination of the individual. He found in these attributes a rare intersection of British and Oriental virtues.

'And, men, as a former captive of the Japanese, I should know the value of these qualities.' Allardyce drew himself to his full height of over six feet. He warmed to his theme: 'I say that because in Camp we all had to pull together. It was that or all die together. And, do you know, those were some of the finest days of my life. Perhaps the finest.'

Behind Allardyce, the chief clerk nodded vigorously, his gold Rolex glinting on his wrist.

The new arrivals were marched out to their desks.

Despite the disorientating effect of Mr Allardyce's speech of welcome, Wallace found he enjoyed going to work. It put some kind of rhythm into his day where before there had just been the interludes between different activities. Employment gave him a sense of purpose; although, actually, there was not very much to do at Department.

To Wallace's uninformed eye, the office seemed over-staffed. There was one clerk who appeared to do no work at all. He kept his head bowed over a pile of completed invoices for hours at a time but produced no discernible results. He was not equipped with either pen or pencil; instead, when the chief clerk was making his rounds, he would pretend to write with his thumb-nail.

Finding himself under-employed at the end of his first month, Wallace went to the chief clerk for more work. As a result, he was kept in over the tiffin hour. He was not actually given anything to do. However, he occupied himself by categorising the requisition forms for stationery he had completed, in triplicate, during the morning. He did it in alphabetical order at first: Envelopes, Erasers, Foolscap, Ink, Nibs, Pencils, Rulers. Drawing-pins and manila envelopes were a little difficult to place. Then he re-shuffled the forms according to the quantity of the requisition. Finally, according to the size of the article. At length he began counting the number of desks in the room. He had reached almost three figures when Mr Allardyce emerged from his glass cubicle. The Englishman walked unsteadily in the long corridor between two rows of desks.

He would have gone right past, had Wallace not spoken.

'Working late, hah, Mr Allardyce?' Wallace was shocked by his own boldness but sensed that his advances would not be spurned.

Mr Allardyce halted. He did not look directly at Wallace for a moment but felt in his trouser pocket for a handkerchief. He gave the impression that he had heard a voice in his own head. His face, always florid, was unusually flushed, making the ruptured veins in his nose stand out more than ever.

'My name is Nolasco, sir,' Wallace prompted.

Mr Allardyce looked down. There was a flicker of recognition in his eyes. 'Ah, yes. Mabel's protégé.'

Wallace was surprised. 'You knew Mabel, sir?'

Mr Allardyce did not seem to have heard him. His drunkard's eyes filmed. 'A remarkable and courageous woman.' He blew his nose drily but explosively.

Wallace steered the conversation to firmer ground. 'Sir, I was real proud to work here.'

Mr Allardyce inspected the contents of his handkerchief. 'I encourage *esprit de corps*. A man of ability could go far here, Nolasco. Look at me, for instance, I'm a self-made man.'

'Ah, that was what you were.'

Mr Allardyce steadied himself with one hand on Wallace's desk. He adopted a frank manner, horribly embarrassing his subordinate.

'Oh, yes, my father was a tobacconist in Romford. Does that surprise you? It really shouldn't. Most of us foreign devils are pretty small fry giving ourselves airs here that we aren't really entitled to. We're aping what we've never known at home.'

Wallace listened nervously. He re-arranged his forms back into alphabetical order, deciding that the conventional way was the most efficient.

Mr Allardyce continued remorselessly. He was no longer looking into an abstracted middle distance but fixed Wallace with his gaze: 'Actually, most of the Chinese outrank us socially speaking, as it were. And they know it, too. It's something I never felt with Indians. We've never really clicked with the Chinese the way you people did. Why, you're almost Chinese yourselves.'

Mr Allardyce folded his handkerchief, controlling his hands carefully. He laughed his genial, healthy laugh, 'Yes, a tobacconist.'

Wallace now said politely: 'So your father a big *tai pan*, hah? He had a big godown he keep the tobaccos in, I bet.'

Mr Allardyce clapped him on the shoulder. 'My dear fellow.' He seemed to have forgotten about tiffin, for he retraced his steps to his office. Wallace heard the clink of glass on glass.

There was one clerk who stood out from the others. He sat on his own near the verandah. It was clear he either chose or imposed isolation on himself since he was evidently popular in a chaffing kind of way.

Wallace was curious. 'Ah, that was Major,' a clerk at a neighbouring desk told him, as if salient traits might be deduced from that information alone.

'Nickname?' Wallace asked.

'Nickname. His real name was Chen.'

Major puffed on his pipe, comfortably aware that he was the subject of discussion.

'Speak to him. He was the mad guy of the office.' The clerk moved on to the water-cooler on the verandah.

Major's dress, when the heat was considered, was more than mildly eccentric. He wore a thick tweed jacket in a violent check. It had leather patches on the elbows. His shirt was striped, surmounted by a white detachable collar that was some sizes too big for him. His legs were hidden in a pair of voluminous grey flannels, which, at the moment, were drawn up to reveal a pair of welty brogues.

Wallace strolled over, wondering whether an opening gambit based on the weather might be considered tactless, but Major spoke to him first.

'You were out of the OK Corral then?'

'Hah?'

'The OK Corral.' He gestured at the chief clerk's compound with the stem of his pipe.

Wallace said waggishly: 'I was the big boy now.'

The remark obviously struck Major as witty for he hooked a spare chair with his polished instep and dragged it over the floor for Wallace.

'I could see you were a man of parts straightaway, Mr Nolasco.'

'Thank you, Mr, Mr, er...'

'Major. They call me that.'

'Ah, Major.'

Major took a pen-knife from his pocket and started to scrape the bowl of his pipe. The knife was thick, bulging with layers of hinged appliances.

'I could see you took an interest in my unusual knife, Mr Nolasco.'

'Wah, I never seen one like it.'

'Yes, I always found it was a good conversational gamble.'

Major pulled out the blades and the wicked looking gadgets, one by one. The contraption looked like a metal sea-urchin.

'This one for opening bottle. This one for filing your nail. This is a fork-and-spoon. And here was my favourite.' Major indicated a dull spike. 'It was for taking stone out of horses' hoof. A gentleman always needed that.'

'Wah, you went·riding at Jockey Club, hah?'

'Not exactly,' Major admitted. 'But you alway had to be prepare. First thing we learn that in the Boy Scout. And anyway you could take off a car wheel with it. Here, you can have a feel of it.'

Wallace hefted the knife and returned it gingerly.

Major pointed at the leg of his desk. 'I use the same knife to record my name for posterity there.'

Wallace was horrified. 'But that was very serious offence: destruction of government property. There were regulation. The chief clerk report it.'

Major clarified the parting in his hair with the horse spike.

Wallace realised he was looking at an independent man. 'You were your own boss,' he said.

Major nodded modestly. 'To all intensive purposes, yes.' He returned the knife to his bulging pocket. 'But I can see you already made your impression on Mr Allardyce. A fine man. He was my model in all thing. The true English gentleman.'

Major's admission emboldened Wallace. 'Major?'

'Hah? I mean yes?'

'If you didn't mind me asking...'

'Ask me anythings you wanted.'

'Well, Mr Allardyce wearing summer clothe but why you still were in winter clothe?'

Major was not at all ruffled. 'That was a good question, my dear fellow. The trouble was my English wardrobes didn't extend to this time of the year. I had my white pith helmet but you couldn't wear it indoor really. Mr Allardyce already ask me where he could buy one from. At the moment I had one pair of short and white stocking on order.'

'Ah, I see.' Wallace was full of admiration for the logic and aplomb of Major's reply. He returned to his desk feeling he had made a worthwhile friend.

Together they took to spending their tiffin hours wandering around the shopping arcades. Major was a knowledgeable and voluble guide. He showed Wallace the little shop where he bought his collars and studs. Through the dusty window they could see an old Englishman in a black jacket and striped trousers putting away his drawer-trays.

Wallace was flabbergasted. 'Eiyah! Englishman work in shop!'

Major was imperturbable. 'Yes, they had Englishmen serve in all the shop in England. You thought they import Chinese man to work for them?'

'You were right, Major. I just never thought about it. Now you mentioned it, I remember they had European waiter at one restaurant in the Central District here as well.'

When they were paid at the end of the month, the first thing Major did was to take Wallace to a jeweller's. Until then Wallace had allowed his pay to accumulate (Mr Poon had refused to take money for his board and lodging). Now Major's arguments convinced him of the need for a particular outlay.

'One of the first thing I notice about you, Wallace, and you make favourable impression except in this one thing, was you didn't have watch.'

Wallace looked uncomfortable. Watches bore unfortunate associations. 'I tell you the truth of it. I never felt the need for one,' he lied. 'You could always tell from the signal gun.'

Major shook his head pityingly. 'And when you were out of range? Or you had ear-ache? No, but that wasn't the point. A gentleman had to have one. How you knew the tiffin break was over, you had no watch?'

On show in the open-fronted shop were a variety of models, glinting in their velvet cases. Wallace was bewildered but Major chose for him. 'You didn't want one of those coolie type: all shiny and one month time all go black. No, sir, what I notice was that all the gentlemen wore them with cloth strap. Don't ask me why, they just did. Another thing, the watch they had was without seconds hand.'

Secretly, Wallace wanted one with an expanding metal bracelet. There was one like that in the jeweller's show-case with three bezels, heavy splashes of luminous paint on the dial, and a black case. But his resistance was feeble. 'I alway thought an airline pilot one was quite nice . . .' His voice trailed away under Major's severe gaze.

Back in the office, however, Wallace's disappointment was replaced by elation. The strap in red, white, and blue (the colours of the Union Jack, as Major pointed out) really went very well with his cream jacket. He worked through the afternoon with a straight back, his left arm resting upright on his desk, fingers on his temple, occasionally shooting the cuff of his writing hand to show his new acquisition to best advantage.

This behaviour, potentially swanking in anybody else, went unremarked in Wallace. He had rapidly become a licensed eccentric. His reputation was due more to his association with Major than any vagaries on his own part. He had moved from his old place to sit nearer to his friend. They were now separated by about fifteen feet of empty space. The cool draught from the fans and the humid in-coming air from the verandah mixed here, creating thermal quirks, miniature gusts that sent paper swirling off desks. It was thanks to this that Wallace and Major had the space to themselves. They took advantage of the air-currents to wing paper aeroplanes at each other when the Chief Clerk was out of the room. Wallace's were simple darts, folded a handful of times at their most ambitious, but Major's were works of art, revealing an instinctive grasp of sophisticated aerodynamic principles. He perfected one design, a diamond-headed bat-like shape, to the point where he could make it circle Wallace's head three times before gliding it back into his own in-tray.

Wallace was unable to compete with such an ingenious harrassment until the day he managed to intercept one of Major's squadrons (Major had taken to sending his planes in three at a time) by the brutal but positive expedient of standing on his desk and seizing one of the wingmen as soon as it came into technical violation of his airspace. This had been pragmatically designated as the area left undusted by the Indian sweeper in the morning. It extended about three feet outwards.

Major's protests were cut short as the chief clerk came back into the room. Wallace had, however, already hidden the aeroplane in a folder.

He smuggled it back to Robinson Path and puzzled over its construction in the fading light. He borrowed pencil and paper from the boys to draft a rough blue-print of his progress. At length the dissected aeroplane became a flat sheet of complexly creased paper. Wallace frowned and flexed his fingers. He used one of Mr Poon's newspapers as the material for some rough preliminary models. After a few abortive experiments he hit on a model that neither nose-dived nor spun but swooped swiftly and smoothly across the room.

The boys applauded. 'Homeworks first,' he chided them. But, encouraged by their appreciation, he made minor improvements of his own to Major's basic design. They amused themselves by sending plane after plane into the nullah until it grew too dark to see the pale shapes ghosting from the balcony into the water-course.

12

The rainy season had begun. Early in the afternoon huge drops, the size of a fifty cent piece, fell from a cloudless sky. It happened without preliminary of thunder or lightning. There was a pattering on leaves, a sudden darkening, then the deluge. The rain fell in stately white columns, winding and twisting in the wind.

Wallace arrived soaked at Robinson Path. He had been waiting with the other clerks in the entrance to the office when the Sikh nightwatchman had shut the building. The clerks were shouting to each other over the sound of rushing water but were still deaf. The road was flooding rapidly. The smaller drains were already choked with foliage. In front of the clerks deep puddles seethed in the downpour.

Wallace's new watch registered one minute after five. The Sikh slammed a long iron grill just behind them, making the runners scream in their grooves and striking showers of sparks in the darkness.

Major shouted in Wallace's ear: 'We got trouble now.'

The Sikh locked the last grill and advanced on the clerks. He had slung his shotgun over his shoulder so that the double-barrels were pointing at the ground.

Greatly daring, one of the smaller clerks shouted from the middle of the huddled group: 'I got my curry but no chicken for my pot.' He mimicked the deep voice of a mendicant Indian. Wallace and Major joined in the laughter.

Wallace said gleefully: 'Those greedy Indian say that to us in Macau too when they come round for tip. They were real crook.'

The clerks pressed closer together, sending one of their number on the edge into a large puddle. The water came over his ankles. He tried to get under shelter again but was unable to find a place. Cursing, he ran off through the downpour.

Wallace's laughter was cut short when he felt something uncomfortably hard in his ribs. He was about to protest to Major when he felt hot, spicy breath on his face. He found the Sikh's swarthy face thrust against his own. The man's fierce black beard prickled. He grasped Wallace by the lapels while his other hand depressed the gun butt. This had the effect of jamming the barrels into Wallace's flank. It was the unpleasant pressure he had felt.

Wallace smiled waterily. The Sikh grinned, an evil, slashing grin. The hole in his beard opened again. 'Such bad guns His Excellency gave us.' He spoke ruminatively. 'They are most unsafe.' He dug the muzzle into Wallace until he feared he had been transfixed. 'They are not even having proper safety-catches.'

Wallace started to wriggle. 'Any sudden movement could set those guns off. Any movement at all, in fact.' Wallace desisted. Behind him the crowd was melting away. 'One day there will be a most terrible accident.' The Sikh's voice was now almost hypnotic. Above the noise of the water, Wallace heard him cock both hammers one after the other. 'Understand me, punk?'

Wallace nodded vehemently.

'Good.' He released Wallace and jangled the keys on his belt. 'Now it is time the water rats are going home, I am thinking. Yes?'

The clerks needed no encouragement. Numerous indistinct shapes were already receding on the other side of the road.

Major had waited. They were soaked within seconds as they dashed up the hill in the direction of the Botanical Gardens. At the Peak Tram station they separated.

May Ling had hot tea waiting for him. She handed him her own towel when his own proved insufficient. He rubbed the harsh material over his back to warm himself with the friction.

Mr Poon returned a little later than usual. He was bone-dry. Outside it was raining more fiercely than ever.

Wallace was going to tell him about the Indian when Mr Poon gestured impatiently.

'The rain come. Time we entertain Allardyce.'

'Hah?'

'Yes, you tell him Mabel invite him. He would come.'

'I didn't understand you. What it had to do with rains or Mabel?'

'Yes, yes. You arrange, Wallace.' Mr Poon was now treating him as he would a fractious Westerner, countering Wallace's embarrassing fetish of the specific with a kind of insistent vagueness of his own.

Wallace gave in. 'OK, OK, I did what I was told then.'

Mr Poon passed his own glass of tea to Wallace. 'Good, son. Any time convenient to him also was convenient to us.'

May Ling spat bashfully onto Wallace's shoe. At the same time she giggled helplessly and averted her eyes, as if to mitigate the disrespect entailed in the act of expectoration. Wallace had explained to her that spit worked with wax to give shoes a lasting patina but May Ling still found the deed fraught with horrendous symbolical overtones. For once, Wallace would have wished her less subservient. When she turned her head a surprisingly generous mouthful of saliva arrived in his trouser turn-up.

This morning he had more important things to worry about. Such as whether he had correctly gauged Mr Allardyce's tastes in entertainment. Once Mabel's name had been mentioned, Allardyce had proved remarkably amenable. They were to meet him at the Star Ferry Pier at eleven o'clock in the morning of the public holiday. What was to ensue was a compromise, struck after long arguments between Mr Poon and Wallace. Mr Poon had not been keen on Western food. 'You always got hungry one hour after you were eating it,' he pointed out. 'Beside, the Westerner enjoy eating our Chinese chow for a change and you could alway make the joke with them about chopstick.' Where *gwai los* were concerned, Mr Poon's social repertoire was a limited one, built up painfully at successive commercial functions where experience taught that uncomfortable and mutually embarrassing silences were best avoided by the exchange of ponderous witticisms, proven successful in the past and rolled into the conversation as required. Mr Poon had been laughing with the same degree of insincerity about the same things for years. His stock of gambits, when time out was included for stage laughter, was just sufficient to see him through a meal and he had no intention of discarding any of his props.

A sea-food meal in one of the floating restaurants in the Aberdeen sampan shelter, followed by an excursion to a taxi-dancing hall or perhaps a discreet visit to one of the superior massage parlours: the Seasonal Playing Centre or the Red Apple Health Club. Such was his tried formula for efficient business entertaining.

Wallace was appalled at the thought of taking Mr Allardyce to a dance hall, let alone a massage parlour. 'He was English gentleman,' he protested, echoing Major. 'He was almost a hero in the war, too.'

Mr Poon snorted: 'Tcha! That Stanley Camp. They were like rat in there. I tell you they beg me for ...' And he halted on the verge of a major indiscretion.

In the end he let Wallace book a table at a European restaurant – the one with Western waiters – but he reserved the right to take his guest where he wished afterwards. 'You were dinner host, Wallace. I took over after.' Chuckling slyly, he added: 'You could spend what you like. Expense no consideration tonight. In fact the more the better. And why you didn't bring your friend from the office you tell me about?' Presented with this last, unlooked for concession, Wallace felt that it would be churlish to quibble about details.

Major arrived at the Star Ferry Pier before Allardyce. Wallace spotted him disembarking from a rickshaw. Major had directed the runner to put him off at the top of a taxi-rank. Oblivious to the tooting of horns behind him, he was paying the man with great composure. The rickshaw-puller, naked except for a loincloth and singlet, removed a white hat from his head and returned it to Major. Wallace signalled to him. Major waved back with his umbrella. It was the type made of oiled green paper, shaped like a coolie hat on a stick. It reeked of varnish.

'Major, I had pleasure in introducing you to my father-in-law.' Major infinitesimally adjusted the rake of his helmet. He was at his most punctiliously correct.

Mr Poon grunted, not uncompanionably.

Further ceremony was obviated by the arrival of the guest of honour.

'Mr Allardyce, sir, may I introduce you to my father-in-law, Mr Poon.'

'I was honour, Mr Allardyce.'

'How do you do, Mr Poon.' He nodded at Major. 'Chen. Ah yes, the elusive sola topee. It should soon be useful.' Major beamed with pride.

If Mr Allardyce was disappointed at the omission of Mabel from his reception committee, his good manners prevented him from looking round, too obviously, over the heads of his hosts.

Wallace bustled his little party along to the taxi-rank. The drivers, perched on the pavement railings, swore cheerfully at Major. His jaw tightened. Getting into the car, Major inadvertently poked Mr Poon in the eye with his umbrella.

Mr Poon was still rubbing his eye when they arrived at the Tiger Balm Gardens.

Wallace leapt out from the front seat to open Mr Allardyce's door for him. Allardyce was simultaneously releasing the handle for himself and Wallace's thoughtful gesture had the effect of catapulting him on to the pavement on his hands and knees. Wallace picked him up and anxiously beat his clothes for him. As it happened, it was the best thing he could have done. His 'little mishap' dissolved Allardyce's earlier stiffness. He became very jolly, examining his scuffed palms. 'No, no. I can assure you it's nothing to a man who has been through the hands of Japanese torturers.'

Mr Poon took him smoothly by the arm. 'Our common enemy, Mr Allardyce, and now with the Red, too. We Chinese, if I could be so bold to tell you, had nothing but utmost respect for your people behaviour in the Stanley Camp.' He guided the big European up the steep path, maintaining a constant flow of conversation.

Wallace paid the taxi-driver from the sizeable expenses Mr Poon had given him.

The constructor of the Tiger Balm Gardens, to whose patented anodyne both the sisters and May Ling were addicted, had been a noted philanthropist. This was quite apart from the relief, real or imagined, that the deceased's pungent balm had afforded to wincing millions all over Asia. The Gardens were his major memorial, along with a somewhat bigger Garden in Singapore, but they were only the most conspicuous embodiment of his charitable work. They were a favourite spot for parents to bring their children. The traditional Chinese mansion the endower had inhabited was near the entrance; it was open to the public on assigned days. The 'Gardens' themselves were a few acres of stunted trees and paths. The real attraction was the porcelain sculptures which were cunningly landscaped into the hillside. There were over a hundred of these, some life-size, others larger. The more mundane showed jugglers, motor-cars, beasts in sylvan and anthropomorphic contexts. These were somewhat leaden in execution and tended to be in drab colours. In competition with the Tiger Balm statues an amateur sculptor had recently won some notoriety by establishing a rival display of his own in a vacant lot opposite the Gardens. Manufactured out of papier-mâché, these had been more enthusiastically realised than their Garden equivalents and were brilliantly painted. The subject matter was commensurate.

For instance, the composition in front of Mr Poon and Allardyce showed a naked woman in the process of being devoured alive by a giant species of toothed snake or amphibious moray eel. One of the creatures had sunk its fangs into the cleft of the unfortunate woman's buttocks; another pair had latched on to her breasts in a brutal parody of suckling twins. The woman's mouth, unhinged in a mute scream, was filled with sweet wrappers and cigarette butts.

'Good God!' Allardyce said.

'It surprise me the first time,' Wallace admitted.

Allardyce, followed by Wallace and Major, gingerly skirted the sculpture in its unfenced pit. They avoided three small boys, brothers in identical shorts and shirts, who were trying to lob more wrappers into the woman's mouth. Mr Poon smiled benignly. He gave them a stick of gum to share, producing a battered packet of Wrigley's from his money-belt.

Wallace and Major, stringing reluctantly along after Allardyce, were already on the next tableau, two trussed victims watching a gang of devils eviscerate them with pitchforks. An ingenious fiend was garroting the men with glistening sections of their own intestines.

Mr Poon arrived, flagging Wallace urgently.

'That doesn't look too comfortable, does it?' Allardyce remarked conversationally. He had always rather prided himself on his powers of social recovery.

Wallace made a non-committal noise and prepared to lead the way up to the Gardens. His guest still mused before the sculpture. 'I wonder what type of double-dyed villain you had to be to end up like that? It's some scene from Taoist mythology, I presume, Nolasco?'

He had originally addressed his question to Major, who busied himself with his pipe. Mr Poon spat on to the path which was liberally greyed with pancakes of hardened gum.

'Yes, yes, that was what it was.' Wallace shuffled his feet. The local interpretation, revealing about its propagators although actually apocryphal, was that the tortured were foreign devils meeting a condign punishment: i.e. just for being *gwai los*.

Uncertain how he had offended his hosts, Allardyce continued uphill. They passed beneath the arch of the Tiger Balm Gardens proper, brushing aside three or four hawker women with their pannier baskets. After a steep ascent through petrified forest glades, deer and hippopotomi, they reached the summit of the hill. Here, at the top of the Gardens, were some panels of scenes from hell, picked out in miniature relief. The servants had brought Hogan here during a badly behaved phase in his early childhood. On the panels the damned were being tortured by fiends, indistinguishable in appearance from themselves, in a bleak early industrial landscape. A lorry, driven by a devil, had run over and almost severed the legs from the trunk of one of the unregenerate. Near this first torture, a woman had been seated on the mouth of a furnace chimney which belched flames and smoke. Someone else was having his head sawn in half. On the fringes of the frieze, fresh squads of apprehensive-looking sinners were arriving in hell from packed pick-up trucks.

After viewing several more scenes of what he still fondly imagined to be scenes from Chinese mythology, each progressively and incredibly more harrowing than the last, Allardyce was glad when they stopped for pickled carrots.

He said jokingly: 'Well, I don't know who'd make worse enemies, you or the Japs,' and was relieved when they laughed but with puzzlement in their laughter.

Major twirled his redundant umbrella, removed his sun-helmet, and wiped his forehead.

'Isn't it just?' Allardyce remarked sympathetically. Fearing his guest was becoming bored, Mr Poon prompted Wallace who said brightly: 'There was more.' Allardyce groaned loudly enough for Wallace to hear but levered himself to his feet.

They descended. Hidden by a grove of giant bamboos on the other side of the road was a menagerie, a commercial enterprise separate from the Gardens. Allardyce was shepherded towards this. A tattered eagle stared balefully at them through meshing and did not respond to Major's clucking encouragements. Wallace called up into a small, doll-sized pagoda. It was painted green with a red roof and was mounted on a pole about six feet high.

'Monkey not coming out,' Wallace informed Mr Poon, who beckoned over a group of beggar boys from the game of jacks they had been playing with pebbles. Money changed hands.

The urchins picked up their jacks and came nearer. A volley of stones rattled into the hutch. A terrified monkey shot out but was jerked short, throttling on a chain. The tallest urchin jabbed it with a long stick. It squealed and capered.

Even Mr Poon smiled. Wallace's innocent laughter spluttered into extinction, however, when he turned to share the fun with Mr Allardyce. The Englishman had a look of thunder on his face. He grabbed the stick from the holder and snapped it in two over his knee, beating the offender with the doubled segments. The other boys fled.

Allardyce was breathing heavily. 'Little blackguards.' He released his prisoner who raced away rubbing his back. The rest of Allardyce's mutterings were lost to Wallace. A vein throbbed thickly in Allardyce's temple. Wallace had never seen him so red, even after the longest of his tiffins. He shrank instinctively from the European, intimidated by his bulk and the rank odour generated by his exertions. Mr Poon and Major also took involuntary steps backward.

Wallace made an attempt to retrieve the situation, standing on tiptoe to pat the monkey which nipped his finger. He jerked the chain vindictively, caught Mr Allardyce's eye, smirked, and stroked the creature's tail. It bit him again.

'You understood the English better than anyone, Major,' he asked as he carefully rinsed his finger in the restaurant washroom. 'Why he got so hets up about just animal?'

Major nodded. He too was confused but had worked out an explanation during the uneasy taxi-ride into town. 'Well, it was like this. It was just monkey that was special. A dog they couldn't care less about or horse. But monkey was special to the English because it remind them of man. Those monkey crafty like anything. You did anything, it didn't matter how difficult, and they could copy you and do it.'

Major paused before continuing with the air of a truthful man who fully expects to be disbelieved: 'I also heard the English believing their ancestor was monkey. Yes, they did. In fact, you could say the boy just there stoning Mr Allardyce great-grandfather.'

'Ah.' The mists cleared.

They returned to where they had left Mr Poon and Mr Allardyce, at a table near the patio bar of the restaurant. They were just in time to see Mabel make her entry, flanked by waiters. The manager kissed her hand with a truncated flourish. Mabel had not troubled to halt or even slacken her pace to allow him to pay tribute but merely extended a long, glittering arm as she passed.

Allardyce leapt to his feet. Wallace almost expected him to salute. 'Mabel!'

'Brian!'

They looked at each other. Mabel gave a brittle laugh and patted her bun. 'So, it was long time no see, hah?'

Allardyce, a man transformed, smiled seraphically over Mabel's shoulder at nothing in particular.

Mr Poon greeted Mabel in standard, terse Cantonese form.

'No, no we spoke English all time tonight. For Brian benefit.' She touched Allardyce's arm lightly as he slid a chair beneath her. 'My, my. I must say this was the gorgeous restaurant. It was French or something?' She gave 'Fraynch' a sophisticated little upward inflection which Wallace noted for future use.

Mr Poon shrugged. 'Wallace knew.'

The manager came perspiring in his wing-collar, pencil poised. 'And so five altogether, lady and gentlemen?' He called to the nearest waiter: 'Giuseppe, cinque.'

Before Wallace could restrain him Major had seized the man by the throat and was shaking him furiously. 'You call me Chink, hah? You call me Chink?' He punctuated each question with an especially vigorous shake. A stud popped into the dish of peanuts on the glass table before them.

More waiters arrived and with their aid Wallace finally pulled Major away. His eyes were wild. Wallace picked up Major's pipe from the tiled floor. Bowl and stem were in different pieces. Major knocked them out of Wallace's hand again. 'I would not stay here to be make an insult.' He buttoned his jacket purposefully.

'No, no Major you must stay.'

Mabel shook her head vigorously at Wallace.

'Of course, if you were insisting, Major.'

At the door Wallace called into the street after him: 'See you at the office, friend.'

He returned with some foreboding but Mr Allardyce seemed to have already forgotten the disturbance. 'Who would have thought he was a Brian,' Wallace reflected to himself as he watched Allardyce squeeze lemon on to Mabel's fish for her. Mabel was behaving like a young girl. Gone was the grand lady Wallace had known. She squealed like Pippy. 'Eiyah, Brian! It gone all over your tie.'

'I daresay the regiment will consider it was in a good cause,' Allardyce responded gallantly but offered no resistance as Mabel dabbed at the stain with a lace handkerchief and then poked the souvenir into his breast-pocket. For all the attention they were paying the others they might have been enjoying an intimate supper at a separate table.

This appeared to suit Mr Poon. He was eating heartily. The rice and noodle dishes served by the restaurant were to his taste. He nodded commendingly to Wallace. Mabel's fish was already a skeleton.

The manager approached cautiously.

Mabel's face became aglow with fresh interest. 'They had good pudding these Westerner.' Her concentration deepened as she inspected the trolley. She tapped the confections of her choice with a taloned forefinger. 'And afterward, I would have fruits and cheeses.'

Wallace was unable to restrain himself. 'Wah, Mabel!'

She smiled brazenly. 'Alway I ate like tiger, hah, Brian?' She massaged his hand, keeping it there while she finished her profiterole.

Allardyce himself had made a poor meal, toying with each course for form's sake. Wallace, who had historical experience of Mr Poon's hospitality, which was tyrannical when it was not stinted, was surprised he had not foisted more food on his guest. So far, however, Mr Poon showed every sign of satisfaction.

Wallace turned to check on Allardyce and Mabel. Mr Allardyce was admiring Mabel's jewellery. She eased a ring off her thumb and showed it to him.

'That's a beauty, Mabel.'

'Very expensive, Brian. Jade, you know. We Chinese say it was the stuff the boy dragon give the girl dragon when they got together and make the baby but it fall on ground and go hard: then it became jade.'

Mr Allardyce looked a little taken aback. 'Really, Mabel. Do you think you ought to say such things?'

Mabel laughed gaily. She dabbed her fingers in a bowl of iced water without troubling to remove her jewellery and dried them on a loose fold of the table-cloth. Neither the heavy meal she had just taken nor the heat seemed to have impaired her vivacity. Coyly, she suggested: 'Coffees at my house?'

Wallace opened his mouth and then shut it as Mr Poon grunted approval. He prepared to summon the waiter but Mabel forestalled him, delving into her sequined purse. 'You were on me tonight, boys.'

Mr Allardyce said angrily: 'No, no. Don't be ridiculous,' and tried to seize the bill which Mabel fluttered playfully just out of his reach. 'You are being a silly boy, Brian.'

Allardyce subsided.

The manager, who had been watching anxiously, relieved Mabel of the reckoning.

She walked through the busy, flickering streets with her arm through Allardyce's, trailed at a discreet distance by her ostensible hosts. In the pack they lost sight of her but Mr Poon did not falter. As they climbed the streets grew darker and emptier. Ahead Mabel and Allardyce waited for them outside a tower block of modern flats. They mounted in a lift walled with mirrors, which showed Wallace that his eyes were bloodshot and his complexion muddy. The lift whined smoothly to a halt and they stepped straight into a room.

Wallace was far too shocked to breathe the 'Wah' Mabel clearly expected as her due but she seemed satisfied with his unaffected hiss. Mr Poon, on the other hand, coolly appropriated the only chair in the room, leaving a pair of battered pouffes to the other men. Mabel unplugged a shining coffee-maker which had been bubbling in a vast expanse of bare floor, deftly twisting the lid and ejecting a mound of pulped grounds. She brought the dark, viscous concoction to the men in three mother-of pearl cups which were ready on a lacquer tray. Her movements were precise and economical. She ministered rather than merely served them. Then she went to sit on the floor with her head resting against Allardyce's knees and absent-mindedly moulded the grounds into pellets, while Wallace wondered where the Tonochy Dance Hall entered into Mr Poon's plans.

'Musics?' Mabel suggested. She slipped a record into a modern-looking gramophone, which apart from the scanty furniture was the room's only adornment.

Allardyce, in his trance, was oblivious to what the others said or did. His eyes followed Mabel dully around the room.

Wallace finished his coffee but found it bitter. Staring around him with open curiosity, he noticed a spiral stair-case at the end of the long ill-lit room. Mabel answered his unspoken question. 'Yes, altogether I had three floor of this building. The lift stopping on this floor. Upstair my husband was . . . resting.'

There was a curious smell, at once acrid and sweet. Mabel put a match to the coffee grounds. She laughed when it spluttered out.

The gramophone clicked itself off and Mr Poon interpreted it as an opportune cue to leave. Wallace obeyed his peremptory summons. 'Thank you for lovely evening, Mabel.'

Still reclining, she tittered. 'No, no. You forgot. It was me who was *your* guest.' But she did not append any thanks or rise and Wallace edged discreetly away. As he and Mr Poon waited for the lift, making a great show of pressing and re-pressing the button, pretending they were already outside in a vestibule, Wallace stole a backward glance. Allardyce sat alone on the pouffe. His mouth hung slightly slack. Mabel was tinkering with something that rattled in the corner underneath the gramophone. The coffee-maker was where she had abandoned it in the centre of the room.

13

Department was busy for the first time since Wallace had known it. From a typing pool, newly created on the verandah, the efficient clatter and ring of the girls' machines came as a cheerful sound. With the pattering of the rain outside, the noise had a soothing effect, concentrating the attention. The chief clerk presided over an animated scene. The clerks worked furiously. Each had an unstable hummock of forms on his desk, kept at a uniform level by constant additions to the pile. Even the man with no pen had found himself a stump of pencil.

It had been raining continuously since the outing. Every morning Mr Poon would switch the wireless on and smile to himself as he listened to reports of flashfloods in the New Territories, their toll of ravaged crops and drowned livestock, and the latest landslides and subsidences on the island itself. The most dramatic of these had occurred half-way up the Victoria Peak where a large section of Magazine Gap Road had collapsed, leaving a wide orange gash on the mountain.

The landslide was visible to Wallace as he worked at his desk by the open French windows to the verandah. He could see ant figures moving over the cut. It was astonishing how fast they closed the lips of the giant wound on the hillside. Wallace imagined the wilderness of mud and splintered timber and the curious carrion reek; it was all so deceptively neat from a distance. The road had collapsed a few days after the day out with Mr Allardyce. The contract for its repair had been drafted from the office. Wallace had dragged his feet over this at first but Mr Poon's newly bland manner had concealed a threat. Or so it seemed to Wallace. The trouble was, apparently, even taking Mr Allardyce out in the first place had been a technical misdemeanour. 'Now you were telling me,' Wallace thought bitterly but restrained himself from saying. Mr Poon's words came back to him: 'Expense no consideration tonight. In fact the more the better.' And then there had been the unexpected invitation to Major. Feeling himself on treacherous ground, Wallace temporarily put speculation about Mr Poon's plans and motives out of his head.

He drafted the road repair contract for Mr Allardyce to sign.

Wallace's part was purely clerical: drawing up the pink form and its pale-blue copy after the Department model. But his initials, he was disturbed to find, appeared on the reference code at the top of the form. Mr Poon was nowhere mentioned. The company getting the work was Mr Yip's, Mabel's husband.

Allardyce duly signed. There was no trouble there. Wallace went into the frosted glass cubicle, under the penetrating scrutiny of the Chief Clerk, and shoved the form under the Englishman's nose. He even put a pen in Allardyce's hand and with a finger indicated the place. A shaky signature but it sufficed.

Wallace had enjoyed plenty of time to prepare the contract. Mr Allardyce had been several days away from work. He had finally appeared in the office late one afternoon. Since then he had been withdrawn. He appeared completely uninterested in what was going on around him in the office. His ruddiness had been replaced by an equally pronounced pallor, a dirty white of the same shade of off-ness as the faces of the devils at the Tiger Balm Gardens. Strangely enough, his walk seemed steadier to Wallace and there were no more clinkings from his office.

Major was not talking to Wallace. Even without the burden of extraordinary work, it was doubtful whether aeroplanes would have bridged the gap between their desks. At first Wallace thought Major's disgruntlement might have been caused by the weather. This hope faded after Major rebuffed his overtures.

Wallace had decided that what he had to say should be propitiatory but oblique. Furthermore, his opening remark should encourage Major to mount one of his favourite hobby-horses.

He cleared his throat. Major did not look up. Wallace was forced to call over. 'Not just the coincidence, hah?'

Major glared at him.

'The weather, I meant.' Wallace touched his matted hair ruefully. 'They must have know it was the Queen Coronation the day we went out and they stop the rain.'

'Who was "they"?' Major demanded truculently. 'And what the hell it matter it was the Queen birthday or the day she get crown? She was a person just like you or me.'

Wallace spent a solitary tiffin in the small, over-crowded canteen. He amused himself by tracing his initials on a steamy window-pane. Condensation trickled down and effaced them as soon as he had removed his finger.

Under these circumstances leaving Department was not the painful severance it might have been. The increasingly earnest office atmosphere, the effacement of Mr Allardyce, and the obtrusive hegemony of the chief clerk were definitely less to Wallace's liking. He hankered after the old care-free days.

There was no fuss with the police. A tip-off from Mr Poon's contacts forestalled that kind of unpleasantness. Wallace supposed Mr Poon's informants to be reliable; they had certainly done well to anticipate whatever trouble there was going to be. There had been, for instance, no clue in Mr Poon's Chinese newspaper, normally so quick to scent matters of this kind. Nor had there been a hint in the editorial columns of the Communist daily, in which a fierce campaign against abuses in the colonial 'bureaucracy' was being waged. Wallace had continued to handle work in the office; he was even being given more responsible assignments.

Nevertheless, he was alarmed.

Mr Poon was calm and sympathetic, a tower of strength in the crisis. He had seated himself on the lion-throne in the reception room to break the news to Wallace. He made Wallace sit on a footstool while he explained the situation to him. Wallace's mouth opened and shut like a grouper in a restaurant tank. Seeing his son-in-law's reaction, Mr Poon had been quick to emphasise that Wallace was not directly involved. 'But it could be . . .' Mr Poon chose his word, 'embarrassing, hah? Your initial on the form, like you say. I would tell them your relative in Macau ill and you went away. Then a little later I gave them your notice.'

Wallace licked his lips nervously.

'Actually only Mr Yip and maybe Mr Allardyce involve. I suppose they might go and fine Mr Yip but no one go and put sick man like Mr Yip in Stanley Prison. He didn't have to worry.'

'Mabel getting into trouble?'

Mr Poon laughed. 'Mabel only his wife. Only Mr Yip name was written. She safe. Like you, Wallace. But maybe you better have holiday, hah? Just in case. Then you could come back when it had all been forgotten. I wrote you letter when. Already I make arrangement for you.'

Wallace levered Mr Poon's thumb up and made a fist around it. 'Uncle.'

Mr Poon patted him kindly on the head. 'You took May Ling with you as well. You would be staying in country village. No one knew you were there. Right at the other end of the New Territory. No road, only ferry boat took you there. It was not my own family village but I had house there. When it would be OK to come back I would send message to you.'

Wallace felt the need to lie down. As he was going, Mr Poon called out: 'And Wallace.' He turned obediently. 'I don't think you knew how much our family were loving you.'

Wallace swallowed a lump. Through watery eyes he thought he saw a shadow or a small animal in the corridor. When he blinked there was nothing.

Part Two

1

A mountain protected the village. It was not a particularly tall mountain, even by the standards of the colony. The smallest of the Nine Dragons, for instance, the uneven, serrated ridge of peaks that gave the British enclave on the mainland its name of Kowloon, would have dwarfed it. Really, it was only the most ambitious of a range of aspiring foothills to the north of the Dragons, but its prospect was unrivalled.

From the grassy plateau that was the summit, it was possible to see as far into Communist territory as British. There was little to tell between the two jurisdictions: the Border was a brown river flowing stolidly through a plain of paddy-fields, identical on each side. At night it was just, only just, possible to make out a glow of reflected lights from the city bounced off the nearest of the Nine Dragons. By day there was nothing.

The New Territories began thirty miles away without warning. Buses, after jerking their way through the peeling tenements of Mong Kok, submerged at reckless speed, roared out of a tunnel, spiralled around a steep ramp cut into granite cliffs, wound around a wooded reservoir, and were suddenly surrounded by ancient fields. There were no suburbs, no preliminaries. Town rudely became countryside. And it was countryside of the most intractable sort, diligently cultivated but cut into the hillsides at crazy angles, formidably manured, irrigated by complex canals to depths in which a child could drown. Carp swam in these fields and the roads ran like causeways above the dank, malodorous cultivation. After a while the invading roads petered into buffalo tracks. One such path wound three miles from the nearest highway, over the scrubby hillsides, to the mountain.

The village itself lay in a depression, shaped alarmingly like the mouth of a volcano, which was contoured into the mountain's landward flank. It gave the settlement a deceptive air of impermanence, as if it were liable at any moment to be spewed incandescent into the valley. Despite what topology suggested, the site had been continuously inhabited for over a thousand years. The network of families who inhabited the village – a clan bearing a universal surname

– took pride in tracing their lineage through to the common ancestor who had founded the settlement a millenium ago. This was a feat characterised more by ingenuity than scrupulousness. Technically, the bulk of the population were usurpers, although of a standing of more than three centuries. Clues to the original trespass persisted in the extent of the village's fortifications. Most New Territories settlements were surrounded by a wall, or at least its ruins, with perhaps an iron gate and in some cases a moat as well. The village exceeded the conventional quota of defences. It was possible to make out the ruins of two walls, with another still more or less standing. There was also a trench, now just a shallow depression, a puddle in the rainy season, which had (according to alternative oral legend) variously contained combustible straw or daubed bamboo spikes. For, once, pirates had preyed on the coast. To the extent that the Imperial government had declared an evacuation of the coastal area, defined within a perimeter of 50 *li* from the sea. The original inhabitants had been forcibly removed, but undeterred either by piratical depre-dations or the proscription of the Canton administration, squatters had moved in. When the owners had returned in depleted numbers a decade later, they had accepted the accomplished fact. Force deployed against the defences reared in their absence would have been pointless. Genealogies had been manipulated and the two groups had located a focal but mythical ancestor in the tenth generation: a sensible compromise.

The village and its defences had never been tested by pirates, which piece of good fortune the villagers had attributed to the beneficent *fung shui* or spirit of the neighbourhood. Geomancers had identified this as a rampant but avuncular dragon near whose forehead the village was by chance or design situated: the eyes to be found by drawing a straight line through a pair of distant peaks which would bisect the village exactly: the protective coils of the creature winding symmetrically round the mountain, culminating in a potent twist on the plateau. In other words, the village was invisible from the sea.

The energy spent in fortifying the village had not been expended, however, in vain. Pirates and brigands were an episodic threat; other villages were a constant menace. The invariable state of affairs between neighbouring settlements was rivalry; each had its particular feuds. The village had been engaged in a vendetta, started by an irrigation dispute somewhere around the time of the Tai Ping rebellion, the details of which were lost in time, against a Hakka settlement seven miles up the valley. The Hakkas, 'guest people', had arrived in the area a few centuries ago. Shortly before the colonial authorities had assumed control of the area, an exceptionally sanguinary battle had been fought in which men of the Hakka village had laid hands on an ornamental cannon, harnessed water buffaloes to it, and fired fearsome home-made grape-shot into the village. Souvenirs of this engagement (three shot had embedded themselves intact in the mud walls) were kept in the chief of the village's five ancestral halls. Conveniently breached in places to allow the passage of carts, the single standing wall still held the thick-roofed houses in a loose embrace. In more modern history (this was a few years before the Japanese Occupation) it had again proved useful against the Hakka foe who on the contemporary occasion had contented themselves with a purely ritual defiance, hurling threats and pulpy, unsavoury missiles over the wall. Both sides had behaved as if the wall were solid masonry, carefully ignoring the existence of the holes. The only safe place during the lobbed bombardment had, in fact, been before the apertures.

The latest immigrants to the settlement had come by ferry. The railway ended in a small market town some miles short of the village. Hoping to confuse possible pursuers, Wallace had decided to disembark at the ferry's penultimate stop; although even the last left a three hour walk along the deserted sand beaches of this remote coast.

The stubby little paddle-steamer had been full of coolies, plastered against the sides of wide-slatted lorries, on their way to the new highway that was being driven from an isolated jetty in a circle back to the city. As the ferry glided into the shallow bay over the rubble clearly visible on the bottom, a gong had clanged, echoing hollowly over the water. Far above the gaggle of sheds on the beach a grey and orange geyser had streaked into the void, blossoming at its summit. The crash reached Wallace as the debris bounced off the hillside, crushing trees and bushes in its path. The whiff of cordite drifted over the water. Wallace had been watching with a professional interest, pointing details out to May Ling. She had laughed defiantly: 'It was only the little bang!' Then, as a hooter sounded, the coolies had driven down the gang-plank, the scratching ignitions of their lorries taking one by one.

At the next stop, there were stares as they disembarked. The village formerly served by the stop had long been depopulated and abandoned. The settlement was now used by the army as a firing-range. Wallace looked dubiously at the black skull-and-crossbones signs on the little wharf, but swung Fong's cardboard case over the side with more decision than he felt. A tanned sailor held May Ling's wrists as she dropped awkwardly onto the planks.

They watched the steamer and its broadside of inquisitive faces skew away. The wheels churned, seeming to get a grip on the unresisting water; then the boat picked up speed, leaving two white rods as its wake.

It was a long, exhilarating walk. The damp sand was hard yet bouncy underfoot, lending a spring to the stride. They took it in turns to carry the light case and were able to spot smoke rising from the mountain-side just as the sun was setting over the sea.

2

Their house was near the walls, in one of the outermost of the settlement's six wards, each of successively later foundation, fanning out in concentric order of seniority and inter-connected by a maze of alleys. In all but one of the wards there was an ancestral hall with its tablets commemorating the dead generations. The major hall was located in the centre of the depression. In addition to ancestral tablets it housed boarded inscriptions celebrating the scholastic attainments of the community's distinguished dead.

The village was not Mr Poon's own birth-place. He had come from a community now over the Border, in Communist territory. Closure of the frontier and a subsequent embargo on trade with the Reds had disrupted the marketing practices of the entire New Territories. Most of the village's produce, for instance, had gone to a large market town over the river and subsequently beyond access on the Chinese bank.

Mr Poon had bought his house as an outsider. This was a flagrant violation of the clan code and had caused mutterings at the time. But custom was a waning force and the headman, who owned the property, had been able to ignore the disapproval of the more stick-in-the-mud elders on the village council. The house, situated next to a Chinese sausage factory (odoriferous) and behind a small Buddhist convent (unlucky), was an otherwise unsaleable property. Before the war such a transfer would have been unthinkable but many old ways had fallen into disuse during the Japanese Occupation. Feasting, around which most of the ancestral rites were based, had not been possible during these years of hardships although some long-defunct ceremonies had been recovered after the war when an Australian anthropologist had been able to reveal to the ritual headman, amongst other pieces of lore, what the strange domino-like markings on the older ancestral tablets represented.

Mr Poon had never been to the house; he had bought it as a kind of insurance against possible unspecified urban disasters. Now, as he had always expected, he had found a use for it.

The building was typical of those built immediately after the British annexation of 1898. It was simple to the point of starkness, the walls

107

poured in a crude mixture of lime, mud, and burnt shells. The roof, made up of overlapping green tiles, was the only extravagance. Seen from the air the housetops looked like a dragon's coiled, scaly back. There was an open cock-loft upstairs for pigs or hens and one room below for living and sleeping, with a recess for stove and pots. The alley separating the terrace from the row of habitations opposite was about five feet wide. Wallace could have toppled from his front door into his neighbour's living quarters. Granite benches had been let into the walls of the houses. Through use these seats had been buffed to the sheen and texture of glass. The old women had a monopoly of their use and would pass the whole day there, smoking water-pipes, gossiping, and eating sweets. At the end of the alley was a brass water-tap, a major social focus for the young women and marauding packs of village dogs.

The newcomers were able to settle themselves in without fuss. The villagers barely noticed them. They had arrived at an opportune moment. The rice cycle was at a crucial stage: at perhaps the most important juncture in the peasant's calendar. The first crop would soon be harvested; the second, germinating in the nursery beds, awaiting transplanting to paddy, was under intensive preparation.

Wallace and May Ling were only the newest additions to a ward of recent arrivals. There was no ancestral hall here, the inhabitants playing little part in the traditional life of the settlement. The heads of families were men from other villages who had married daughters of the lineage but were themselves excluded from membership of the clan. Formerly substantial land-owners, they had left their natal villages when the Communists had taken power. Now they lodged on suffrance. They cultivated vegetables or kept poultry. These were ignominious modes of agriculture, scorned by rice-cultivators. The villagers rented out sandy land on high ground to the immigrant farmers. Low terrain would have been more suitable. Naturally, the newcomers had no voice in the running of the village.

They had grown beyond an embarrassment into a major threat to the stability of the settlement. They were both a nuisance and a tool for the headman. When they first arrived three years ago he had hoped to use them against his traditional enemies in the village. But things had not quite worked out that way. Now he had two groups of trouble-makers where before there had been one.

★

The headman's position was basically unassailable. He owed his present strength to the Japanese who had formally instituted the post of headman where before the war he had been merely the most influential member of the village council. On returning, the colonial administration had retained him in the post. His influence had grown. As well as having powers of probate, he meted out rough justice to wrong-doers. Bodies would occasionally be found in road-side ditches miles away from the village. The government turned a blind eye to these judicial murders. Fiercely independent, the New Territories people were due to revert to the jurisdiction of China shortly before the end of the century, according to the terms of the lease of 1898.

Under the Manchu empire the headman's family had supplied generations of scholar-administrators. Over the years they had gained control over numerous segments of the richest clan lands. The headman had added to an already comfortable income by conniving in the clandestine trade carried on over the Border with the Reds. Along with his henchmen he controlled the political economy of the entire village.

By a process of skilful delegation, including the institution of countervailing checks against the more ambitious of his associates, he was able to live a life of leisure such as his forebears had enjoyed. Occasionally he varied the regime of village life by paying a visit to the concubine he had installed in the market town.

His single major enemy was the proprietor of the village tea shop, which doubled as a gaming house. The owner was a corpulent individual in stained apron and greasy clothes. He was a total contrast to the headman, a spry but dignified figure with his grey, stringy moustache and neat tunic suit and cloth shoes. Besides revenue from gamblers, amongst which number the headman was occasionally included, the tea shop owner was also head of the night watch. Those wishing to enter this organisation of village security had to purchase office from him. Thereafter he drew a percentage of the protection money they collected. This ranged from moneys paid to the watchmen for *not* beating their gongs every hour during the night, as they were supposed, to conventional tips given at the major festivals.

Any advantage the tea shop owner derived from his headship of the night watch was purely financial. The watchmen were a neutral force, composed of adherents from both camps. As well as defending against possible invaders, the watchmen also acted as the village police force. They would punish minor infractions of the community code with a light beating with bamboo poles. Those chastised were unable to harbour a grudge as their heads were placed in a sack as a preliminary to punishment at the hands of unidentifiable assailants.

Although unable to exert political leverage in his position as titular head of the only cohesive armed force in the village, the owner of the tea shop had been able to make capital out of a string of reverses the village had suffered in various spheres since the war. The slump in fortunes had been most noticeable scholastically. Learning was no longer, as it had been in the old days, the avenue to political power. But the poor examination results gained by the younger generation of villagers had compared unfavourably with the success of candidates from the Hakka village. Crops had been poorish, there had been a resurgence of mosquitoes, and a spate of stillborn children. Most sinister of all, shrines to minor earth gods and water spirits on the village boundaries had been curiously desecrated. At the insistence of the headman (who had flattered himself that he denied his enemy a chance to make propaganda here) the nightwatchmen had mounted a vigil but had not been able to catch the culprits. In the morning, stones had been found dislodged from the cairn they had guarded.

Despite all efforts made by the headman to stamp on panicmongers, the old women began to circulate stories of evil spirits. By now the headman had resigned himself to the expense of a major exorcism to be undertaken by Taoist priests or Buddhist monks. He planned the ceremony for the month after the harvesting of the second rice crop. This was a traditionally difficult time of year for the headman when the rice farmers had abundant time to make life awkward for the rulers of the settlement at village councils or assemblies in the ancestral hall – only supposing incentive was provided. The charge for the exorcism would be met by the headman himself, who was nothing if not astute. He consoled himself with the thought that the village would have been due for one of its minor exorcisms, held every ten years, in the near future.

3

The first nights were not easy. The very casualness of their arrival and induction contributed to Wallace's anxiety. He felt like a trespasser in the musty old house and waited to be evicted in the night. Ridiculously co-existing with and feeding this fear was another, contradictory, obsession: that his presence had been forgotten or not remarked at all. There would be fire, earthquake, a tidal wave; the house would collapse, burying the two of them, and no one the wiser to their plight. Wallace would rap on the wooden bed with agitation and then the knocking would remind him that the headman had installed that dolorous couch on their behalf. Until now he would never have imagined that a bed could be less forgiving than the spartan canvas contraptions at Robinson Path. Now they seemed almost decadent. A prickly straw mat, thin as paper, was the only padding between his body and the hard timber. It added an irritation to, rather than subtracted from, the general level of discomfort. And the porcelain pillow was the last word in refined perversity: a monstrous entrapment.

It was noisy, too, in the countryside. So much for those lying poems the boys did for their brush-stroke exercises. When the cicadas stopped their rasping early in the evening, the frogs began to croak. Once they had desisted long enough to encourage a degree of somnolence in their audience, they would begin to croak again with enhanced enthusiasm. Wallace was able to resign himself more easily than May Ling. He drew consolation from the effect that his balancing of the pros and contras of their situation had on her, precluding as it did from the existence of frogs the presence of rats. This made it impossible for May Ling to sleep at all. She kept imagining a large black rodent nibbling at her feet in the darkness. Then, one night a week, the Buddhist nuns would organise gambling amongst themselves. The slap and crack of their dominoes and starling-like twittering of their voices carried over the alley as Wallace cursed and turned.

And at dawn a rooster crowed, shatteringly.

Eldest Sister's anti-social ablutions palled by comparison.

There were also smells. Mercifully, these seemed to be at their strongest in the day. Evil fumes issued from the adjoining sausage factory. Wallace suspected the final pork product of being heavily compounded with unmentionable substances. The shrivelled red bundles of tough meat, speckled with creamy knots of fat, hung like leprous penises on lines at the side of the factory.

Stronger than the smell of the sausages – omnipresent – was the odour of the fields. The manure was made up in unequal proportions of night soil and rotting fish. The human leaving was the most important component in the formula. It was zealously collected and re-applied to the paddy in an endless cycle. It was, in fact, the basis of the entire rural economy.

As the wind blew, the smells could be ripe, sharp, sour, or even sweet and sour. When it was calm, the different odours lay in zones. There was a thick belt on the lower levels of the hillside, near the flat paddy and the larger terraces. This smell seemed to lie solidly on the palate, almost a taste in the mouth. Higher up, most noticeably on the walls, the smell was thinner, rancid, apprehended through the nose. Curiously, it was more offensive than the richer stinks of the valley.

Wallace sniffed the warm air cautiously when they first scaled the village walls for the view.

This was panoramic to the point of artificiality; it might have been a scroll-drawing. The morning sun glinted off water as straw-hatted figures moved in bowed lines, never straightening. In the far distance only the massive sixty foot brick watchtowers of the rival village could be seen. (The Hakkas' system of village defence operated on a different principle: the eagle as opposed to the porcupine.) The fields were neat squares except where they followed the contours of the river. Some of the divisions were a brilliant green, others a deep chocolate. They resembled a checker-board or a much-patched garment: and indeed the rice had the effect of binding and conserving the silty, ancient soil. The contrasting colours of the fields were not noticeable from the ground. It was a transformation and contrast that came with height. From the level of the nursery terraces, even, the shoots were thin on the paddy, almost invisible against the grey water. It was possible to make out fish swimming in the stocked ponds, dark, mobile patches in the soupy water.

'You never would live to be old in the city.'

May Ling wrinkled her nose rebelliously. 'Poo! All their ar-ar I could smell!'

112

Wallace said severely: 'It grew the rice we ate.'

Nevertheless, he had been breathing stertorously through his mouth. Now he tried to disguise this from May Ling.

'What was the raise-up little field down there?'

The seedlings were almost ready for transplanting from the nursery beds. During the last three weeks they had been densely fertilised with a particularly concentrated mixture to a point well beyond the threshold of olfactory tolerance of any city-dweller.

Wallace equivocated. Following the rebuke he had just administered to May Ling, he was not keen on having to live up to his own standards. 'The baby rice grew there before they put it in field,' he answered uneasily.

'We could see?'

'Er. Maybe they would get angry, hah?'

'Why they would get angry, Wallace?'

'Maybe they think we wanted to pull it up or drop poisons in.' A scrap from the *Reader's Digest* came to him. 'You knew how animal got fierce about their baby. Same thing.'

May Ling was not satisfied. 'Silly, Wallace. Wah, look they took it out now.'

Three women in black pyjama suits and straw hats had arrived with short hoes, terminating in sharp-looking crescent heads. They began to lever some of the young plants out, with what even from a distance, could be seen as extreme gentleness.

'Look! Soon they would put it in field, Wallace.'

'How you knew that, May?'

'Old women outside house were telling me.'

'Ah.' Wallace did not like her pert manner. The reply had smacked of smart-alecry and he did not care for her forming associations behind his back. It was impossible to say anything, though. He glanced imperatively at his watch. 'OK, time we go.'

'Going where, Wallace? You didn't have anythings to do here.'

'You didn't mind where, May.' He seized her grimly by the elbow and frog-marched her down the slope to where the wall ended in one of its abrupt gaps.

'Eiyah! You hurting me, Wallace.'

Appeased, he released her. She rubbed her biceps ostentatiously on the way down. At the main gate a group of naked children – some with a string around the navel – surrounded them. They stared solemnly. The boys pulled their uncircumcised tassels reflectively. Growing bolder, some of the older children tried to touch May Ling. Wallace shooed them away. May Ling smiled as they continued their stroll; she enjoyed being a focus of attention.

While the territory was still new to him, Wallace took May Ling on rambles beyond the village walls, over the green hills. The highlands were still the home of wild animals, of species almost extinct elsewhere in the colony: barking deer and wild pigs included although tigers and leopards were no longer among them. They followed old tracks and pathways. Occasionally, they came across rocks which had been daubed with blood and chicken feathers or had clumps of half-burnt joss-sticks stuck in the soil. Wallace surreptitiously crossed himself as they hurried past these.

The countryside became familiar to them. One day Wallace decided to strike out on a slightly longer expedition, to the very margin of village lands. The longest possible walk lay on the east side, so far unexplored by them. The boundary here was five miles away, marked by a thick grove of giant bamboos. On the other side was Hakka land. The boundary had once lain at a large, lichen-covered rock a mile beyond; before that, it had been a half-mile back at a small stream. These shifts in location reflected the balance of power between the settlement and the Hakkas. The current position had remained unchanged since before the war when the villagers had been able to advance their claims, following an alliance with the fierce Man villagers (symbolised by a gift of mildewed leather armour from the village and a reciprocating visit to the village by the Man's Lion dance team at the lunar New Year).

But after the war, when the village's luck had started to deteriorate, some mysterious incidents at the boundary had resulted in the villagers voluntarily remaining well behind the old markers.

Wallace held May Ling's hand as they picked their way over the flat rocks in the fast-flowing stream. May Ling hurried over; she knew a flashflood had come roaring down the dried course some years ago and drowned a group of village children. She was relieved to pass this small obstacle, so innocuous-looking now.

They had bought cold pork dumplings and preserved black eggs with fiery yolks at the tea shop. They ate these in the shade of a tree, cracking the eggs with difficulty on the yielding bark of the trunk. They pressed on with renewed vigour until, coming over a hillock, a wall of green poles appeared before them.

'Better go back, hah, Wallace?'

He nodded. 'OK. But first I got two walking stick for us.'

She clapped her hands. 'Good. But you thought you were strong enough to break it?'

'You bet I was.'

As he seized the nearest bamboo with both hands and threw his weight on it, turning his back to get better leverage, he was struck lightly on the shoulder. He grinned to himself. 'You wait till I had this big stick.'

Something else struck him on the knee and immediately afterwards a cloud of missiles, stones, fruit, nuts came out of the thicket, clattering against the brittle bamboos.

'What the . . .' They retreated to the top of the hillock. There were a few rustlings in the bamboos. Wallace thought he saw something, then all was still in the grove.

'Real strange. Maybe there was some Hakka children or animal hide in there.'

'No, no, Wallace. What animal could learn to throw thing? It was evil spirit.'

'Well, he was sure a good shot if he was.'

He stared at a peeled banana lying on the turf of the clearing.

'You got mess on your trouser, Wallace.' May Ling knelt and wiped the remains of a squashed persimmon off the cuff with her handerchief.

At home a slight, but persisting, sense of unease did not prevent Wallace from enjoying his first night of sound sleep since their arrival.

By now they were adjusting to the routines of the village. They retired shortly after dark and rose early. Mr Poon had been generous with Wallace's expenses. In the day they had enough money to indulge themselves with what delicacies they pleased at the tea shop. May Ling cooked in the evening. Every day she went to a stream with the other wives and beat her husband's wet laundry between stones. Afterwards she lounged on a warm granite bench in the alley and listened to the stories the old women told.

One of her favourites concerned the wife of a headman who, kidnapped by pirates a century ago, killed herself to save her husband the price of a ransom.

May Ling liked, in turn, to entertain her husband with these tales after they had eaten. He listened avidly, even to those he found too fantastic to believe. Such as her account of the rise and fall of the chief families in the village.

Apparently, there had once been a slave class in the community. Whole families had been born into and died in this form of bondage. The beginnings of the system went back to the time of the Tang emperors. At some unspecified point in the evolution of the lineage, roles had been reversed. The slave families had somehow enriched themselves, bought their freedom, land, and prospered inordinately. At length they started to employ descendants of their former masters as servants. The owner of the tea shop was said to have come from such a servile family. The ritual headman, an impoverished frail old man, dependent on alms, fed at festivals (it was a wonder to Wallace how he had survived the Occupation) came from a line said to be related to the Tangs themselves.

Wallace scoffed. 'You think the big-shot go and let themself be took over like that? May, you must be more stupid than I thought. You thought I could make myself boss of your father house just like you were saying? Thing just didn't ever happen like that.'

May Ling was quite obstinate. 'No, it could happen.'

Wallace could not be bothered to argue the point. He found it amusing how prickly May Ling could be sometimes. 'OK, May, have it your ways.'

4

Since the big rains of a few months ago it had been hot and dry. The air was clear and although the sun was far fiercer than it had ever been in the city the effect was nowhere near as debilitating. They developed tans, richer than those of the field-workers. As a joke at first, they took to wearing straw Hakka hats fringed with black cloth and found they enabled them to move, even at midday, without discomfort.

Then the weather turned.

After a bright morning, as clear as any of its predecessors, the afternoon began thick and humid. May Ling who had been energetic, sweeping throughout the house, suddenly drooped. Her lassitude infected Wallace. He joined her on the bed. It supported his back reassuringly. He stretched, careful as always not to touch her. It was silent in the alley. The air in the house was suffocating. Wallace decided it would be cooler in the open. There were some stones on the mountain-top, with trees on the top to give shade.

May Ling caught up with him at the village gate. 'I kept you company, Wallace.'

'You were good little wife, May.'

It was hard work, but worthwhile once on the summit. They walked across a surprisingly flat plateau, inhaling a mixture of sweet herbal scents and salt from the sea. It was far breezier than conditions on the ground might have suggested. Wallace's jacket cracked in the wind. The world seemed empty. Wallace ran ahead exuberantly. He suddenly tripped, vanishing as if through a trap-door.

May Ling ran over in alarm, snagging her ankles in the long grass. A short jump beneath her was a broad ledge, ending in a steep drop to the sea. Wavelets washed against the cliff bottom. Boulders of regular size had been rolled around the edge of the platform in a circle too symmetrical to be the result of the weather's vagaries. Wallace was perched on one of these. May Ling slithered down onto the flat. Wallace pointed to the bank and drew a gasp from her. 'Wah! A real cave-hole.'

It was not so much a cave as a rock arbour. A snaggle-toothed cluster of stones roofed over, the gaps in its side plastered over with flaking red sandstone, with a recess gouged into the bank at the far end. Although a sizeable edifice, it had mellowed into the hill, and was invisible from a distance.

'Maybe pirate gold in there, May. We took look?'

She was dubious.

'Don't worry. I would make sure there was no snake inside.'

Her brow cleared.

Flushed with the reconnoitring zeal of his forebears, Wallace swaggered in. Once out of the light, he prudently waited for his eyes to adjust to the darkness. It was colder inside, chilly with a dry cold. He moved further in. Where the darkness was deepest, in the far reach of the excavation, the distance shortening and receding in the uncertain gloom, he imagined a swimming paleness, gone and then evident again as a slow, heatless burning on the eyeballs. He struck a match. The flame was reflected in a heap of smashed crockery. Puzzled, he struck more light. It showed shelves in the far wall. Each shelf carried a row of blue-veined jars, the size of the dustbins at Robinson Path. Straining, Wallace levered one from its repose and removed the lid. From it, he took what was unmistakably a human femur.

He dropped it with a hiss of horror. The match expired. In the new and utter darkness he howled softly, beating a fist against his forehead, wiping the defiling hand on his trousers. Striking another match, he located the bone, replaced it in its casket and grated the icy porcelain over its rough shelf. Then he swept the floor for his dead matches.

He pinched the last one off the grit. As he rose, his elbow smashed against another, lower jar. After what seemed a long pause, there was the sound of crockery breaking. He took a step forwards and there was hideous crunching underfoot. To more of the appalling sounds, he fumbled his way to the light at the entrance.

He flopped onto one of the pieces of the rock circle.

May Ling panicked. 'What was in there, Wallace? Hah? Tell me, tell me.'

He groaned, head in his hands.

'You could tell me. I would not be frighten.'

Wallace's breath escaped through his throat in a thick rattle. 'It was my bad lucks. It just my bad lucks to go and do it. Now I would be curse man. They would drink my blood all up. I could never escape from them.'

'Who is them, Wallace? Who want to drink your bloods? We go and get policeman, hah?'

'You didn't understand, May. It was where they keep their ancestor bone. I go in there and spill their bone all over the floor and then tread them.'

'Eiyah!' May Ling recoiled. She sat on the side of the semi-circle facing land. After a while Wallace started to pace about. He threw pebbles over the drop but because of the overhang was unable to see them splash into the sea. He consulted his watch in the gathering darkness.

'Eiyah! My hand watch stop.'

'What time it said?'

'It say half past three. I must have just knock it now in the grave.' He kicked a clod of sandstone over the cliff.

'Wallace I had idea just now.'

He spat over the edge. 'Tell to me.'

'If we give Mr Spirit a present that would make him more friendlier to you and then he would not want to drink all your bloods up.'

Wallace thought. 'Same thing as in the bible. Only we didn't have a goat or a sheep, and I wouldn't want to throw you over the cliff edge.' He laughed.

May Ling delved in her bag. 'There not much treasures here. Just a Tiger Balms and a comb. What you would give the spirit for present?'

'I only got moneys with me your father give to me.'

'No. It would have to be somethings of you.' She saw the gold glint on his wrist. 'What about you were giving him your watch?'

Wallace leapt to his feet again. 'What? It was very expensive watch.'

'Then it would please spirit.'

Wallace had to admit the logic of his wife's case.

In a clump of scrub out of sight of the ossuary he found soft earth to dig a hole. Shielded from the wind, he thought he could hear the sea slapping and sucking below. May Ling fell to her knees and scraped the earth with her comb. They placed their offerings in the rough trench and covered them. Wallace patted May Ling's head. 'I said it again: you were being good little wife to me this day. I would not forget.' May Ling swelled.

'Now we better pray. Come on.'

She joined her palms but the sea distracted, compelling a hideous fantasy of Wallace drowning below the cliffs, dashed against sharp rocks, spun in whirlpools – she, unaware, failing him – as he was sucked to the bottom to be released, pinioned in the rent shroud of his jacket. She heard the breeze whistle through the grasses. She concentrated again but the sea mumbled insidiously. There was the sound of rain pattering. She opened her eyes. Wallace, his back to her, was urinating ferociously into the bushes, thrashing down the leaves in gouts of gold.

'War-less,' she reproached him giggling.

He looked sheepish. 'Wah, I need that like anything. All that tea I was drinking at tea-shop this morning.'

They emerged from the shelter of the break into a stiff wind. There were black clouds coming in low over the sea. Breakers were smashing into the rocks below the cliff.

'It got real dark, hah?'

'I think it would do big rains, Wallace.'

'We better get down fast.'

They descended without mishap, although on the exposed defiles the wind was treacherous, banging them into each other with its force.

The village was packed with muddy-legged workers, carrying their tools. Animals – bullocks, pigs, a flock of squawking chickens – were being driven down the alleys by their owners.

Wallace flattened himself against the wall of a house to avoid the wheels of a buffalo-drawn cart.

'My God, it got more dangerous than Nathan Road. You were OK, May?'

Inside they lit their oil-lamp. They waited for the storm. From the precautions the villagers were taking Wallace suspected it might be a fully fledged typhoon. He sipped cautiously at the boiling tea May Ling had made.

The headman's glass, still full, had long grown cold. A daughter-in-law tip-toed up to replace it with a fresh infusion. The headman was depressed. Not by the prospect of the typhoon. The village weathered these annually. In the crater it was noisy but safe. The mountain deflected the brunt of the winds which howled over the rim of the depression. Subsequently there might be the risk of flashfloods but with foresight and care these could be avoided. In fact, the classic cause of fatalities in the typhoon season was flower-pots falling on the heads of unwary pedestrians, and there were no tenements here.

What made the headman gloomy was the prospect of at least four hours in the company of his animals and women. On the whole the animals would behave themselves. Their initial fright over, they would lie down in disciplined peace in their separate groups. Not so the women, who were given to squabbling bitterly amongst themselves. The daughters-in-law (the headman was uncertain how many of these there were) proved the shrillest every year. The arguments were petty but vehement. The headman would sit alone at a table while the controversies went on behind his back. He knew the women were really arguing in advance over the dispositions he would be found to have made after his death. Sometimes the headman thought the women actually looked forward to the typhoon season. In the event their rivalry was pointless. The headman had long ago designated his entire personal fortune, as opposed to the clan lands he held in his lifetime, to endow a trust in commemoration of himself. There was a certain ironic consolation to be derived from the contemplation of this during his imprisonment in the house. He smiled for the first time as he warmed his palms against the sides of his glass.

5

The typhoon was unprecedented in its ferocity and duration. It raged for five hours with a lull of an hour when the eye was over the colony, followed by still fiercer winds for another six. Later, fortifying a retrospective sense of adventure that had been totally absent at the time of the action, Wallace discovered that the Royal Observatory in Kowloon had measured wind speeds in excess of 180 miles per hour.

May Ling had placed wooden storm shutters over the apertures pierced in the concrete of the walls. She had found them stacked under the bed by some provident predecessor. Even before the real winds arrived, the shutters rattled ominously but, secured by two simple wooden pegs, they rose to the challenge, becoming fixed under the pressure of the big gusts. Wallace passed some time explaining the physics of the phenomenon to his wife.

Rain slashed into the mud outside, carving rivers which flowed down the slope of the village, becoming waterfalls on the steps between the rings of houses, then rushing down to the big drainage hole in the centre of the village in front of the main ancestral hall.

Wallace could hear the roaring water; it was so loud it drowned the impact of the heavy drops on the roof.

It was dark inside but, denied real blackness to compete against, the oil lamp threw a pale glow which could not combat the grey light trickling through chinks in the planking.

Wallace felt safe, inaccessible, and dry.

May Ling had been scratching on the floor with a piece of tile. Now she unhooked the lamp from its bracket and placed it on the floor. She rummaged in a wooden box she had been keeping secret from Wallace. (He had looked in it one day when she was in the alley with the old women; it contained shells, stones, some preserved leaves, and a sheet of paper on which she had been practising her signature.)

She dropped a fistful of Tiger Balm tops on the floor and started to arrange them in rows. 'OK, Wallace, you were ready to start?'

He stooped and saw that she had drawn a game board on the stone. He counted the squares: '. . . seven, eight. Wah!'

May Ling flushed with pleasure. They began.

Wallace's sense of peace, strongest when the typhoon was at its wildest, evaporated as the winds died. It was as if they had been a protection against encroachments on his little sanctuary.

The shutters began to chatter and then were still. Wallace removed them and looked out into the alley which had become a canal. A man was splashing around the houses in knee-deep water.

The headman had survived the last hours without being unduly inconvenienced by his women. They had been terrified into silence by the extraordinary strength of the winds. At the height of the tempest a big, solid blast of air had flung a dead sea-gull against a rotten storm-shutter and smashed a jagged hole in it. The bird had landed in the lap of one of the younger wives. The general consternation had suited the headman. During the lull, he left under pretext of taking stock of damage after leaving stern instructions that no one was to stray from the house. The strident voices rose behind him as he picked his way across the square to the ancestral hall. A few tiles were missing from the roof but there was no obvious external damage. He continued his tour through the wards. Sounds of cooking came from the houses. He saw tableaux of families at food, frozen briefly in light as he went past in the dark. The puddles got deeper in the outer wards. As he emerged from the fifth ward a large raindrop struck him on the back of the hand. He hesitated. The outermost ward was one for which he hardly felt responsibility. A lighter breeze ruffled the flooded surface of the alley in front of him. He thought of the competing voices in his house, given full rein in the lull, and entered the alley.

Wallace stuck his head out of the narrow aperture as the headman waded past. The sounds of his watery passage echoed from wall to wall after he was out of sight. No lights showed from the dark sides of the terrace opposite. Wallace climbed off his chair full of admiration.

'You just hear a real hero going by, May, and you didn't even know it. It was real dangerous to go out but all time we were here he was looking after us.'

'Like Ah Dairdee.'

Wallace stamped, crushing a Tiger Balm top. 'No, not like Ah Dairdee. Get it into your head. We was here alone by ourself. No Dairdee, no family, no nobody. We did it ourself, hah?' His temper had not been sweetened by losing ten consecutive games of checkers to May Ling who now saucily said: 'What about headman you was telling me about, hah?'

For the first time in their marriage, Wallace hit his wife. May Ling rubbed her ear reflectively. It had not been a hard blow. Wallace twitched his fingers in embarrassment. He was uncertain what to do next. They looked at each other over an uncomfortably short distance. May Ling tittered propitiatingly. She said: 'There was bogey in your nose, Wallace.' He grinned awkwardly while she wiped him with a handkerchief she had hung to dry in the morning. They sat on the bed and he put an arm round her meagre shoulders. They did not notice the passing of the typhoon.

By dawn the typhoon had blown itself out. In the morning Wallace splashed his way to the walls, leaving May Ling asleep after the excitements of the previous night. Neither the deep puddles nor the glutinous red mud he encountered prepared him for the sight from the ramparts.

The marshy fields had become a lake, an inland sea with real waves pitching sluggishly in rolls and hollows. The flood lapped just below tree level on the mountainside, considerably diminishing the elevation of the village. There was no sun and, unfaceted by light, the moving khaki water shrouded the valley as far as the eye could see. Aesthetically, it was a drab, mournful spectacle, unredeemed by any natural splendour. Practically speaking, he knew he was looking at a disaster.

He spotted a group of figures at the edge of the water and slid down the greasy slope to join them. The elders were huddled in a disconsolate little group. Wallace did not attempt to join it but loitered on the outskirts.

A dead rat floated on its side in the water, its long, scaly tail brushing land while its snout pointed over the Border towards some destination never to be gained. Wallace prodded it with a stick, releasing a burst of extraordinarily noxious bubbles.

The elders exclaimed angrily. The headman shook his finger at Wallace and they moved down. As if this was a pre-arranged signal in an ambush, frogs commenced croaking from close but well-concealed positions in what Wallace construed as a mocking pitch.

★

The first crop had been totally destroyed. The rice plants could withstand minor flooding, of the type produced by heavy rains. The fields were drained by a complex system of dykes and sluices, constructed over centuries. This time, though, the water had risen to an unparalleled level. And it was not the swampy stuff which normally irrigated the shoots. It was salt water; the ocean. The fierce winds had piled up the sea at the river mouth, forcing it up the estuary, where it had gone over the brimming banks to swell the cascades of fresh water pouring off the hillsides. Only the fish had benefited. The floodwater had risen over the top of the stock-ponds, enabling them to swim to freedom.

Wallace had originally hoped that the typhoon might eliminate unwelcome interest in his misdeeds in the clan tomb; he had surveyed the drowned fields with a mixture of despondency and relief.

This was not to be the case. The incidents reacted upon each other, dramatically. Later, Wallace could see that their conjunction had set off the whole long history that was to follow.

The ritual headman discovered the desecration the day after the typhoon. His two young grandsons, who had helped the old man make his routine climb to tend the tomb, raced back ahead of him. They alerted the villagers who had been occupied in clearing storm debris from the muddy streets. The village watch, armed with staves, had been summoned to the main gate. They met the old man as he stumbled down the lower slopes.

Wallace heard the alarm gong beat fuzzily from the centre ward. There was passionate shouting and the slap of bare feet in the alleys. Hurrying to the wall, he saw the crowd around the ritual headman disintegrate and the watchmen engage in a race up the mountain.

He found May Ling on an alley bench and took her back to the house, running the gauntlet of hawking dowagers. Nervousness made him rougher with her than he had intended. 'You never saw nothing, you never hear nothing, and you never would say nothing, OK?' His fear communicated itself to her; she nodded dumbly.

'They kill me and maybe they would kill you, too, if they only knew. They did what they want out here. No one found out. You understood me?'

May Ling nodded again. This time she plucked up the courage to speak: 'Only one thing, Wallace. Who had broke up the pot before you go in?' Wallace shrugged his shoulders; he had not troubled himself about this.

'Then it really was evil spirit, like we saw in the bamboo.' She spoke almost with satisfaction.

But there was to be no investigation. Wallace's fears for his personal safety proved groundless. The villagers saw both typhoon and spoliation as separate manifestations of the same maleficent fortune. An exorcism was what was required, and in the opinion of some it was long overdue.

The headman submitted to majority opinion at a mass meeting convened in the main ancestral hall. There were times when it could be expedient to bow to democracy.

6

The exorcists arrived in a wallah-wallah boat, one of the small craft that normally plied for hire in Victoria Harbour in competition with the official ferry services. There were three exorcists. Nothing had been left to chance. There was a Buddhist monk, a Taoist priest, and a professional geomancer of flexible persuasion.

The little boat lurched in the oily swell. It had to plough its way into the bay. The exhaust bubbled and snorted as the stern rose and fell in the waves. An area had been cleared amongst the rotting jelly-fish, timber, and weed that the typhoon had thrown up on the shore. Three of the sturdiest nightwatchmen waded out and carried the holy men to shore on their backs. The headman and ritual headman led them up to the village. As the exorcists passed through the gates they looked straight ahead, ignoring the files of villagers on each side. They were taken straight to the headman's house for a private briefing, emerging after dark for a dinner at which they were guests of honour. A trestle table was set up under a tree outside the tea shop. A crowd of spectators gathered, May Ling and Wallace positioning themselves unobtrusively at the rear. Being slightly taller than the average villager Wallace was able to keep May Ling informed of what was happening.

'They got one of those Tao priest with tall black hat on that got sort of long ear at the side and there was one of those monk fellow in dark robe. The other fellow just got on a old-fashion Chinese suit like headman had.'

Standing on tip-toe with her hands on her husband's shoulders, May Ling could only see the priest's tall hat. It disappeared as he addressed himself to his bowl of bird's nest soup. By the time the dessert of sweet peanut stew and lotus seed dumplings arrived, the crowd had thinned considerably.

The priest started to roll a huge, unwieldy cigarette. The monk stood up and turned his fold-up chair back to front. He sat fork-legged, parting his skirts with circumspection. Trousers showed underneath. Wallace was irresistibly reminded of a key scene from the film he had taken the boys to see at the Sheraton cinema, when insurance had been sold to a reluctant tradesman.

The monk adjusted his robes, exposing a chunky gold wrist-watch and bracelet. He sketched a figure, possibly necromantic, in the air and conjured up a handful of long needles which he stuck with deliberation into the back of the headman's chair. Then he began sheathing them individually, up to their bobbles, in his wrinkled scalp.

There were impressed murmurings from the remnants of the crowd.

The monk withdrew the pins and came to the point. 'The *fung shui* of this village is disastrous.' His two colleagues nodded in agreement.

The crowd drew in.

'It is very obvious that ritual has been stinted: insufficient food left at the graves, too few joss-sticks burnt. But all this is really beside the point. These are minor issues. The recent bad luck of your village has come about because of evil forces in the mountain. My colleague is better equipped than I to explain.'

The geomancer gracefully acknowledged this compliment by pouring tea. He elaborated to the headman: 'There are two dragons in the mountain, one good and one evil. The evil one has awakened from a long sleep and is destroying the good work of the one which has been your traditional protector. What is needed is an exorcism. When was your last?'

'Nine years ago,' the headman informed him. 'The ritual headman officiated.'

The exorcists shook their heads. 'Too long. And these things should be professionally conducted.' The geomancer looked at the ritual headman with disfavour. 'Apart from your general run of bad luck were there any similar disturbances? Strange noises at night, for instance?'

From the front row of the crowd Wallace gave vent to a hearty affirmative, choked off into a grunt. The headmen looked at him with surprise.

The geomancer pursed his lips and observed that the younger generation could often be more sensitive in matters of this kind than their seniors. The priest and monk nodded at Wallace approvingly.

And had there been any unexpected deaths?

The geomancer looked gloomy when informed that fortune had here so far spared the village but brightened as the priest reminded the headman of the urgency in that case of prophylactic ceremonial.

Confronted in publc with this kind of diagnosis it was difficult for the headman to quibble over the fee. His mortification was compounded when the owner of the tea shop, provider of the banquet, also offered to pay half the costs of the exorcism.

The charges settled, the geomancer continued: 'There is a a rock six miles to the north-east of the village which used to be on clan land, is there not?'

The crowd hissed corroboration.

'The spirit of this rock,' the geomancer revealed, 'is an eagle. You should release it by building a shrine on the top in the shape of a sphere. The evil dragon will believe this to be a pearl. As you know, dragons are attracted to pearls. The dragon will try to take the pearl but the eagle will fly away with it in his claws. The dragon will chase the eagle and leave you alone. Your troubles will be over. Of course, these events should not be given a literal construction. To human eyes the rock and the shrine will appear to be in the same place as always.'

He held his hand up modestly as he received a spatter of respectful applause from the villagers. 'There will also have to be additional prayers and sacrifice offered at your ancestral tomb in the usual way. These will eradicate any of the minor disturbances you have been troubled with.'

The exorcists finished their cigarettes after which they were escorted to the village guest house to rest and prepare for the next day's work.

The villagers assembled in front of the ancestral hall in a grey light. The men carried field-tools with them. They would march behind the exorcists, headman and elders. Behind the men were the boys and in the rear the women and small children. The priest, who would play the major part in the exorcism, was aided by three small village boys, two carrying poles with long belts of red fire-crackers attached. A third carried a bulky cylinder, wrapped in white cloth. Behind them were two bearers with a banner inscribed in red and gold: 'The United Clan of Mountain Village Visits Its Graves'. There were a pair of flautists and also a ceremonial two-man gong. At a cautious distance from the gong, six elders staggered under the burden of three trays each with a glazed whole roast pig, specially barbecued in the tea shop.

Wallace yawned as he pushed May Ling into the crowd of old women. The crones gave her a cackling welcome. The young wives of the village carried babies in cloth slings on their backs.

As the first cock crowed, the village marched out of the main gate to a fearsome cacophony. The procession snaked around the twisting paths to the foot of the mountain. There the head split off from the rest of the body. The priest and his boy attendants took a steeper, little-used way to the summit which wound up from the sea-shore. Banner flying, gong beating, flutes piping and cymbals crashing, the main group continued to ascend. The flautists still managed to keep an even stream of sound issuing from their pipes during the steepest stages of the climb.

The village waited for the priest above the mouth of the tomb. There was quite a long wait before the priest's tall black hat became visible over the long grasses, moving smoothly above the waving vegetation. His two colleagues awaited him at the entrance to the tomb. He emerged from the grasses, making what was under the circumstances a dramatic entrance.

Purifying fires were lit with paper while the holy men entered the tomb with joss. The monk was swinging a censer of a type Wallace had last seen in use in a church in Macau. There were scrapings and clinkings, amplified in the narrow confines of the cave. Wallace closed his eyes and visualised the scene.

The ritual headman had laid out the pigs at the entrance and was prostrate behind them in a position not dissimilar to those of the roasted carcasses themselves.

The exorcists re-emerged. The geomancer signalled to one of the priest's boy attendants. The priest himself began to read a text from a bone-handled parchment scroll which he shook out of his sleeve. The nasal chant droned on. The attendant with the cylinder struggled to unsheath it. There appeared the legs of a tripod, half uncovered, and finally an arrangement of plumes and peacock's feathers, surmounted by a mirror.

Wallace recognised the instrument as a *fung shui* reflector. Its mechanism was elegant, economical, and neatly retributive. Evil spirits saw the reflection of their own hideous faces in the mirror and were stampeded in fright. The more malevolent the spirit, the nastier his fright. The concept was uniquely Chinese and Wallace imagined it effective only against suggestible Cantonese devils.

The priest paused. Mistaking this for the end of his spell, the boys lit the fuses of their fire-crackers with the stumps of smouldering joss sticks. The rest of the incantation was blotted out in a series of amazingly noisy explosions. The priest's mouth stopped moving but the fire-crackers went on bursting. The belts at the end of the waving poles were slowly consumed from the bottom. Wallace's ears sang in the silence and he imagined any devils to have been frightened away long ago when the two-man gong boomed behind him.

The geomancer took the *fung shui* reflector, the tripod looked like an item of photographic equipment, and jabbed the legs into the sandstone on top of the tomb. The sea breeze ruffled its feathers. The geomancer gave the device a spin and it began to twirl slowly in the wind, flashing into the eyes of the villagers as it caught the rising sun. It began to whirl with accelerated revolutions. Wallace saw his own startled face considerably magnified before the changing images blurred.

There remained the construction and consecration of the shrine on Eagle Rock. The task was of a more delicate nature, involving an act of technical trespass on the Hakkas' land, and a small band of young men were despatched at dusk. They took hoes and flails with them for defence, as well as the actual building. Passing through the groves of giant bamboos and over the Hakkas' fields, they did not meet with any interference. They completed their work and returned before light.

7

The flood had not come up to the level of the nursery beds and vegetable plots. This meant that the immigrant farmers still had their crop intact while the villagers' own livestock had also survived in their houses. Rent from the vegetable allotments would ensure there was no actual starvation in the settlement but there would have to be serious economies, not least the further reduction of ritual. This was a vicious spiral: it was precisely such stinting on ceremonial expenditure that was generally reckoned to have brought about the present situation.

The young rice plants in their nursery still survived, on higher ground. There was irony to this, for unless transplanted soon they would die. But the water in the valley showed no signs of falling. The headman had markers placed on the hillside; they showed that the water had marginally risen. To add insult to injury, the Hakkas' fields, never so severely flooded, had drained. In fact, their water appeared to have run down the valley to the village.

May Ling was washing the bowls.

'You was sure they could do nothings about it, Wallace?' She was positive that some aspect of the situation might have been overlooked but at the same time she wished to avoid irritating Wallace by any intimation of superiority.

'There was no chance, May.' He flicked a grain of rice moodily across the table to a cockroach. 'The water never go away in time to plant number two rice. The old drain system all block up. It was too deep and dirty for them to dive without getting drown. And they never got enough stuff to put on field and make it good for growing again.'

May Ling sighed. Wallace felt he had disappointed her. He said grandiloquently: 'I would give them money to buy new field.'

'But you didn't have enough.'

'No.' Wallace had to admit this. 'But if I did it would be secondary consideration, hah?'

'Ah.' May Ling seemed impressed.

'You see.' Wallace swelled out his chest as if the presentation were already a matter of record.

When May Ling said: 'I was sure you could do somethings,' she reverted to serious discussion a little too quickly to be utterly respectful and he was curt with her. 'So you had brainwave then, you were so smart.'

Immediately May Ling's lively face became stolid and pasty. Wallace prowled the room.

Becoming bold again, May Ling ventured: 'But you was engineer, Wallace. You trained before for it, hah?'

Wallace, despite himself, laughed. 'That was different. I didn't study all that hydraulic stuffs.'

'You didn't have to use dirty languages.'

'Hah?'

A not unfriendly silence ensued. But she had set his mind working and in the morning, after sleep, there was a result.

Wallace articulated his 'brain-wave' in the tea shop over their morning congee. He snorted half-angrily, half-contemptuously, but nevertheless with some admiration for his own ingenuity.

'What it was, husband?'

He shrugged modestly, in the wriggling movement of a snake shucking its skin, causing his fold-up chair to creak dangerously. 'No. It was nothing. Also it wouldn't work.'

'But tell.'

Just to show off his fecundity, inapplicable though its stratagems were to the real world, he told her. When he had finished her eyes glowed. To prevent frustrating speculation, he immediately said: 'Of course there was no bomb to make hole and I couldn't really see how the field was all looking underwater.'

May Ling jigged up and down out of her slippers in her excitement. 'The coolie, the coolie.'

It took a moment to understand. 'Wah!' Then the rest came to him almost unwilled.

In places the water was so shallow that the boatwoman had to punt the tiny sampan. Unshipping the long oar at the stern, which doubled as rudder and propulsive unit, she did this as effortlessly and economically as she rowed.

The boat and the services of its owner had been presented to Wallace by the headman. He had given Wallace a courteous, mystified hearing before instructing four men to carry the boat up from the beach to the flooded valley. The boatwoman, a widow, had come from a small fishing community up the coast and married a village man; now she earned a living by fishing in the bay.

The creak of the oar's rattan bindings and soft ripple of water against the sides were the only sounds. The boatwoman did not splash as she undulated the oar from side to side, her toes gripping the greasy planks with assurance. May Ling sat in the centre, acting as ballast. She had strict instructions from Wallace not to move.

According to his improvised sounding-line, it was deeper at the sides of the valley than in the middle. This instrument was May Ling's clothes-line, knotted at measured intervals, with a roof-tile lashed to the end. Wallace threw it ahead, standing in the bows, with a swinging, underhand movement. They circled randomly at first, Wallace pointing the boatwoman from sounding to sounding.

Somewhere in the centre of the valley, when the village had dropped out of sight behind its mud ramparts, which in turn blended into the mountainside, the boatwoman stubbed her oar against a solid object about five feet beneath the surface. Wallace tried to peer through the opaque water. His line brought up weed; on a repeated attempt a wood board with holes drilled in it. It was a piece of sluice-gate, the centre board from the biggest drain. Wallace made a mark on a piece of paper he had squared into a grid. Bearings taken, and the depth ascertained, they moved on. He marked the site of the various sluices with pomelos, anchoring the buoyant fruit with string and stones.

Fish swam lazily a few inches down.

By stages, they arrived at the limit of the flooding. The sampan ground against a mud-bank. Wallace leapt out, landing high and dry. He paced from end to end. On the distant mountain-top there was a flash of silver, intermittently repeated. The women waited patiently. The boatwoman squatted in the stern, moving her oar fractionally to keep the craft stationary. At length Wallace clambered back on board.

Wallace found the return voyage much shorter than the outgoing. He was still calculating when they bumped at the spot where he had first gone down to the flooding. The rat, he saw, had disappeared.

He was some distance from the boat when May Ling called. 'I could move now, Wallace?'

At home, using the empty stove as a desk, he brushed his calculations onto rice paper, borrowing what he found in May Ling's little box of effects. He worked on into the darkness, collating large figures from small sheets and transferring them as crabbed calculations onto a master draft. He was immune to distraction. Food May Ling had prepared filmed with grease. When at last he finished and turned out the lamp there was a pale light outside.

He had a basic plan, crude but logical, which incorporated more commonsense than expertise. His course at Foochow, such as it had been, had included rudimentary demolition and the principles of flood control. Now he wished he had studied in a central province on the Yangtze, Honan, perhaps. He had picked up most of his sketchy knowledge of this specialisation in the field. He remembered how a reservoir had been drained outside Macau. He would just have to imitate from memory.

Basically, small charges were necessary to clear the silt from the sluice-gates. But large bodies of water would also have to be drained before this could take effect. The drains flowed into the river and its course was blocked. It might be possible to blast out a section of the valley wall, where the incline from the centre was gentlest, and create a gap for the water to run through down to the sea. Then the lake would subside enough for the river to run, recognisably, within its banks again and do the rest of the work naturally. Later, charges would have to be set to create a landslide to dam the hole up again or the next problem would be drought.

Fortunately, the area to be blasted was neither of *fung shui* significance nor cultivable even by the vegetable farmers. There seemed to be nothing to lose by trying.

But he could not get through to the headman. His calculations meant nothing to the old man.

May Ling came to the rescue, unsurprised. 'Of course he didn't understand sum, Wallace. Why you didn't make little model for him, like playing at beach?' Wallace just looked at her and nodded, with lips pursed.

They found the children by the main gate, making a pair of cicadas fight. Wallace led them to a virgin morass, near the rice nurseries, where the experiment could be set up discreetly. He located a mound from which he could direct operations to advantage, while May Ling worked with the children.

An hour into the project, one of the older girls in the gang, standing back to wipe mud off her eyebrow with the back of a hand, exclaimed sharply. She called out to the others, pointing out the salient features of the terrain taking shape before them in miniature. The architect beamed, then sternly ordered the labourers back to work. Efforts redoubled.

At one point an inquisitive water-buffalo had to be pelted away with mudballs but it lumbered past without damaging the burgeoning earthworks.

Wallace organised a bucket-chain and soon had a mimic lake lapping at the base of his model mountain. The scale was faithful. The village wall was perhaps the most realistic detail, consisting of the same raw material as the original. May Ling had stuck two forked twigs on the mud pie that represented their house and went on to suggest as a centre-piece the delineation of a group of people working on a replica of their surroundings and within that ... Wallace interrupted her: 'Some people, May, was too clever for their own good.' She subsided meekly.

The headman was beyond measure impressed. He walked right round the construction with his arms stiff at his sides, his neck locked at right angles to his marching body. Wallace was equally gratified by the reactions of the other elders.

In accordance with the instructions a boy was sent to bring the fire-crackers left over from the exorcism. Wallace snapped the red tubes in half, tapping the coarse-grained black powder into the headman's water-pipe. He sealed the chamber with Tiger Balm, ran a fuse down the spout and sank the crude mine at the head of the valley at a scale point one thousand yards from the village and some three hundred feet below it. The onlookers fell back.

Wallace leaned over the lake in the attitude of a fencer, holding a smouldering joss-stick at arm's length. A cascade of sparks gushed from the spout. He jumped back to join May Ling who already had her hands over her ears. Too late, he worried about the transformation of pipe into shrapnel. There was a profound subterranean belch; large bubbles; smaller bubbles; from which, bursting, smoke was released across the agitated surface of the lake. Then a neat segment of the West side of the valley was breached. The mud crumbled at first, rather than being swept dramatically away. Water trickled between the cracks, forming puddles; the trickles became rivulets, the rivulets a stream, the stream a torrent. It shot with some force through a square section of the valley wall.

The villagers stood, as if hypnotised, in the path of the approaching flood. The water hissed past, lapping around their ankles. Still they stood there, while the children laughed and jumped.

On his overseer's mound, where he had been joined by a proud May Ling, Wallace was above the flood. He splashed through the water to receive the headman's congratulations.

After the undeniable impact of the demonstration, the real thing came as something of an anti-climax. To start with, there were not even bubbles to see, still less a scaled-up dam burst of raging white-water racing down to the sea.

The nightwatchmen had, as May Ling first suggested, purloined explosives from the coolie workings down the coast. They had found these deserted in the aftermath of the typhoon. Wallace had tamped quantities of gun-cotton into wine jars the village council had, following an eloquent address from the headman, commandeered from the tea shop. Then the bulk of the explosives were sunk in a giant sap under the part of the valley wall Wallace hoped to bring down. Subsidiary charges had also been laid in the sluice-gates, under water, with the surplus explosive concentrated on the central sluice.

Wallace had been hoping for something more spectacular; tall, creamy fountains erupting from the surface of the water to collapse thunderously after the effect of a Hollywood depth-charging, at the very least.

The fuses were lit and there was a suspenseful wait. The water winked in the bright sunshine. Not a ripple disfigured the flat mica-like surface. Turning his head, Wallace waited for earth to burst out of the hillside, for rock splinters to be scattered in a sheet of flame. The twin set of explosions were approximately synchronised.

He had used bamboo pipes to carry string fuses to the small charges on the sluices. A powder-train had been scattered over the hillside, leading to the main mine, and it had spurted impressively away from the walls. They lost sight of the fiery snake going around a rock.

The interval extended itself.

'Oh God, nothing happen.' Wallace's voice was hoarse. His eyes started to film with moisture.

There were mutterings from the spectators. Wallace caught the headman's eye and looked away quickly. The walls emptied.

★

The small charges on the sluice had gone off, as Wallace discovered when he punted out, by himself. So much was evident from the splintered timber and dead fish on the surface. 'The sun shine too much so we didn't see it,' he rationalised to May Ling when he got back. But there could be no doubt the main stock of explosives had failed to detonate.

He walked nervously to the site, aware of the risk of delayed blast. He steeled himself to walk over the planked hole the nightwatchmen had excavated. The powder fuse had been consumed. He looked down into the dark funnel leading to the mine but saw nothing.

That evening he took food in gloomy silence.

In the middle of the night there was a shattering roar. The floor trembled and a fist seemed to punch through the centre of the hard, comfortable bed.

Wallace's heart pounded. 'You stayed here, May.'

'No, I came.'

The nightwatchmen were already on the ramparts. Wallace could not see anything but there was a rushing sound and a faint, swampy whiff. He was barred egress at the gate but the nightwatchmen slapped him on the back and grinned broadly. They chattered excitedly amongst themselves. He puffed politely on the home-made cigarette they offered him.

'It was dangerous to go out,' he explained to May Ling. 'Like flashflood, hah? You might get sweep away when you couldn't see in the dark. There must have been spark or something live down there and it just bomb up.'

They could go out at first light. Most of the water had already drained. The valley was choked with mud, piled in whorls and drifts. In a sort of cup, at the bottom of the mountain, parallel to the village, there was a pool of deep-looking water about a hundred yards in radius. But the inland sea was no more. Instead, there was the river again, meandering weakly through uncertain banks. It seemed a little farther over to the Red side than usual but Wallace was prepared to dismiss this as an optical illusion.

The section of the valley wall which had been demolished was a thin slice, unlike the wide slab taken out of the model. The rush of water had left the steep sides smooth. There were patches of green slime on some rocks, and a few puddles. Seagulls were perched on the higher rocks. Wallace calculated the strength of the flood which had shot through from the dry patch on the beach immediately below. Most of the flood-water had discharged straight into the sea, which was clearly visible through the cut. The sea was exceptionally calm and, if anything, Wallace imagined he had improved the *fung shui* with his emergency landscaping.

There would be no need for further blasting. A small landslip had created a rough dam at the end of the new ravine. It would only be necessary to fill in some gaps to have effective control of the water level in the paddy.

Wallace was chaired back by the jubilant nightwatchmen. He grinned and gave them a thumbs-up sign.

He found May Ling walking around the outside of the walls. She ran her finger down a deep crack that spread out into smaller fissures like the veins of a leaf. There were others running continuously round.

'These not here before, Wallace.'

'No. You just were never noticing them before. They were real old. Maybe the Hakka cannon make it.'

'They came from big banging you make.'

Wallace felt obscurely flattered. 'Maybe, May, maybe. I should have put more dynamites down and make them really to fall over, hah?' He laughed boisterously and the nightwatchmen joined in, although uncertain of the joke.

Quails' eggs were roasted in enormous iron woks at the celebratory dinner. But Wallace and May Ling declined the headman's offer of a grander residence in the centre ward. The little room with its cock-loft and kitchen was a home to them.

Wallace said to his wife: 'Actually, I didn't even mind those damn frog anymore.'

These had somehow survived the ordeal of wind and water and, following the extinction of their enemies, the rats, had within a few nights of the draining multiplied with miraculous quickness, making the darkness lurid with their roar.

Thousands of the bloated creatures were crushed every day beneath the bare feet of the villagers as they planted the second rice crop. The corpses rotted in the paddy but were left there by the peasants, who believed they would enrich the soil. Still, there seemed to be no end to the infestation.

8

The Gurkhas came in a helicopter. They flew low over the sea, then the machine shot up the cliffs to the mountain-top. It hovered on the plateau, manoeuvring with difficulty in the tricky cross-wind. The Gurkhas swarmed out of its belly down a rope ladder.

Although conventional aircraft were now a familiar overhead sight in even the remotest parts of the New Territories, it was the first helicopter seen in the village. Until then Wallace had only seen photographs of 'choppers', as they were laconically designated by the caption-writers of the *Tiger Standard*, operating in the Korean theatre. Nevertheless, he was able to adumbrate their principles of flight and stability to May Ling.

'They use them against the Red. They were clever because you could easy stay where you were in them: not go forward, not go back: just one place all the time.'

'But just now he was going forward and then back again,' May Ling pointed out.

'That way it was more fun. Anyway, you couldn't really stay in one place and it was same in the end.'

By the way she put her arms akimbo May Ling showed she was not satisfied.

The British officer in command of the Gurkhas came down with two riflemen and a radio-operator, who staggered under the weight of the apparatus on his back. The long aerial whipped over the Gurkha's head.

'Walkie-talkie,' Wallace remarked in an effort to regain ground lost.

When May Ling did not rise to her cue, he said aggressively: 'Real tough guy, those Gurkha. The Jap frighten of them like they was tiger or something.'

'Huh! They got short leg like anything.'

Wallace gritted his teeth.

The officer was armed only with a stick, which he carried in his arm-pit. He saluted the headman without dropping it. By gesture, he politely declined an invitation to enter the walls. They stood together a while, the headman shaking his head in response to the officer's arm-waving.

The soldiers returned to the summit, the Gurkhas taking two steps to every one of their commander's.

Faint sounds of hammering drifted down from the plateau in the dusk.

Wallace guessed that an observation post was under construction. 'It serve them right for selling stuff to the Red when they shouldn't,' he speculated to May Ling.

Next morning he was climbing the hummocks of white sand and coarse grass which separated the lower slopes of the mountain from the beach, on his way to inspect the dam in the cut, when he saw something shining. He picked up the officer's stick. Engraved on the silver were the words: '2/LT. RODERICK J. McINTOSH'. He thumped it reflectively into his palm. He turned and set off up the mountain.

The Ghurkas were lying on their stomachs, looking over the Red side of the border along their rifle sights. The officer had a large pair of binoculars to his eyes. It was difficult to spot them at first under their camouflage net. For preamble, Wallace cleared his throat.

Ten rifles covered him before the breath had left his chest. He said: 'I bring back your stick, Lieutenant.' He held it upright. A squat Gurkha depressed it again with his rifle barrel. The radio operator stroked the handle of his kukri.

'You shouldn't really have come up here, old chap, but never mind.' The officer rolled back onto his stomach and adjusted the focus of his binoculars. No one else moved.

'Incidentally, we pronounce it "Left-enant". The Americans say "Loo-tenant". And I'm a captain anyway.' He had been speaking as he swept the border below. Now he sprang upright and brushed the grass from his sharply creased trousers. He issued rapid, incomprehensible instructions to the Gurkhas in their own language. They relaxed perceptibly. While Wallace and Captain McIntosh sucked scalding stew from billy-cans, the Gurkhas cut grasses and added them to those already on the net draped over their position. Equipment surrounded them in neat piles. Already the post bore the air of something more permanent than the mere bivouac it was.

Captain McIntosh rinsed his fingers in the water his orderly poured from a felt canteen. He stretched on his bed of trenched grasses.

Wallace could not resist saying: 'You soldier sure knew how to make yourself comfortable.'

The sybarite looked amused. 'An old campaigner's knack.' He offered Wallace a cigar, which was declined. Captain McIntosh blew the smoke methodically around them. 'Gets rid of the mosquitoes. The only other way is to get in the water. It looks good swimming here, too. A damn sight cleaner than Sheko or Repulse Bay, although I don't suppose for one moment you've ever been there.'

Wallace occupied himself with pouring more condensed milk into his steaming tea. He carefully caught the drops of white syrup on the tin's jagged lid.

'You speak pretty good English for a country boy.'

Wallace pouted unassumingly.

Captain McIntosh flexed his baton between two hands. 'Now, look. I can see straightaway you're an intelligent sort of chap. Why don't you help us and help your village at the same time? We can do each other some unofficial favours without any fuss.'

'You meant like what, Captain?'

'Look, we know what goes on out here. Red platoons come over from time to time. A little smuggling goes on. We're not fools, we know it does. We allow it. The embargo will soon be lapsing, anyway. But technically it's still illegal and you can be punished for it, savvy?'

'Ah.'

Having made his point, Captain McIntosh unbent. 'Between you and me, we don't like to upset our friends over there too much. Live and let live. And so far they've fallen in with it. So we were a little disturbed to hear they'd been getting up to some funny business lately. Personally, I have to say, I found it a little out of character.'

'Like they did what, Captain?'

'You must have heard the explosions? It was all clearly audible at the firing-range, so don't pretend you didn't hear it.'

Wallace's expression managed to suggest guarded admission without at the same time irrevocably committing himself.

'That's the smallest of things, though.' Captain McIntosh dropped his voice. 'We think we might be onto a spy ring. Someone has been flashing heliographic messages over the frontier. They seem to have been flashed from up here. What got staff so worked up was the fact that the messages seem to have been top secret as they were sent in a highly complex code and at a hell of a lick by an expert operator. Hot stuff, whatever it was. We haven't been able to decode it so far. It looks absolutely random but when we crack it, you watch out.'

A Gurkha refilled their billies.

'Now the thing is: are there any notable Communist sympathisers in your village who might have come up here with a mirror and flashed those messages?'

Wallace giggled. Captain McIntosh raised his eyebrows frostily.'I wouldn't have thought there was much to laugh about.'

The radio operator tapped him on his gleaming boot and passed him the binoculars. Wallace crawled over and aligned his gaze in the direction of Captain McIntosh's body.

Far below, the villagers were still at work in the paddy. Wallace saw nothing out of the ordinary at first, then spotted the dinghy being paddled over the river. Captain McIntosh spoke urgently into his wireless set. Wallace picked up the abandoned binoculars and focussed them. His eyes watered, then the dinghy and its occupants sprang into definition. The Liberation Army soldiers, in their tunics and forage caps with red stars, were being steered by a man in a fur hat, wearing a leather holster. Wallace consigned the popular myth, concerning the lack of external insignia of rank amongst the Communist forces, to his growing stock of exploded legends.

Captain McIntosh snapped orders. There were metallic snickings, sounds which, without turning, Wallace could identify from innumerable films as rifle bolts being worked.

'Twelve hundred yards. Three rounds rapid. And make sure you miss widely.'

The Gurkhas got their shots off in a single continuous tearing. Wallace watched, binoculars on the boat. It seemed quite a long time later, the pocks erupted harmlessly in the river. Through the glasses, they seemed to be very near the boat. The expressions on the Chinese soldiers' faces changed comically. The dinghy turned around and made rapidly for the bank.

Seconds later, someone whistled, following up with a cough.

In a moment Captain McIntosh had dived on top of Wallace and depressed his face into a patch of saw-toothed grasses.

'Mortar!'

There was a soft crump on the other side of the plateau, at the cliff-edge. The ground quivered. Wallace wriggled free of Captain McIntosh's protective carapace but kept his head low. In the fields, the dots worked placidly on.

The Gurkhas had vanished. Here and there the grasses swayed, in the direction of the prevailing breeze.

'Hold your fire.' Wallace was reminded of an Audie Murphy film that had enjoyed a long run in Macau some years previously. He was tempted to raise his head and immediately buried it again in the grasses as bullets thrummed directly overhead with the fluttering sound made by injured birds.

143

The Reds appeared satisfied with the extent of their retaliation. Then the Gurkhas were under the netting again.

Wallace felt the scratches on his face. Captain McIntosh called for iodine and personally attended Wallace before striding off to the cliff edge for a 'dekko'.

The bomb had landed directly above the ossuary. 'Smack on', as Captain McIntosh put it. Porcelain shards stuck sharply through the powdered sandstone. Skulls, rib-cages, pelvises, had been widely dispersed by the blast but seemed for the most part to have survived it intact. Wallace yanked a piece of rotten shoring from the tomb. He began to make a pile of bones. The jars would have to be put together jigsaw fashion, assuming key pieces had not been totally pulverised. As he turned his attention to some fragments of burial jar, it occurred to him that the task was pointless. The order of the interments had been totally confounded. He held a skull in one hand, a femur in the other: orb and sceptre. He pondered; he could be putting two separate spirits into the same repository. And what if they had been enemies in life?

Captain McIntosh poked a finger bone with the toe of his boot. 'The dragon's teeth, what?'

'Yes, but the bomb go and kill ancestor as well as bad dragon.'

Ironically, the *fung shui* reflector was still intact, although the feathers had been stripped from it and the mirror was filmed with dust. It lay on its side, away from the rubble. Wallace picked it up by the tripod. It was lighter than might have been expected. He hefted it experimentally behind his shoulder. He took a few paces to the cliff-edge and with a stiff arm lanced it out into space. It fell rapidly into the sea, hardly making a splash.

When they returned, the Gurkhas had struck camp. The radio operator was patting the flattened grasses into shape again and another Gurkha was turning the ashes from the cooking fire into the earth with his bayonet.

Wallace watched them descend into the valley. He felt slightly disappointed not to get a chance to see the helicopter at close quarters. The soldiers skirted the workers in the paddy and headed up-valley around the Hakka settlement.

9

Party headquarters in Hong Kong mobilised quickly. The demonstrators arrived the next day, having ridden a branch line of the Kowloon-Canton railway to the market town five miles from the settlement. Walking the rest of the way along stone-flagged tracks, over the swelling hillsides, cautiously skirting the new landslips, they found the paddy empty, the crop taking.

Now that they had finished the work of transplanting the shoots, the villagers had time to contemplate the latest events in their saga of misfortunes. A meeting of household heads was planned in the ancestral hall under the direction of the elders. It had been convoked on the suggestion of the tea shop owner.

The headman stayed in his house. He had not emerged even to inspect the ruins of the tomb. He took stock of his position in the light of the most recent auspices and found it distinctly deteriorated. Even the funds he would have got from completing the latest sale of contraband to the Reds had been snatched from him. His daughters-in-law crept around the house. They did not try to bring up the subject of dispositions, even obliquely.

The chanting of the demonstrators floated over the walls to the tea shop like the buzzing of a giant swarm of irate hornets. Wallace was cool enough to pour more peanut oil and soya sauce onto his cold *cheong fun* but smoothly swallowed the flat, white noodles whole. He was in time to get a place on the ramparts.

The view had always been panoramic. Now, with spectators along the length of the entire wall, Wallace knew the fortifications reminded him of the football bowl at the South China Athletic Association.

The demonstrators were forming on a flaking mud-flat at the edge of the paddy. The crocodile was composed of several distinct groups. In the rear there were the party cadres, recognisable by their blue cotton uniforms, red arm-bands, and brown canvas shoes (these last manufactured in the work-shops of a leading left-wing businessman). The corps was composed of hired help, including wiry coolies, dockworkers, and rickshaw men. In the van, conspicuous for the graphic ferocity of the slogans on their banners and the ardour with which they shouted them, were the senior pupils of the Communist Academies. The boys, holding hands, came in advance of the girls whose long blue cheongsams and ankle-length white socks were heavily splashed with mud. The cadres gave the order to squat, and tidied up the fringes of the crowd.

The alert came from a nightwatchman, posted on the seaward side of the walls. A partial view of both the bay and the valley was commanded from where Wallace stood. A boat was coming in from the horizon at high speed. At first it was visible only as a white bow break, then the hull materialised, thrusting out of the waves, and finally the varnished superstructure. The launch, a large Chriscraft, was powerful enough to surge straight into the bay without having to turn across the current. Soon it was bobbing off the beach. A speedboat with an outboard motor was winched off the stern by uniformed sailors. They ferried passengers to shore.

These stepped awkwardly out onto the shingle. All Chinese, they were led by a man in a blue tunic suit, similar to those worn by the party cadres. The others were dressed in Western lounge suits and ties. They walked towards a knoll on top of the beach, from which there was a good prospect down the valley. The sailors followed with boxes. From these they produced a folding table and deck-chairs. A candy-striped umbrella suddenly sprouted from the centre of the table. A hamper materialised, and the party bosses settled down to their buffet. Wallace's early hopes for a passive, Mahatma Ghandi-style demonstration, encouraged by the protagonists' adoption of sitting postures, evaporated. The appearance of the 'Fat Cats' meant real trouble.

After the recent shelling, the frontier still presented a picture of bucolic tranquillity. It was difficult to imagine a spot from which the Reds might have done their mortaring undetected.

The demonstrators remained seated when the police arrived, but broke out into renewed chanting. The police marched in at the double, three abreast along the narrow track. They carried round wicker shields and long riot sticks as well as their usual revolvers. They formed into ranks on the hillside, a hundred yards above the demonstrators. Four sergeants, in black rain-cloaks, held up a sign inviting the crowd to disperse. The reply came as louder, more insulting slogans: 'running dogs', 'imperialist lackeys', 'murderers of the nation'. There were murmurs of agreement from the villagers. Their dislike of the police was, in fact, completely unideological. There had been an episode a few years previously when the police had tried to levy an unofficial tax on gambling in the tea shop but had been driven away by the nightwatchmen. Later, an insulting gift of dried mushrooms, the amputated stalks signifying demotion, had been sent to the rural police station in the market town.

Suddenly silencing the murmur of conversation on the walls, a huge mechanical voice boomed out from the beach-knoll. The sound cut out and the valley reverberated to a hum which intensified into a piercing electric shriek, and was followed by the crackle and tearing of static. The voice returned and the party bosses began to issue their orders of the day.

In response the demonstrators rose. The cadres herded them into a solid formation. Concealed weapons – iron bars, poles, bottles of acid – were produced and waved in the air.

The police shields came together and overlapped into a phalanx. The khaki ranks were favourably placed on what was obviously about to become a battlefield. The demonstrators would have to run uphill if they attacked, whereas the momentum of a police charge would be enhanced.

At a barked command from the megaphone, the demonstrators shifted position into the paddy to face the police at an angle across the lowest part of the slope. The police phalanx turned as a unit, without a single gap appearing in the tortoiseshell of shields.

The demonstrators steadied themselves, then charged, splashing through the paddy and up the hillside. They appeared to bounce off the shields before retreating down to the paddy and regrouping. The police followed and halted just before the water.

During this time the megaphone had not ceased to relay a continuous flow of invective against the police, and exhortation aimed at the demonstrators.

After gathering themselves, the demonstrators attacked once more and were repelled in a cascade of spray. They withdrew deeper into the paddy, many limping. Several lay where they had fallen.

It had been a confused mêlée of gyrating legs and milling arms. The villagers watched in a gloomy silence.

The police stepped into the paddy. They began to beat their truncheons against their shields, producing a deep, drumming note.

The megaphone had been silent for a while. The 'Fat Cats' could be seen disputing amongst themselves for it. At length the official in party uniform secured it.

The metallic rantings became distorted beyond comprehension.

The original possessor strolled over to the buffet where he used chopsticks to pincer up a dumpling from a wooden basket and convey it to his mouth.

In the paddy a third charge was being prepared. The rank and file appeared to be reluctant to risk a third confrontation and were being harangued by the party cadres. One blue-tunic in particular was distinguishing himself. He was slightly in advance of the others, carrying a flapping red banner. He rested the butt on the ground and with his free hand gestured to his comrades to follow. He might have been striking a pose from one of the Reds' propaganda posters.

The police fell silent.

With a roar the demonstrators charged.

The police rushed to meet them, whooping and drumming, and as one man the crowd broke. The standard bearer skidded, saw the backs of his fleeing comrades, took one look at the oncoming police, dropped his banner and ran. Encumbered with their riot gear, the police made slow progress in the water and glutinous mud but this was counterbalanced by the crippled condition of many of the stragglers. Wallace was able at a glance to compute which of the hobbling malefactors would evade arrest and which would not, rather like the game of risk so popular in the casinos of Macau in which toy horses stuttered over a moving felt belt in a race whose outcome was determined well before the halfway stage was ever reached. The late standard bearer for instance, despite being handicapped by a tardy start, was showing the police a clean pair of heels and overhauling his injured comrades one by one. Many of these, for their part, had been in the rear of the charge and had enjoyed a sufficiently early start to guarantee escape. Others, less fortunate, were cut down by their pursuers. Little knots of policemen stood over the fallen bodies, their flexible truncheons rising and falling in rhythm. The last fugitive was brought down by a single policeman yards from the brush of the lower hillside, into which sanctuary the standard bearer crashed. He was the last to escape.

Wallace heard the deep concussion of marine engines taking. Smoke drifted over the water from the exhausts of the Chriscraft. The speedboat was already being winched onto its parent.

Before the police had regrouped, the launches were surging out of the bay at full throttle.

The police did not try to enter the village. They herded their prisoners onto the foot-track. After a brief period of recovery, the march set off.

Once the procession was out of sight, the nightwatchmen unbarred the main gate and began to comb the hillside for demonstrators who might have eluded the police. Fortunately for these, they all appeared to have been either apprehended or to have escaped from the immediate vicinity.

After dark Wallace went down to the beach. He sat where some knife-edged grasses met the sand. The full moon cast mobile shadows. Soon he began to imagine sounds. He thought he heard rustlings in specific but changing areas. He threw a stone at random. Someone cried 'Ow!'

Wallace snapped: 'You could come out with your hand up.' He was appalled to hear his summons obeyed. He retreated some way down the beach, thrusting a suggestive hand into his jacket pocket.

Someone came into the moonlight. Even with the head cropped to give the look of a pineapple, there was no mistaking the familiar face above the unfamiliar stock collar and tunic.

'Major!' Wallace was unable to believe the evidence of his own eyes. He approached and prodded the apparition in the chest to check that he was not dealing with a phantom of his own imagination.

Major was solid enough. He brushed Wallace's hand roughly aside. 'I might have known it was you, Nolasco, playing silly game the whole time. You didn't change.'

Wallace refrained from the obvious riposte.

'Anyways, you didn't mind, it was Comrade Chen, actually.'

'Ah.' Wallace looked carefully at him. 'But Major you were hurt.' Blood was indeed seeping from a superficial cut over Major's left eye. 'It was those police, hah?'

'No, it was you go and throw big sharp stone into bush. You could kill someone that way.'

'I was sorry.' Wallace saw that Major was carrying a folded red cloth. 'Eiyah! It was you with big red flag.'

Major looked pleased. With a flash of the friend Wallace remembered, he said: 'Custer last stand, hah?' Then he recollected himself. He said severely: 'Those mad running dog would pay when the revolution come.' He appeared to be setting himself for a harangue.

Wallace said hastily: 'How was Mr Allardyce?'

Major semed happy enough to be diverted. 'I thought you would have known. Allardyce dead.'

'Chut!' Wallace swallowed.

'It was a stroke the doctor say.' Major spoke brusquely. 'He was imperialist.'

'He was good man to you.'

They were silent for a moment.

Major offered Wallace a packet of Lucky Strike. Wallace hesitated, then accepted. 'Those imperialist was wicked but they sure made good cigarette.' For a moment Wallace thought he might have gone too far. Then Major laughed; they giggled together like a pair of guilty schoolboys.

'Major, I heard you people also couldn't drink.'

'You didn't want to believe all you heard.'

Wallace picked up a handful of sand and let it trickle through his fingers.

'So you disappear rather sudden, Mr Wallace.'

Wallace opened his palm and the breeze scattered the last grains of sand.

'But you wouldn't want to see that fat chief clerk all grinning, anyway, hah?'

'What he had to grin about anyway?'

'Really you was out of touch here. He was first Chinese head of department now.'

'HAH?' Wallace's voice echoed round the bay.

'Shh!' Major looked round nervously before continuing. 'Yes, he succeed Mr Allardyce. Now your wife father was good friend with him. Together they got all the contract going for themself. Everyone knew that.'

Wallace stood up, then squatted on his haunches, repeatedly stabbing his fingers into the sand. 'A frame-up, hah? They were just wanting to get Mr Allardyce out of the way? And they get me to go away because I maybe become his friend? What a pair of crook.'

Major said: 'That was what we Red, I meant Communist, was fighting against.'

Wallace ignored this. A discrepancy struck him. 'So why the two-face old devil bother to get me out here? Why he just didn't let the police get me?'

Major looked genuinely shocked. 'He couldn't do that. You were in his family. He had to look after you.'

'But ...' Wallace looked for the word, '... he made me fall-guy.'

'Sure, but that was different. He could do that. You still got to respect him. He was your wife father after all.'

This argument was too subtle for Wallace to grasp. He pursued the enquiry in a different direction. 'You said everyone was knowing, hah?'

'Of course.'

'Then why they didn't arrest Mr Poon and Chief Clerk?'

Major smiled. 'It was all rumourings in small place like Hong Kong. Anyways, he was first Chinese head of department and with all the riot now it was good thing to have him.'

'So it was you Red he could thank?'

'You could say it like that.'

Wallace shook his head in disgust.

'Don't take it personal, Wallace. Actually, you could go back any time you wanted now.' Major stood up. 'And I better had get going, too. It would be unsafe in day.' He added self-importantly: 'They got patrol out for me, you know.'

He crashed into the bushes. After he had gone, Wallace walked up and down the beach in the moonlight.

10

In the succeeding days Wallace made himself as inconspicuous as he could. He was not sure himself why he might be blamed for the recent spate of misfortunes but he was the victim of an obscure guilt, and he feared his own sense of culpability would communicate itself. He took to his long expeditions again, striking along the line of the coast, rather than penetrating inland as before.

He left May Ling at home. He assumed she would pass the day in gossip in the alleys and relied on her for intelligence reports. He was to be frustrated in this. When he returned in the dusk he would try to quiz her about her day but she would be evasive. Once, trudging back along the sand, smoke rising out of the mountainside ahead of him, he thought he saw her strolling on the beach. He followed the slight figure, a quarter of a mile ahead, but lost sight of his quarry as she entered the walls.

May Ling was waiting for him in the house. After food he noticed a little pile of sand on the floor but it was too late to determine whether he had brought it in himself.

'You were doing anything today, May?'

'Doing nothings.'

He still found it odd that a village woman should have been walking aimlessly along the coast. He was sure it had not been the boatwoman's stocky figure ahead of him.

Again, he tried to pump May Ling about village affairs. He had hardly seen one of the inhabitants since the confrontation in the valley. To his intense aggravation she was as obstinately unforthcoming as before.

'What you really did, May, hah?'

'Doing nothings.'

Then he fumed.

He was sure she was deliberately suppressing something. Yet, loyalty apart, it was in her interest to pool information with him.

At length curiosity got the better of him. He went down to the paddy the next morning. The fields had become one enormous scarred quagmire. He knew already that the crop was beyond saving. Ravaged at a later stage, it was just possible that the shoots might have survived. In the short space since their planting it had seemed they might be flourishing despite the unpromising soil.

Wallace returned quickly. Alone in the wasteland, he felt like a fly on a piece of rotting meat. There was an ominous silence over both the fields and the village. He jumped in the alley as a shutter banged.

Indoors the sensation of conspicuousness, of physical vulnerability was still there. As he rested his head in his hands he brooded on the thinness of his skull. He tapped his cranium with a knuckle. The expression of concern on May Ling's face was gratifying. It gave him the appetite to manage a sesame seed cake, of which she had laid in a store from the tea shop.

'I tell you, May, it was just like cowboy ghost town out there.'

The villagers had been out destroying the new shrine at Eagle Rock. This had been done on the headman's instructions. It was his last expedient. The arrival of the demonstrators and the repercussions of their visit had actually given him valuable leeway. The loss of the second crop had numbed the will of the farmers. The meeting in the ancestral hall had never taken place.

In this interval the headman had written to the geomancer for a second opinion. The answer, delivered by a messenger on a rusty bicycle, was clear and plausible. The eagle had renegued. It had not only taken the pearl constructed for it by the villagers but had snatched all the remaining good fortune of the settlement and flown away with it to other villages. So much was evident from the fact that the three other settlements within a radius of twelve miles from the mountain had not suffered serious damage to their crops. In fact, it was now generally known, the Hakkas had produced a bumper harvest of sugarcane and had enjoyed unprecedented examination success.

There was only one thing to be done and the village had done it. The entire population of the settlement, excluding the immigrant farmers, crossed into Hakka territory and smashed the shrine. There was nothing stealthy about this raid which was undertaken in broad daylight. The village watched as the young nightwatchmen scaled the outcropping and threw down the pearl. The women fell on it with sickles and poles, crushing the ball of mud and lime into dust. The rock itself could not be destroyed but token punishment was inflicted on it with the tools available.

Wallace was disturbed when he found out about the latest episode in the village's evolving *fung shui*. But at least the enraged villagers had not thought of taking the last of the gun-cotton from him.

Wallace got the idea from the children. They had been playing around the pond which had been left after he had drained the fields. Some of the older children had lashed a few logs together into a raft and had floated themselves out into the centre.

There was nothing strikingly original in itself about the idea of a marina.

As a child Wallace had been to the boating lake at Lai Chi Kok amusement park. The inhabitants of Shatin village, situated on an estuary close to the city, also rented out bicycles for exercise on a dusty and otherwise unproductive area by the river. It was the novel combination of ideas already extant which made Wallace's scheme so genuinely exciting. No one had ever thought of siting a recreational centre so far out in the most inaccessible part of the agricultural, the – as it were – functioning New Territories. At a stroke he converted disadvantage into distinction. The commercial possibilities of the idea were rapidly apprehended by the elders. The owner of the tea shop was a particularly enthusiastic advocate, and as a result Wallace was given a free hand.

Fortune, for once, was with him. No substantial dredging was required. The pond was of an even, adequate length. Only the boats needed building and there was timber in abundance on the hillsides.

There was debate over their design, though. Wallace inclined towards miniature paddle steamers, motivated by pedals. 'You had to have something different,' he argued. 'They already had row-boat at Lai Chi Kok.'

Unfortunately, the task was beyond the capabilities of the village carpenter. Instead he produced a facsimile of the boatwoman's sampan. Further versions of the same basic design followed. These were adequate. As Wallace pointed out: 'Like you didn't want to row all the way to Macau in them.'

But there was still something missing. He put it to May Ling: 'You were coming all the way here and then you did what, hah? You sat in your boat like you gone stupid or something, just turn your head around and look at nothing.'

154

And yet, at the same time, taken as a form of recreation for the Cantonese, the whole arrangement was also insufficiently passive. Too much, in fact, like work.

May Ling suggested: 'Let village people do rowings.'

'But then the visitor really got nothing to do.'

'Maybe you put fish in pond and they could do fishing.'

'May, that was real brain-wave.'

As a final touch Wallace decided to turn the pond into a classical water garden, with an island, wooden pagodas, silhouette bridges, and a spinning water-wheel and falls. Some bamboo shoots rapidly thickened at the water-side and he ran out a little plank pier. The mountains made a perfect setting: nature blended harmoniously with artifice. And when the frogs migrated to it they bestowed upon it the final touch of authenticity.

It remained to bring boaters to the boats. Wallace had two options open to him. Either tourists could come by ferry: in which case a jetty would have to be built off the beach. Alternatively, they could come by land, across the same track taken by police and Red demonstrators. It would be easier to build the pier. The trouble here was, end and means were insufficiently variegated. He sounded May Ling: 'It was bit funny, hah? You came on ferry and then you were here, you got on boat again.'

She saw the point.

The track was three miles from the nearest metalled road. It was still safe even after the rains but the surface had been lacerated by the unusually heavy traffic. The flagstones, where they existed, would have to be re-laid and strengthened. Widening the path throughout its entire length was at present beyond the capabilities of the settlement. However, Wallace took his remaining chunks of explosive and blew up a big tree-trunk which had partially blocked the way a mile outside the village. He did it to amuse his labourers; it could just as easily have been rolled away. But they did good work, putting shoring up on the narrowest parts of the walk and tidying up the earth falls. It would have to do: Wallace did not anticipate a sudden influx anyway. 'These things took time,' he cautioned May Ling.

To help things on their way, he had placards painted in Chinese characters and English letters, advertising the attractions of the water garden. He wrote the English legend himself, below the ritual headman's stylised ideograms. The boards were nailed to stakes and driven in to the shoulder of the highway leading to the market town. Wallace had reasoned that cars would have to slow down here from the suicidally high speeds prevalent in the New Territories.

The road and its vehicles alarmed Wallace. He had grown unused to it. Most of the traffic was commercial: sputtering ramshackle lorries, with a few private cars. He positioned the signs as advantageously as he could. The lorries passed perilously near, with a rush and a rattle. The drivers blared their horns in a continuous blast that rose into a crescendo, were suddenly past and wailed away.

As they were returning, he looked back from the brow of a hill, where the track dipped out of sight, and could see the vehicles jockeying for position. A slow-moving lorry was blocking the path of a car, sliding across to prevent it from overtaking every time the driver came alongside. Horns honked furiously.

Better results might be hoped for from the posters put up in the market town by the headman whenever he visited his concubine. One of the main tourist routes from the city to the frontier passed through the town.

Wallace also considered placing an advertisement in the *Tiger Standard* but rejected the idea as too expensive. If the water garden was the success hoped it would generate enough profit to plough back into expansion.

Community funds were by now low. But there had been additional help from an unexpected quarter. The immigrant farmers had donated nails, tools, and caulking for boats. They had a large stock of these commodities which they used for building poultry coops and crating their vegetables for the waggon-trip to market.

'Real nice of them, May,' Wallace pronounced.

'Of course. Their wife go tell them. They got brother and sister and mother and father in village. All family good to each other in hard time.'

'You had a lot to learn, May, you knew that?'

The four cyclists came bouncing down the track a week later. They swooped down the slope to the lake, glided round on their momentum, taking in the boats bobbing at their moorings, the pier and the pagodas on their rock islands, before beginning to pedal up the slope again.

Ever afterwards, Wallace wondered whether they had been among the first tourists to embark on the water, having first reconnoitred the spot. No cyclist ever used the track again, at least not while Wallace was resident in the village. But he liked to think they had returned without their machines.

The first trickle of customers began to come in shortly afterwards. The first group was a party of students from the Chinese university. All the men wore spectacles. The girls were in long cardigans and tartan skirts. They were heavily encumbered with hiking paraphernalia: portable radios, walking sticks, knapsacks, field-glasses, ropes, which they left on the pier. They hired three craft and were poled out by nightwatchmen, trained by the boatwoman. From shore, Wallace observed them carefully for signs of boredom or disappointment. But they toured the sights with interest before casting lines in the centre of the lake. Full satisfaction was guaranteed when one of the girls hooked a fish, although in the ensuing excitement it slipped back overboard. They finally left the water with five fish and had their catch fried over a brazier behind the pier, a stroke of entrepreneurial genius on the part of the tea shop owner. By chance, a consignment of wind-dried sausages was being sent to market in a cart by the immigrant farmers. In their dehydrated state the sausages were virtually odourless and made good back-rests for the passengers.

And so two more refinements were added to the original conception.

In the following weeks the cook-stall and carts provided an ancillary source of revenue that was not to be despised. Later, the villagers began to hawk sugarcane, straw hats, leaf aeroplanes and a kind of pea-firing bamboo popgun, operated by a plunger, that had been a traditional village toy for generations.

A certain routine now linked the days into larger units. For the first time, the village had to accommodate itself to the seven days of the urban cycle – in reverse. For five days the lake would be quiet, with a handful of customers monopolising the water. The other two would be frenetic as a mass of holidaymakers from the city competed for the limited facilities.

The commercial success of the lake had the effect of considerably simplifying the chain of relationships which perpetuated life in the village: the ratio between hands and mouths; the transformation of the stinking human input to the soil into the land's sustaining output; the whims of wind and tide and the control exerted over them by the operation of ceremony.

Henceforward, the question of subsistence conformed to two sides of an equation of elegant clarity: keeping a maximum number of boats

157

on the lake while allowing a minimum period to elapse before turning the protesting customers round.

There had been trouble here, with boaters arguing over the precise span on the water to which they felt their fare entitled them. In the early days the issue had on the whole been satisfactorily regulated by natural forces of supply and demand. Basically speaking, if there was a surplus of craft over hirers, time on the lake had been unrestricted. With the increasing popularity of the spot, however, this kind of rule of thumb was no longer an adequate measure. Angry scenes had taken place. One boat-load of tourists, just embarked on a trip, had been hooked in and forcibly ejected under the mistaken assumption that they were the previous occupants stealing more time. The hirers of the other craft had succeeded in staying out the whole day, hiding behind rocks and tall weeds, or manoeuvring themselves into the centre of a crowd of other boats.

It was an interesting problem: a profitable dilemma for the village. Wallace could wish other difficulties as enviable.

He considered issuing individual time-pieces to each boatman. This idea was soon discarded. Quite apart from the expense, craft with hired polers were no longer a majority, so rapid and wholesale had been the transformation in customer attitudes. To have had different boats coming in at equal but randomly staggered intervals would also have created logistical jams, opportunity for further unseemly incident.

The tea shop owner's brother-in-law, a ship's chandler at Tolo Harbour, was able to put the village in the way of what was required. This was a giant clock for measuring boxing rounds, with a bell loud enough to cut through the hubbub of a gymnasium or across greater distances over water. It was smuggled off an American aircraft carrier in an orange-box. The mechanism was simple and robust enough to survive the rigours of clandestine transportation and the vicissitudes of exposure at the lake. The workings were adjusted to ring at longer intervals and the boats sent out and brought back in unison. It was natural that the queueing customers should wish to take tea.

After the early turmoil had been sorted out, Wallace was again able to take pride in his creation. As he and May Ling floated on their own one morning after the weekend rush, he said: 'They could thank me for all this.'

May Ling pressed her knee against his. She had been trailing her hand over the side and now brought in a spiral of orange peel and a transparent newspaper.

11

The first signs of trouble came when four of the boats upturned for the night on the shore, with keels in the air, were found with their bottoms smashed in. Three more had been sunk at their moorings and rested in the shallow water, just beneath the surface. The carpenter had them all patched and caulked well before the two busy days. But it was disturbing, ominous.

The nightwatchmen mounted an ambush in shifts. At dusk they left the village with their heavy bamboo poles over their shoulders. Swinging at the end of these on loops of string were pyramids of cold rice, wrapped in lotus leaves. The boats were all pushed to safety in the centre of the lake. Just before dawn the shift was relieved by new sentries.

On the fifth night of their vigil, they were rewarded.

The three Hakkas were severely beaten, placed in pig-coops, submerged in the lake, pulled out again, beaten, re-immersed, extricated, and finally left sprawled face-down on the pier.

Water gushed from their mouths and nostrils as they were struck across the shoulders by the nightwatchmen. When light broke, one was still lying there. The body was removed.

The Hakka war-party came in daylight. It looked like the entire able-bodied male population of the settlement.

Wallace joined the village men as the tocsin gong sounded and they rushed out of the main gate. He considered any attack on the lake as of direct concern to himself.

Apart from tools, the Hakkas mustered several antiquated fowling-pieces. One pock-faced peasant, all gold teeth with a milky left eye, toted a double-barrelled weapon, heavily wired around the hammers. The breech plates had once been chased but were now orange with corrosion. Both tubes were loaded with bamboo arrows, barbed with glass. He held the weapon by the neck of the butt, as if it were a pistol.

The two groups met at a bend of the river. The nightwatchmen grouped themselves around the headman at an order from the tea shop owner and tightened their grip on their poles. Others slipped round to the Hakkas' rear to complete an encirclement.

Dogs from the village patrolled the space between the bands, snarling at the strangers, their scant fur bristling.

A number of the more excitable Hakka youths adopted exuberant but impractical fighting postures, feet wide apart, hands moving in slow, graceful circles in the air. In turn their actions produced a series of statuesque counter-demonstrations from the village youths. The nightwatchmen made minute adjustments to the distribution of their weight.

When a pair of the more enterprising village mongrels snapped at the shins of an armed Hakka, the situation further deteriorated.

The Hakkas' guns, at least as dangerous to those behind as to those before, began a slow descent from the perpendicular.

Wallace seized the headman and propelled him into the narrowing gap between the two front ranks.

The Hakkas listened, suspiciously at first.

Translating individual game strategies and expressions was difficult but the headman displayed fidelity to the concept, if not the details, of what Wallace whispered into his ear during pauses. Considering the immediate pressure they were both under, they did well to get the basic idea across.

The contest Wallace proposed was not recognisably, even in its externals, the game played by Goan Indians at the Kowloon Hockey Club, but it would serve its purposes as a form of restricted warfare.

A rendezvous having been arranged, the Hakkas left – under the circumstances – amicably.

At a meeting held under an awning, with the rival elders seated on rocks, it was decided to stage the contest over the area between Eagle Rock and the small stream which formerly marked the limit of village land.

Both parties had stipulated that the field of play should be equidistant from the two settlements. This had excluded several topographically more suitable sites. It was an uneven sort of pitch, which favoured the village over the Hakkas, in that they would be defending an uphill slope with the formidable obstacle course of the haunted bamboo grove as a final defence. To counterbalance this, however, the goal they must capture, Eagle Rock, was considerably smaller than the stream they guarded. Wallace tentatively suggested changing halves at an indeterminate point in the game but his proposal was vetoed by both sides: it would have flouted the whole principle of territorial propriety around which the game was predicated.

A purist of sorts, Wallace had been loth to jeopardise the fundamental convention of limiting play to a single ball but was flexible enough to concede a point and permit two. These were to be manufactured of rounded pebbles from the sea, thickly wrapped in hides.

Where, however, he remained adamant was in permitting only thirty men a side. And after decisively arguing that to field any more representatives would be a self-defeating exercise leading to full-scale hostilities on the field of play such as the game itself had been designed to circumvent, he was able to restrict the number of participants to fifty a side. This left a hundred players, give or take a few dogs, to be absorbed in an area the size of ten conventional pitches or three average segments of lineage land.

In the absence of other suitable materials, sticks were to be of bamboos not longer than the tallest men in the respective villages. Again, Wallace would have preferred equipment of standard dimensions but was forced to yield under joint pressure from the contestants. To his surprise, the Hakkas abided by the decision even when the biggest man in their village – in despite of the Hakkas' reputed Northern origins – was found to be a head shorter than his counterpart.

Even treated with heat, the bamboos could not be warped into a curve and had to be left in their natural condition.

By this stage absolute verisimilitude had long ceased to be the issue. Wallace was concerned with efficiency, and with both teams composed of novices he expected a frightful prospect of hacking, harrying, and chopping without, perhaps, any accompanying progress on the part of the ball or balls.

The inexperience of the players raised the question of an arbiter. Wallace, reluctant to place himself in a potential cross-fire from the protagonists, hoped (he knew too optimistically) for a degree of constraint and self-regulation from those involved. But the Hakkas and the villagers were again at one in electing a panel of six arbiters, three from each community, with the headman, ritual headman, and tea shop owner acting as village representatives. Wallace was given a roving supervisory role, similar to that of a linesman, although there were no provisions for a ball going out of play as such. Given the possibility of play taking place out of sight of the elderly arbiters, largely confined to one spot, Wallace's was an important role. The firing of a green rocket would signal the scoring of a Hakka goal to their supporters in the plain.

Wallace was able to secure a seven days' interval before the trial, during which he planned to initiate the villagers into the mysteries of the game as understood by himself.

He trained them on the beach, on damp sand, firmer than the powdery white stuff he kicked up in plumes on his long trudges.

. From the first session he was struck by the quality of the play. No individual was particularly outstanding for his skill or strength and there were many swiping misses at the ball before a burly nightwatchman connected flush, splintering his bamboo and sending the ball whirring lop-sidedly into a wave.

It was the co-ordination between the players that was impressive. In fact it was excessive. Wallace had difficulty in convincing the members of the two trial sides that they should not pass the ball between each other to facilitate the scoring of goals. Once this misapprehension was eradicated, progress was fast. There were no sustained displays of charismatic dribbling – such as the Goans would dazzle spectators with – but equally there was not the factionalism within teams which, Wallace remembered, had often sabotaged the Indians' best efforts, with the jealous stars fighting each other for possession. The nightwatchmen in particular shuttled the balls back and forth amongst each other as if born to the game, covering yards of the beach in swooping passes.

They preferred to play with one hand, prodding rather than paddling the ball before clouting it upfield in a swiping stroke to be trapped, briefly swizzled, and slung onward to a new receiver. The action reminded Wallace of the reaping stroke of the fields, but the hunching figures were no longer stationary in lines but moving forwards in patterns of deepening complexity.

From the position of discrete adviser, Wallace soon found himself in the part of goggling spectator. Formations gathered, broke, re-assembled, dissolved again before him to execute manoeuvres the tactical import of which he could only guess, until at the moment of fruition the meaning became apparent. There seemed no limit to the

162

players' fecundity: the ploys, offensive and counter-offensive, were generated and discarded in the moment, each phase of play blending into the next.

The strategy was positive. In the conventional sense of the position there was no goalkeeper with a delegated function of entrapment. The size of the 'goals' precluded such an arrangement; instead, by a process of natural selection, the slower players, that is to say the older men, gravitated to the ends of the beach where once they had stopped co-operating by helpfully flicking the ball to approaching attackers, they began to put up an effective spoiling action.

After Wallace had added the second ball to the game, however, thereby endowing an entirely different order of creative permutations, they proved no impediment.

The practices were carried on out of sight of the few midweek tourists, while the lake was supervised by the womenfolk.

By the end of the week, the village team had attained a remarkable degree of facility with the ball and a mutual understanding that was almost telepathic.

On the day of the tournament the village team met in front of the tea shop before dawn and were fed hot gruel. Crates of brightly coloured carbonated beverages, a successful new line in lakeside refreshment, were stacked under a tree, ready to be packed in panniers and slung on buffaloes. It was going to be a hot, arduous day for the contestants.

Wallace had expected the whole village to go and support their champions. At the last moment, however, after conferring with the tea shop owner, the headman delegated a number of young men to staff the lake in anticipation of customers (it was the third day of the cycle) and in case the Hakkas should have a treacherous attack planned while the village was empty.

By comparison with the Hakkas, who had just harvested their second rice crop, the village appeared to be in heavily depleted numbers.

The nightwatchmen, nucleus of the side, warmed up together, flicking a practice ball leisurely between themselves. They loped up and down the length of the plain. The rival supporters stood in two distinct camps, moving in and out like buffers in relation to the development of play.

Wallace made sure May Ling was behind him and would not allow her to stray.

He would have liked to have seen the two sides bully in dead centre of the plain for possession of the ball, but with two being played simultaneously, this was clearly impracticable.

In the end the Hakka and village teams each retired to their base line, and the biggest men on each side teed off.

The balls rocketed down the pitch off the bamboos, bouncing in the dust. With wild whoops the two teams pursued their respective advantages. The villagers' projectile – and as the day wore on it grew increasingly difficult to recognise as balls the ragged, irregularly spheroid objects lashed at with splintered staves – had ricocheted off a boulder a few hundred yards from the ruined shrine on Eagle Rock. The village attackers raced after it. The Hakkas had made the mistake of committing their entire manpower to the offensive and there were no defenders to oppose the villagers.

For their part the village defenders had trapped the Hakkas' ball. Switching it from player to player, they trotted up to meet the mass of Hakkas. As they closed, the Hakkas whirled their sticks in the air and the villager caught in possession looked in imminent danger of decapitation. There was the crack of stick on stick, indistinct oaths and – when Wallace looked again – dim figures lurching and swiping in thick orange dust. A villager, not the original possessor, emerged from the cloud with the ball and jabbed it upfield. Caught off-balance, the Hakkas skidded and lost valuable time in reversing their forward momentum before they could give chase to the elated village defenders, now become attackers.

Meanwhile, the village forwards had caught up with their own ball and scored against the lichen-covered side of Eagle Rock. They received the second, originally Hakka, ball from their defenders and smacked it against another part of the unguarded goal to register a double score. Wallace, who had been standing anxiously by the goal, was showered with splinters and powdered moss; he brushed chips of stone from his eyebrows and lobbed the balls back into play.

Doggedly, the Hakkas re-formed. The villagers had not given them their ball back and they showed no signs of wishing to recover it. This was only one of the *ad hoc* conventions that were to be evolved in the course of play and meticulously observed by both sides.

The villagers teed the balls off again from the middle of the plain; they hurtled down the pitch on different trajectories: one skeetering along the ground, raising puffs of dust, the other spinning slowly in a high, lazy parabola. Both landed at exactly the same distance from their point of origin but on different wings of the plain.

The Hakkas trapped the balls and moved into the attack. However, it was noticeable that they had left a rearguard by Eagle Rock.

A fierce struggle for the balls developed in mid-plain, culminating in a hive-away attack by a group of young Hakkas who had succeeded in detaching a ball from the ruck and stealing away with it unnoticed.

The village onlookers shouted unheeded warnings. The attackers remained ignorant of the battle raging behind them. At length the young Hakkas eluded the elderly village defenders. They proceeded up the slope, skirted the side of the bamboo grove and disappeared from sight. Minutes later, distant shouts indicated that they had succeeded in placing their token in the stream. A rocket rose from behind the hill and burst over the plain in a flash of orange and green smoke.

The elders under their awning were presented with a problem. Should play terminate for both balls to be simultaneously returned to a new cycle of play? Or should action with one continue while the other was driven off anew?

In the event the game went on while the Hakka forwards were returning from the stream. Their defenders, although heavily outnumbered, succeeded in thwarting the attacks of the villagers until they returned.

Play settled down with neither side able to maintain a decisive superiority. The village held on to its early lead but could not build on it. At the same time they foiled the Hakkas' fierce and increasingly disciplined attacks. Occasionally there would be two balls in play in the same half of the plain but these instances of local superiority were short-lived.

As the morning wore on, the light intensified, bleaching the dust which had caked on the players' perspiring bodies. Through slitted eyes Wallace checked the position of the sun, now a glowing white orb directly overhead.

On the moment, the village's two-man gong boomed. Play ceased. The contestants trooped off to different sides of the plain to rest and take refreshment. The Hakkas sat in the shadow of Eagle Rock, the villagers near the bamboos. They drank thirstily, smashing the necks of the bottles on stones. There was a stack of sugarcanes, green and purple sticks, which they chewed, spitting out the mangled fibres. The women chafed the shins of the injured, rubbing Tiger Balm into the bruises until they shone with a waxy veneer. Wallace swilled Green

Spot Orange around his mouth, expelling it in a thin stream through whistler's lips. He could still taste dust in his mouth.

The gong sent a flight of birds screeching from Eagle Rock.

In the afternoon the game dragged. It had developed into a dour test of stamina, all inventiveness drained from the play. The settlements both registered a goal immediately after the interval, taking advantage of each other's early lapses of attention. The offensive capacity of both teams clearly outstripped their capacity to defend themselves. The village, however, clung to its marginal lead, gained in the morning.

The balls shuttled monotonously back and forth or were wildly hacked at in panting, unruly scrimmages. They had become stained a deep brown by dust, the one which had been soaked in the stream a darker shade than the other. Repeated blows had distressed the surface of the hide wrappings; they now looked like shaggy pelts.

Eagle Rock's shadow elongated. When it tipped a white-washed stone in the middle of the plain, the game would end.

The Hakkas suddenly gained control of a ball, the lighter-coloured one, and headed for a gap in the village defence. The village rearguard emerged from their band of shade near the bamboos. The old men were at once dazzled by the sun's dying glare. Hakka after Hakka flitted through the gaps in their defensive cordon, while the defenders lumbered helplessly amongst their own huge shadows.

This time the Hakkas went by on the other side of the bamboos.

Another rocket went up, indicating that the score was tied.

Wallace eyed a warm-up ball jettisoned in the lee of a crate of Green Spot and considered hurling it into play. He rejected the idea: the consequences would have been too unpredictable. He hesitated only fractionally before kicking it away.

The shadow was almost touching the stone. Wallace calculated that there were another five minutes left in the game. A win for the village would have been satisfying but a tie would at least enable the lake to continue functioning without interference.

The villagers' ball was now in the middle of the plain, in a group of swinging players. The Hakkas appeared to be finishing slightly stronger than the villagers.

Shadows were lapping over the plain in blots and pools. Dying light briefly dappled May Ling's face and shoulders. What had been a quivering fretwork of light and shadow on the ground became a lake of pitch.

Suddenly the ball shot out of the vortex of struggling players. A stocky Hakka on the outskirts of the scrimmage took aim at it on the move and sent it bouncing over the plain. The players broke and gave chase. The ball continued rolling. Wallace, fresher than the players, was able to outdistance them from the side without undue exertion. The Hakka contingent that had just scored in the stream to even the match were returning. They spotted the slowing ball and raced towards it. Wallace arrived at the level of the ball at approximately the same time. In exuberance, the leading Hakka struck the ball with more force than necessary. It careered erratically up the slope to the bamboos, deflected off rocks and bumps.

The sun was now low, just disappearing behind the top of the mountain. Its last rays struck Wallace in the eye, not strong enough to dazzle, but still distracting in the gloom in front of him. He lost track of the ball momentarily. When he blinked, the sun had set but he was unable to locate the ball. Its eccentric course made it difficult to deduce a probable line from its previous path. Wallace screwed up his eyes. And caught sight of the brown, furry ball. It seemed to have accelerated: swerving, sliding, slipping, even – Wallace observed incredulously – zig-zagging, the ball appeared to have a life and volition of its own, in defiance of the laws of physics as Wallace had been taught them. And there was another. And another. All scurrying or loping, as the nature of the changing terrain dictated. The ball had multiplied itself.

They disappeared – without trace – into the bamboos.

The Hakkas had converged on the spot. Wallace looked at them. They had the glassy, comically stunned eyes and open mouths of a school of gold-fish. He shut his own with a faint pop.

12

There was to be no more trouble between settlements. The Hakkas retired undramatically from the field and the villagers made an orderly withdrawal to their own land.

To Wallace's mind the contestants had solved nothing. But to judge by the egregious behaviour of the villagers, the game had been cathartic at the least. There were no more night patrols and the boats were left casually beached after the day's use. In short the villagers behaved as if they had just won a signal victory.

Winking bonfires up the valley indicated that the Hakkas were celebrating with barbecued pigs. Rockets burst soundlessly in the night, fired from the tall Hakka watch-towers.

The news spread.

Emigrants from the two settlements staged marches through the market town on the same day, with banners and firecrackers, carefully avoiding each other's routes. There were no incidents.

Wallace was not sure about the propriety of all this. He believed in meriting one's victories. But both sides seemed to be happy with the arrangement; and certainly it had the advantage of saving face all round. The boundaries remained unchanged.

With the dispute settled and the lake a solid success, Wallace was free to speculate about events further afield. And out of a passing interest in developments in the outside world he began to feel for the first time a certain staleness and dissatisfaction. He was, he realised with awe, home-sick. Home-sick for the Poons!

May Ling, too, had been spending less time in the alleys. Once, as he passed under the walls, he had seen her in the dark, staring at the competing shimmer of night and paler shadows on the nearest of the Nine Dragons. He observed her for a while before moving on. In her own secretive way she was as restless as he was.

Mr Poon's promised summons came, therefore, opportunely. It arrived in the village by bicycle messenger and was delivered personally by the ritual headman. The village's new prosperity had resulted in lavish spending on ceremony but he looked as lean as ever.

Wallace left the envelope on their bed and went to look for May Ling.

He found her on the beach.

She was wearing tight countrywoman's trousers rolled up to the calves. Her feet were buried in sand up to her delicate ankle-bones, which were sprinkled with fine white particles. She approached him with her hands jauntily on her hips by turning her toes in towards each other and out again. She banged her hip against his and came to a halt. She put her arm across his neck.

Wallace grinned awkwardly. He stooped and by way of distraction came up with some flat pebbles which he started to skim across the waves.

May Ling knocked his store of ammunition off the flat of his palm. She pulled her blouse over her head. Wallace looked hurriedly up and down the deserted beach. She peeled her breeches off, staggered as they snagged her legs. She reminded Wallace of a deer caught by a bolas. She tugged one leg free and kicked them off. They sailed over her husband's head, blinding him with sand. When he had rubbed the grit out of watering eyes, he saw May Ling running into the waves in her underwear.

A cold wind blew. It was long past the season for sensible bathing.

He followed warily onto the damp sand. It turned into orange shingle just before the water's edge, the waves rattling in and hissing out. The sea-floor along this part of the coast was known to shelve sharply a matter of a few feet from shore, plunging treacherously into tide-scooped wells.

Wallace called to her but went unheeded as she plunged into the base of a swelling wave. He had already unbuttoned his shirt when she re-appeared some distance from land. He cupped his hands but the wind blew away his warning.

May Ling began to strike out parallel to the line of the beach. The strong current abetted her. Wallace had to walk fast to keep up with her. After a while May Ling swam across the current to her husband, judging the amount of deflection precisely. But she had not finished. Still some twenty yards from the beach, she reversed direction and returned the way she had come. She was obviously familiar with the intricacies of the currents for she moved as quickly as before. Hers was not an elegant stroke: with a chin tilted nervously back on a stiff neck and hands urgent under the surface. She spat frequent mouthfuls of salt water, pulling wry faces as she did so. Having re-attained her original point of departure, she came in dog-like: a resemblance given substance by the matted coils of hair which hung like the ears of a bedraggled pekinese. She halted in knee-deep water as Wallace came to greet her. A look of cunning passed over her dripping face and as quickly vanished. She bent, as if to scratch her leg. Wallace took all the water she could hold in her cupped hands full in the face.

His soaked shirt stuck to his chest in the chilly wind.

He was hit by another deluge. And another. May Ling tittered. He opened his mouth and tasted the bitterness of salt water. May Ling began to kick spray at him in a continuous curtain, using alternate legs. His shouted threats had no effect on her. He remonstrated, appealing to her good sense. He retreated slightly. 'May, I got good news.'

She closed in, kicking lightly. He begged weakly: 'You stop, I would tell you something to please you.' The splashing stopped.

'I bang my foot on stone, Wallace.'

He was instant solicitude. 'Show.'

She hopped upon one leg. Wallace bent. This time there was shingle as well in the cloud of spray.

Wallace chased her up the beach. Despite himself, he was laughing. May Ling moved awkwardly but managed the feat of picking up her clothes without breaking stride.

She was reading the letter when he came through the door. She had already laid out a fresh shirt for him.

They were able to return by road. The link-road started by the coolies had been recently finished and curved at its nearest part to within two miles of the village. The way to it lay over difficult ground but a guard of honour acted as bearers and conducted them to the bus-stop. After that, it was easy going.

Part Three

1

Mr Poon had shrunk. Wallace was barely able to dissemble his shock. When his father-in-law made the motions of rising to him, the old man's trousers had sagged, grotesquely enormous at the waist. Mrs Poon and Fong were with him in the reception room. Like Mr Poon, it seemed smaller. Fong had gently pushed him back down again. His money-belt, notched to the nearest hole, had risen well beyond the emaciated outlines of his rib-cage until it encircled his arm-pits. Instead of compensating for the thinness of his limbs, the disappearance of his comfortable belly made those appendages seem gawky. His bald dome no longer shone.

They saw him surreptitiously adjust his money-belt under his blankets and quilts. Wallace proffered his hand and had to wait as Mr Poon fumbled before extending a veiny claw through his coverings. He did not ask them questions about their stay in the village nor did he refer to the circumstances of Wallace's departure.

After the formulaic courtesies there seemed little else to say. Mrs Poon nodded benignly at the couple, indicating the audience was over.

The sisters were unfolding the camp beds in the bedroom and stowing the cardboard cases underneath. The sacks of root-ginger and peanuts presented as a farewell gift by the villagers had already been taken to the kitchen.

The sisters bustled happily. They smiled shyly at Wallace. Immediately on the defensive, he glared back. They retired, hands folded, eyes down-cast. As they were rounding the corridor, he called out for tea. It came with a quartered orange and two steaming, perfumed flannels.

Wallace sucked the acid fruit noisily. Acting with the tea, it scoured the film on his teeth, leaving them like silk. May Ling wiped his mouth for him with her own flannel and then drew the drapes across the window. 'Time for siesta, hah, Wallace?' She joined him on the edge of the two beds he had pushed together.

The boys had been away when they first returned: on a camping trip organised by the school, so the sisters had informed Wallace. The school's long summer vacation was, apparently, just about to end.

'The boy almost ready to do their exam,' he had remarked conversationally to Ah Lung. There had been no reply.

Wallace was genuinely looking forward to seeing the boys again. 'I was their idol, you know,' he boasted to May Ling, who nodded matter-of-factly. Ah Lung just spat into the cuspidor and rustled his newspaper in front of him.

Wallace was taking a mid-morning snack with some of his former associates from Department when the boys returned early on a Sunday.

He was alerted by the familiar khaki satchels, somewhat more stained and faded, slung from their customary pegs in the corridor. The boys, however, were not to be found in the house.

There were shouts from the playground, audible through the balcony windows. Glimpsed fleetingly through the thinning foliage of the trees, two heads flashed down a slide. This was deserted by the time Wallace had crossed the nullah. From the centre of the playground rose shrill screams. Wallace hurried over. Standing on the edge of a little pit, he looked down on a strange scene.

Clarence and Hogan, shoving from out of a crouch, heads between their arms, were sprinting around the pit, causing the merry-go-round it contained to revolve at high speed. With every other revolution Clarence would leap onto the platform, balancing on one leg as he struck sparks from the ground with the nails in his other shoe. Smaller children, who had now stopped screaming, clung desperately to the railing.

The whole contraption dipped up and down, clearing the ground by a few inches. Clarence jumped off and brought the wheel to full speed again. The children began to cry.

'Ah Kei! Ah Chung!'

The boys looked up; they did not recognise Wallace immediately. They jumped onto the merry-go-round slowing it with their combined weights.

They spun round a few times before Hogan stuck out a foot to bring it to a final halt. He was wearing a fur hat with a beaver-tail, of a type worn by frontiersmen or trappers in the Rocky Mountains in the early nineteenth century.

The children ran off. The boys swarmed up the steps of the tiny amphitheatre.

'OK, Uncle?'

This was not quite how Wallace had envisaged re-encountering his nephews; nevertheless, he made the best of the circumstances.

'Hullo, boys. You both grew big, hah? I could see straightaway.'

Hogan, who had been the one to greet him, sneered. His manner implied that Wallace would have to do better than that.

Clarence extracted a green plastic pistol from his trousers pocket, put the muzzle to his mouth and ejected a purple lozenge onto his already stained tongue.

'PEZ, Uncle Wallace?'

'Wah, thank, Clarence.'

Hogan blew and aggressively popped a pink bubble.

'Going home for lunchtime, I suppose?' Wallace was hinting, rather than ordering. They went back over the nullah, Hogan stamping in front, Clarence walking with his uncle. When they reached the road Hogan waited for a break in the traffic before loping across, emitting a shrill war-cry and fanning his open hand before his mouth. Clarence followed suit, leaving Wallace sedately in the rear.

The boys and their father were apparently ignoring each other. Beyond unavoidable encounters at the cross-sections of alimentation and sanitation – made impersonal in any case by the publicness of life at Robinson Path – there was no contact; certainly no communication.

Even had the boys still brought back homework with them when school resumed (which they no longer did) it was doubtful whether they would have tried to enlist Wallace's help in their present recalcitrant frame of mind.

He tried to bring up the issue of homework one evening after food, only to be met with fish-looks from the boys.

The weight of curricular emphasis at the school had been radically re-apportioned, the boys explained.

Their father butted in. 'They didn't trust the little bastard not to cheat at home. But maybe you thought they were just lying and leaving it behind, hah?'

Wallace smiled sympathetically at the boys.

Hogan let out a prolonged, rattling belch, expertly re-cycling his store of air. The sisters tittered faintly.

★

A month after their return, with the weather cool and dry and the slides in the playground covered in yellowing leaves, Mr Poon took to his bed, where he was ministered to by his daughters.

He had begun to absent himself from meals soon after Wallace had come back, almost as if he had been holding a position until relieved.

This had necessitated a readjustment of seating arrangements to fill the new power vacuum.

Ah Lung, who had grown a moustache, had wished to assume his father's place at the round table, next to the wireless. It did not occur to Wallace to challenge him. He had nodded to Ah Lung and placed himself, as he had been doing, in his old seat.

Ah Lung twiddled moodily with the knob of the wireless.

The amahs arrived with the soup rather earlier than usual, as the rest of the family were filing in. Ah King negotiated the narrow space between the back of Ah Lung's chair and the wall, holding the tureen at arm's length over her head.

Ah Lung stroked the thin pile of his moustache with satisfaction.

Ah King insinuated herself past him and placed the dish with its brimming marrow-shell in front of Wallace. Mrs Poon moved from her old seat to flank Wallace and removed the ladle from her son's grasp. May Ling pressed her knee against her husband from the other side.

Ah Lung's eyes bulged.

The sisters passed their shell-pink bowls to Wallace, the one inside the other. He served them soup. The family waited. At length Ah Lung passed his bowl to Wallace. He stared challengingly round he table.

Wallace averted his eyes.

The amahs removed the limp marrow. In came eggs. The others waited while Wallace took first peck with his chop-sticks, dip-lomatically choosing white rather than yolk. On such compromises were dynasties founded.

Afterwards May Ling served him a glass of tea in the reception room.

A few days later Mr Poon summoned Wallace to an audience in his sickroom.

He was lying on his back on his bed, propped up by a teak chest. Eldest Sister was preparing an unpleasant herbal infusion for him. It was difficult for Wallace to reconcile the shrivelled old man before him with the domestic tyrant he had once feared.

The old man motioned to him to sit on the edge of the bed. Wallace rubbed the bronze Buddha's belly with his forefinger before perching himself uncomfortably on the edge of Mr Poon's couch.

'No, no, son, you were coming nearer.'

The old man flapped his hands languidly. Wallace heard the door close softly behind the sisters.

'Business very hard now, Ah Wallace.'

'Ah.'

'I would hide nothings from you. I needed your helps now in all thing. I knew about the thing you could do. So no need for modest. You already prove yourself. I ask you to return so you could look after thing for me.'

Wallace turned down the corners of his mouth and rocked modestly on his haunches.

'Actually it surprise me.'

Wallace's startled eyes met Mr Poon's which remained expressionless, black as the beads of his abacus. They both started to laugh, Mr Poon silently, wheezing.

Two anxious heads appeared around the door, one over the other. Wallace ordered the sisters away. Mr Poon nodded approvingly. 'That was the good way.'

From then on Wallace had the keys to Mr Poon's desk, drawers, and chests; all except the teak coffer, which Mr Poon kept in his room. He installed himself at the desk in the corridor, raising the barricade of newspapers even higher around himself. He sat in a stockade. He sifted the invoices, correspondence, schedules into neat piles, using Department classifications and procedure.

At first Mr Poon sat by him in a rocking-chair, advising, informing, and warning by turns. Wallace was astounded at the breadth of his father-in-law's commercial interests. A whole network unfolded before him. He was not surprised to see that Mr Poon had once held a directorship in a fireworks manufactory; something of no particular significance, although, reading between the lines of the flat legal phrases, the parting with the other directors did not seem to have been amicable. However, he was intrigued to see the name of the Chief Clerk at Department cropping up amongst Mr Poon's contacts from a relatively early stage in his career.

On this point, though, Mr Poon reacted with a touch of his former asperity and Wallace tactfully abandoned his enquiries.

After a few weeks Mr Poon began to emerge from his bedroom less frequently and when he did sit in his supervisory capacity would spend long hours staring into the kitchen. Then he stopped coming altogether, and Wallace forged on alone with increasing confidence. One evening, sitting in the flannel pyjamas May Ling had chosen for him in the Wing On department store, in the throes of coping with a problem in mental arithmetic, he had recourse to Mr Poon's abacus. As he flicked the black beads he dislodged a small key underneath the frame. Memories revived. He put the key to the top tray in the bureau. To his enormous surprise, there was a fob-watch in there, identical in all respects to the one he had pawned. He swung it by the chain and wound it. It ticked sweetly. He dropped it into the breast-pocket of his pyjama jacket. Before going to sleep he set it by the church clock at midnight.

While Wallace occupied himself in the corridor, May Ling seemed happy to consort with Fong. Mrs Poon sometimes joined them. Wallace could eavesdrop from his desk, leaving him wondering how much Mr Poon had heard him say in the old days.

May Ling had a fund of folk-lore brought back from the old women of the village and her coarser bucolic anecdotes proved the ideal counterpoint to her foster mother's dramatic tales of southern court life in the silver age. The sisters, still given to ritual hair-braiding, attended on each other in a corner of the room, pretending not to listen. Soon they gave up this pretence; they would laugh or gasp at appropriate junctures while they sat with their backs turned, looking out of the window. Later, they would demand explanations or elaboration of interesting details. But they always began the session at the far end of the room, furtively edging their stools down like the children in the playground in their game of freezing in motion as they stole up on a playmate in a corner. If Fong or May Ling moved at all – and they never looked behind – the sisters immediately halted. Half-way through the morning they would prepare refreshments in the kitchen, passing Wallace with eyes averted.;

The days passed peacefully. Mr Poon was now rarely seen. Wallace took to sitting with May Ling and Fong in the playground during the evenings. The air would be fragrant with charcoal and garlic from the houses down the valley, over-powering the staleness from the nullah.

Once the three of them took the cable-car to Victoria Peak to enjoy the view from the summit. They walked from the windswept little station with its whining cable-drums and bright lights out into the darkness.

May Ling leaned far out over the railing at the edge of the precipitous granite cliff, kicking her legs behind her dangerously. Far below, the illuminated waters of the harbour glittered and beyond rose the mountains on the mainland.

'Wah, Wallace, you looking hard you could see the village light from here.'

Wallace patted her rump affectionately. 'No, you couldn't.'

'You tried hard you could.'

He humoured her. 'Eiyah! I thought that I could.'

She jabbed him with her elbow. They stood there watching the lights on the ships in the harbour until they were cold. Afterwards, they had English cream cakes at the Peak Café, and milky tea. Wallace sent back the dish of sliced lemon which arrived with the hot-water jug and milk.

Mrs Poon's grand mah jong parties had been in abeyance for some time. Now they resumed. Fong appeared extensively versed in the game. May Ling, of course, had acquired a crude working knowledge during her adolescence at the sessions at which she had assisted in the capacity of mascot.

The women began by playing amongst themselves, idly clattering the tiles together on the same table the boys had once used for their home-work, pushing and pulling with flat hands in movements reminiscent of the bridge-work of a particularly histrionic concert pianist or, in the shuffle's concluding phase, of participants in a seance, with tentative fingers on the same gyrating glass. The bright lights playing on the table, however, and the crash of tiles, like muted gunfire to Wallace in the corridor, would have been sufficient to daunt any spectres thus summoned.

Mrs Poon originally brought out the pieces, which had been part of her dowry, to illustrate the point in a story. The tiles were beautifully crafted in bamboo, ivory, and jade. Once out it had been a short step to demonstrating their use on the table and, after the tiles had been shuffled, to arrange them in a two-tier wall. Dice were thrown. Then a lop-sided but earnest game of three players was initiated, with Mrs Poon taking the part of a fourth player.

By the end of the week invitations had been sent out. Mabel Yip was amongst those first requested to make up a foursome. She arrived by taxi in the early afternoon, sending out the driver to pull the bell-rope for her. Wallace heard her climbing the dark staircase without faltering. She greeted the sisters graciously. He half-rose from his desk in the dim hallway. Mabel's tight sheath-like cheongsam glowed but her face was shadowy. Her thighs showed pale through the deep slash in the sides of the dress. She was carrying something in her arms.

'The big-shot now, hah?' Her tone was, nevertheless, friendly. 'You were already quite famous.'

She swept into the reception room, trailed by the sisters, also in cheongsams for the occasion, although of a less clinging cut than Mabel's.

Wallace followed and saw May Ling and Fong leaning over the balcony, giggling. They were swinging the taxi-driver's fare just out of his reach in the provisions basket. Fong whispered to May Ling. She dropped the provisions basket and they advanced on Mabel, still flushed from their game.

Mabel let out an excited yap, through some ventriloquist's trick seemingly produced from the region of her chest. Totally, at variance with the rest of her behaviour, although he had seen Mabel in her kittenish mood with Allardyce, this puzzled Wallace until he identified the emitter as a small lap-dog she was cradling. Mabel dropped it, scrabbling, on the throne.

'Sausage dog, hah? What his name called?'

'Mitzi.'

Wallace produced a 'nugget'. 'There was one dog they got you could put it in cup it was so small. They came from Mexico.'

Mabel did not bat one of her mascara-loaded eye-lids. 'I knew. We had one of them when we live in Jardine Look-Out but the next door house Alsatian go and eat it one day when I didn't look. People up there had guard-dog and they didn't give them foods so they would go and eat burglar.'

'Atchoo!' Wallace clearly enunciated the sound, cleverly disguising the expulsion of air itself.

'You had cold?' Mabel enquired solicitously.

Wallace was apologetic. 'Sorry, Mabel. Your perfume quite strong.'

May Ling ushered Mabel to her place at the table. Mrs Poon, seated, awaited with the seriousness of a sacrificial high priestess. Both May Ling and Fong were wearing blossom behind their ears. Mrs Poon had draped a black cardigan over her shoulders; she was obviously anticipating a protracted session. The cold that came from a sluggish circulation was the major source of discomfort in the terminal stages of such proceedings. Without permitting further small-talk, in fact without addressing a single word of greeting to Mabel, Mrs Poon began to mix the tiles. May Ling just had time to flip open a black box and push it over to Mabel. It contained coloured cigarettes.

Wallace retired to his desk.

He hoped the sounds of play were not keeping Mr Poon awake. He had been sleeping a lot recently.

When he returned it was already dark outside. Clouds of smoke had settled above the mah jong table, twisting and billowing in the bright light. The players' faces shone. Wallace positioned himself behind the sisters who did not appear to have moved since he vacated the room. Mabel rose, removing the mauve cigarette from her holder and stubbing it in her tea-saucer. She indicated to Eldest Sister that she should take her place. After coy protestations of inadequacy, tinged with genuine apprehension, she did so. The others had been continuing, regardless of the small interruption.

Mabel took Wallace to the open window with her, where she reloaded her cigarette-holder.

'The old lady play you hard, hah?'

Mabel rolled her eyes. 'We hardly began it yet. Some party I remember went for three day and night. Actually, I was so happy to come. I was just lonely old woman now, Wallace. Only Mitzi to keep me company.'

She placed a bejewelled hand flat on her chest and looked sideways at Wallace to judge the effect of this confession.

'No, no, Mabel. You had Pippy you could be proud of. You make that girl everything she had.'

Mabel sighed. 'Now that Pippy marry she forgot old woman like me.'

'Marry?' Wallace simulated polite shock. The news, though unexpected, was not totally surprising. He hazarded a guess. 'Her English soldier boy-friend, hah?'

Mabel confirmed this. 'She gone "home" now for a leave. Sometime I got a letter from her but not for a few months now. It happen quite quick.'

There was a commotion at the other end of the room. Second Sister, hands lifted in horror, was endeavouring to separate Mitzi from the throne. May Ling giggled. 'Mitzi go and have a accident in Hogan Davy Crockett hat.'

Mabel excused herself and went to relieve Second Sister. She proceeded to the corridor where she could be heard rebuking the dog in pidgin English.

When she returned Wallace was encouraged by her previous flexibility to bring up the potentially difficult subect of Mr Allardyce.

'Ah! Poor Brians.'

'It was sad he go and die sudden like that.'

Mabel looked quizzically at him. 'Die?' She began to laugh. 'Poor Brians just disappear.'

'Ah, that make me happy to hear.'

Mabel's journeying eye had summarised developments at the far side of the room. 'Tcha! I better get back before Ah Jik could maybe make me lose game. I enjoy my talking to you Wallace. We could see more of the other.'

Rarely had Mabel been so gracious. Wallace called after: 'I sure wish I could have met Pippy husband.' He intended it as an oblique compliment to herself and as such it was taken.

2

Then Mr Poon died. It was an event greeted with considerable surface agitation but which actually caused minimal disruption to the fabric of everyday life in Robinson Path. In his last days Mr Poon's will once evident, so uncomfortably evident, in even the most minor aspects of the household economy, had diminished to the point where he was no longer felt even as a brooding background presence. Encouraged by Mabel, May Ling had quite brazenly patrolled the house wearing provocative applications of Western cosmetics. To Wallace this had been unseemly, to kick a man when he was down. But he had held his peace.

Eldest Sister broke the news. She had gone in alone to Mr Poon with his morning refreshment a week after the party. She found him on the bed, his eyes open. After the body had been taken away, Wallace saw the tray where she had left it on the teak chest. The blankets had been folded on the bottom of the bed; there was, of course, no indentation to mark the body's place.

The Joy Geen funeral home was in a remote part of Quarry Bay where the tenements thinned along the side of the highway until they were succeeded by a quarter of desolate wharfs and godowns. Tall green trams ran clanking down the straight, able to put on a rare spurt of speed before they coasted to take a corner and rumbled on around the bend to Shaukiwan, the Tai Koo dockyards, and the fishing communities beyond. Juddering dangerously from side to side in the narrow iron grooves, the drivers pinged their tinny bells as they thundered along; it seemed more from exuberance than the desire to warn pedestrians, of whom there were few in this sparsely inhabited area.

Just before the bend and the shipyard there was a quarter of larger warehouses and nightwatchmen's houses, with a few cook-stalls huddled around a kind of compound by the main godown. Here, partially hidden by the looming walls of the biggest warehouse, was the funeral home. It was a six-storey block built at the beginning of the century, originally as a coastguard station in the days before the mass spill-over from Victoria to Causeway Bay and the building of squatters' shacks on the hillsides.

The harbour lapped at the back of the building, where a blank wall reared from the water. All the windows had been bricked in. The sealed apertures had been painted black, like eyepatches. A frame for block and pulley jutted just below the flat roof; it was rumoured to have been a device, not a gallows exactly, from which captured pirates had been depended upside down by the leg, prior to formal decapitation on a defunct and now rotting jetty to the east of the funeral parlour.

Wallace had accompanied the women here. Ah Lung and the boys had preceded them earlier in the day in a hire-car.

Mr Poon lay in state in a coffin lined with plum-coloured satin. He was dressed, at the last, in the same European-style lounge suit, white shirt, and tie he had worn to the dinner with Mr Allardyce. The room smelt overpoweringly of flowers, lilies mostly. Wreaths festooned the walls and were also flung haphazardly on the floor. The petals of these had been squashed by careless feet and the dried sap had glued them to the floor.

Ah Lung advanced on the latest arrivals. He had been using the skirt of his jacket to polish the brass handles on the coffin. His crêpe soles squelched loudly. He halted and held up one shoe across the opposite knee to form a human figure of four and peeled a strip of vegetable gum from the sole.

'Where the hell you been, Nolasco?'

Wallace decided to ignore the provocation; distraction came in the shape of the women. Eldest Sister, red-eyed, chaperoning Second Sister and Mrs Poon, negotiated a passage through the leafy obstacles on the floor.

The chamber they stood in was one of several leading off a main thoroughfare in the building. They were not alone. Other parties passed up and down, visible through the wide, doorless opening to their room. One of the home's attendants appeared in traditional costume and piled more wreaths on the floor.

Electric candles flickered by Mr Poon's casket. The larger wreaths had been distributed around the coffin. Above him, on the wall, were nailed some white bed-sheets, with black ideograms painted on them. The dye had dripped from some of the more complex characters.

In death Mr Poon's usually stolid features had taken on a

complacent cast, illusion produced by the mortician's art: in life the man, resourceful, sometimes ruthless, but always an adversary to respect, had never been that.

'You had to say that about him.'

'Hah?'

'Nothing, May. Just saying a little prayer.'

The family arranged themselves on the row of chairs opposite the door. Wallace hopping around the room in a kind of goose-step, attempting to land in the centre of the floral rings on the floor as he trailed Ah Lung, expected at any moment a photographer to appear and snap the seated group. Their faces bore the look of glazed expectancy peculiar to subjects of professional portraiture. Only the boys were missing. Ah Lung appeared to be looking for them.

'They go and explore, Ah Lung. Like all boy wanted to do.'

Ah Lung went back to polishing the coffin handles.

Wallace's stomach rumbled noisily; they had left the house in a hurry. He settled down to the latest issue of the *Reader's Digest*. Halfway through the article there was a disturbance in the corridor.

Wallace joined Ah Lung at the door.

Clarence and Hogan, each in the grip of an outraged adult custodian, were being carried down the corridor in what looked like a parody of the classic Hollywood lynch scene. They were released at the door but seized by their father as they tried to find sanctuary in the funeral chamber. The crowd was only partially mollified by Ah Lung's stuttered apologies and did not disperse until he had simultaneously rapped both boys on the head with his clenched fists. He drew a hollow, wooden echo from their scalped heads.

Apparently, they had been caught pilfering from the other party's sacrificial baked meats.

'You little bastard, you had no respects?'

'Father, we hungry.'

Ah Lung aimed kicks at them, which they avoided. They retreated behind the amahs.

The afternoon and early evening passed desultorily; no one of any significance would be paying their respects until the next day. The family dozed off on their chairs. The boys had gone home with the amahs, still officially in disgrace.

Refreshment, licit this time, arrived at midnight. Wallace ate with Mrs Poon, the only other person awake. She ate heartily.

May Ling had her face buried in Fong's shoulder. Mrs Poon put her coat over both of them. She indicated an empty seat next to her own chair. Wallace shook his head. He went into the corridor. Lights still burned. More tributes to the dead man had arrived in the afternoon and had been stacked outside by the parlour attendants. A large wreath from the Amoy firecracker company had slipped off the pile. Wallace replaced it gingerly. Mrs Poon had dozed off when he returned.

He took this opportunity to inspect Mr Poon more closely, remarking that a dark shadow had appeared beneath the granulated powder dusted onto the face of the corpse. He looked around. He could not quite nerve himself to put flesh in contact with flesh; metal, either keys, coins, or watch-lid, would have been too abrasive. A new bank-note, folded lengthwise, proved the ideal medium for scooping and retaining a sample, a large flake, the removal of which unhappily left the face of the deceased in the same condition as the older enamelware in circulation at Robinson Path. Bristle, dark and persistent, gleamed in a white crater of exposed flesh. Wallace scraped his bottom teeth over the stubble on his own now perspiring upper lip. He decided against embarking on any kind of make-shift patching-up operation; there was an iron law to the effect that only worse could follow. Instead, he rucked up the folds of plum satin in a kind of ruff around the dead man's neck. The electric candles, although giving off heat in uneven pulsations, were overpowered in the illumination from above. Artificial light was not, in any case, the best thing for complexions, as he remembered. The image of his own yellowed face in the lift to Mabel Yip's penthouse came back to him. Mr Poon had been positively benevolent that evening. Wallace was sure the old man's spirit would interpret his actions according to their non-sacrilegious intent.

'I bet you make me wipe it off you, hah?' he whispered softly now, patting down the lining. 'Actually you were once dead they thought they could do anything to you. I bet you real glad your whisker grow underneath.'

He went to his chair and closed his eyes.

Later, came the sounds of cleaning: buckets clanking, the scrape of stiff wet brush-heads on dirty concrete sounding in his half-comatose condition like the preliminary to some massive expectoration.

The lights in the windowless room were fractionally dimmer; otherwise the airless cell might have been designed – for instance by Red brainwashers – to insulate occupants against the sensation of elapsing time. He decided it would be in May Ling's best interests to have some air.

The dawn was grey and a little chilly. The jetty, smothered in orange lichen and protected at water-level by a coating of slimy green moss, creaked in the swell. It had the appearance of a raft, floating on the surface of the water. By the Tai Koo dockyards a dredger began to stutter, its wheel and buckets picking up speed from a lazy start. An Indian nightwatchman appeared from the complex of godowns, carrying his huge leather sandals. Coolies and stevedores at the Tai Koo yards had already been working long enough to have a break. They squatted on their haunches, eating thick slices of bread smeared with condensed milk.

'Plenty of trouble-maker there,' he remarked. He accentuated the last syllable of the compound noun like a Rediffusion newsreader.

'They had big strike there before war.'

May Ling nodded sulkily. She resented being brought out so early. He brushed the corner of her eye delicately, rubbing the secretion away between his thumb and forefinger. 'You had piece of sleeps there.'

May Ling slapped his hand irritably. On the way to the parlour she had a change of mood. 'You know what I was real hungry for? A piece of coolie bread with sticky milk.'

She ate it at the cook-stall, sucking her slim fingers zestfully.

'You were funny sometime, you knew that, May?'

They went in, both chortling over her newly discovered eccentricity.

Ah Lung ambushed them on the third-floor landing. 'You sure found a good way to show respects to dead peoples.'

Wallace straightened his black tie before joining the family.

The amahs brought the boys at midday and filed between the candles to pay their respects to the dead man, after which Mrs Poon gave them red envelopes.

After tea, it fell to Wallace to escort the boys to the ablutions in the basement. These were reached through a trapdoor in the ground floor. Cubicle after cubicle, laterally partitioned but frontally exposed with no door, extended on both sides for fifty yards. Even the boys were silenced. Then they sprinted down the aisle, letting out their Commanche war-whoops in a fierce treble.

Huge concrete foot-platforms, criss-crossed with cuts for better purchase, flanked the shallow pits. Bluebottle flies crawled torpidly over toppings of stained newspaper. Wallace calculated that the basement must run from the funeral home well under the big godown protected by the Indian watchman, perhaps even under the harbour.

It might have been a storage chamber for confiscated contraband.

The boys came back. Hogan straddled two of the raised footgrips and launched himself into the alley, landing on all fours. Clarence had his turn. He was unable to match Hogan's prodigious leap.

Wallace checked they were alone. He landed well beyond Hogan's mark.

'Eiyah!'

'Don't forget I had the longer leg than you, boys.'

He seemed in some measure to have regained his former ascendancy over the younger members of the household. They went up the stairs holding his hands.

Ah Lung had started his obsessive polishing of the casket handles again. Locked in savage reveries of his own devising, he was oblivious to the others. He came out of his trance to beckon Wallace over some time later.

'You saw this?' He stroked the wood of the casket. 'Five thousand dollar. Five thousand. He had no need to feel ashame inside there.'

Wallace assented nervously. The concealing folds had slipped slightly from the neck but Ah Lung did not seem to have noticed anything amiss with the corpse. He breathed on the buffed teak, rubbing it this time with his elbow.

'I would watch the fellow who carry it. They didn't care if they drop it. They would even break it they might be so jealous.'

There were heavy bags under Ah Lung's eyes. He kept flicking a mutinous strand of hair off his forehead. The muscle in his cheek twitched rapidly as he glared around the room, as if he was establishing a monopoly on access to the dead man.

'Eiyah!' Ah Lung recoiled from the coffin, omitting to release his grip from the handle and almost tipping the box from its trestle. He looked from the disfiguration on the face of the corpse, then to Wallace; he seemed to be checking that it was not some contagious blight spreading around the family.

Hogan prised Wallace's legs apart and crawled through. He had his hands knocked off the coffin by the sisters. Mrs Poon sucked sharply.

Wallace withdrew. He found Fong still seated; she was chewing a square of dried beef. She put the last fibres in her mouth and wiped her hands with deliberation.

The boys pulled Wallace's sleeves. 'You thought the devil had try and catch Grandfather spirit, Uncle Wallace?'

Impelled in his role of unofficial mentor to exceed the limits of what he himself might in cooler moments have regarded as strictly prudent, Wallace offered the boys an explanation. Without invoking the paranormal, it still offered elements of unusual interest for the boys. They seized on it with relish.

'Uncle Wallace say the big black rat go and eat Grandfather face.' Ah Lung advanced on Wallace, fists clenched.

At that moment Mabel Yip made her entrance. She was with the elusive Yip himself, a key, almost a mythical, figure in the advancement of both the Poons' and Mabel's personal fortunes. Wallace had never seen him before, not even on his brief visit to Mabel's penthouse, but he had not the slightest difficulty in identifying him. Palsied, wizened, supported by a pair of bare-foot amahs (rumoured to be Mabel's sisters, hired at slave rates; in fact, her second cousins, formerly employed by her in her Macau operations), Yip tottered into the funeral chamber. He was guided to the coffin where he stood, was kept upright, somewhat longer than might have been regarded as obligatory, contemplating his former business partner. Wallace tried to guess his thoughts; he found something triumphant in the set of the addict's back.

Mabel brushed Ah Lung out of her way. 'Alway want to show off. At his father funeral too.'

She abandoned Wallace with the minimum of formality before embracing Fong and May Ling, her finger nails enamelled in black, shown to advantage with the fingers extended straight down the girls' spines. She was dressed with her usual elegance, her cheongsam slightly more severe in cut than usual, as well as of a darker colour. She wore sun-glasses which she did not remove while she was in the room.

Mabel clicked her tongue reprovingly as Mrs Poon bestowed largesse, but allowed her servants to accept.

'See you downstair when the ceremony was beginning, Wallace.'

Mabel referred to the eclectic rites governing Mr Poon's physical departure from the family, for which the deceased had laid down elaborate and detailed provisions in his will. Execution of this otherwise highly secret document was known to depend on discharge of these obligations; otherwise, so it had been hinted to putative beneficiaries in the author's lifetime, all the money would go to Mr Poon's Kowloon concubine and her family.

'So those crafty so-and-so would get all the money if our hard work had gone wrong,' Ah Lung had explained to Wallace.

Nothing was left to chance at the service. As the noonday salute crashed out over the harbour, taken up by an ancillary battery in the haunted barracks off Garden Road, Mrs Poon led the way down the uncarpeted stone stairs to the home's big hall.

Mr Poon had been winched down in his casket a few hours previously. Aided by attendants, the family slipped into the traditional hooded white gowns of mourning. Wallace felt like a lower echelon member of the Ku Klux Klan in a film of the American South he had seen at the Roxy. They knelt on a low stage. Mrs Poon was seated on a chair in front of the others. The family received an interminable train of visitors, who came to bow and pay their respects to the dead man's photograph. Tedious hours passed. Wallace surreptitiously massaged May Ling's calves; she had complained of twitching cramps in a whisper. He kneaded her legs, one hand on the floor, the other working behind his back. Mabel, seated in the front row with a prayer-book clasped demurely over her knees, nodded at Wallace. Yip was in a row behind, in between the two servants. He had relapsed from his earlier interest in the accidents of the external world into a condition of helpless narcosis. Wallace winked at Mabel.

The queue of attenders came to an end. There had been several false alarms and Wallace had not altogether been able to dissimulate his impatience. He had been chastised for his fidgeting by several painful hacks in the small of his back from Ah Lung. Three men now approached Mrs Poon. Wallace groaned and quickly arched his spine but there was no retribution.

May Ling touched him. 'Wallace!'

'I saw, May. I saw.'

The Taoist priest established himself in the row in front of Mabel. He appeared on comfortable enough terms with the Catholic priest beside him and, of course, the Buddhist monk.

Wallace remembered the words of Mr Poon: 'You could be better safe than sorry,' and thought it one of the deceased's sounder mottos, typical of the man as he intended to remember him.

Then there was communal Christian hymn-singing in which the Taoist priest joined lustily and with familiarity; outdone, however, by the ringing baritone of the Catholic father. The mourners around him leaned forwards and sideways in attitudes of frank curiosity; there was some open sniggering, which continued during the reading of separate texts by the representatives of the separate denominations. Despite Mr Poon's Baptist connections, no representative from that persuasion was present.

The service concluded with the attendants carrying the coffin out to an inadequately loud march played on an upright piano behind the Poons.

Outside a hearse ticked over fruitily. Ah Lung jumped into the vehicle and minutely supervised the insertion of the massive casket, now nailed fast. The attendants struggled with the inert weight. It eased in. They stood back in anticipation of reward and wiped their hands on their trousers. Their expectation was indefinitely prolonged as they waited for Ah Lung, who appeared to have seen the coffin almost too securely lodged. He scowled ferociously as he squirmed behind an apparently insurmountable barrier. There was sufficient space for him to slip an arm through the channel between the glass sides of the hearse and the coffin but no more. He tried – Wallace had the idea at the same time and could imagine the reluctance with which Ah Lung faced up to the solution – to climb over the top of the coffin. Even after sweeping off the wreaths on top of the chest, the clearance was too narrow. Ah Lung pressed his face to the glass and mouthed through it at Wallace, who dug into his trouser pocket. He had exhausted his resources after buying Green Spots for the boys just before the service. He shook his head. Ah Lung produced a sheaf of banknotes and screwed a couple around some coins. He slid them down the coffin to be neatly caught by Wallace as they dropped over the edge. The coffin-bearers said their 'Dojehs' matter-of-factly, leaving Wallace speculating as to the uniqueness of Ah Lung's predicament.

Meanwhile, the different parts of the funeral train were being marshalled behind the hearse. The brass band in their blue uniforms and white naval officer's caps were raggedly warming their instruments. The band-leader fixed a blown-up photograph of Mr Poon into a socket at the end of a long pole. It was a portrait taken some years previously which showed Mr Poon with hair and sporting spectacles of the heavy horn-rimmed type. He was unrecognisable to Wallace.

The hired mourners fell in behind the band. They were composed mostly of off-duty coolies from the docks, rickshaw men, and beggars. Mabel, delegated as representing the family, was distributing partial payments, the residue to be collected at the cemetery. A thin, scar-faced coolie with the bulging calves of a rickshaw man jostled an old woman out of his way to reach Mabel. Several of the mourners wore brown canvas shoes, down-trodden at the heels.

It was Wallace's turn to pull May Ling's sleeve. 'May.'

'I had seen, too, Wallace.'

They joined the others in a hired black limousine of German make as the band, hesitantly at first, then with rather more exuberance than was appropriate, struck up the march. Ah Lung glided past them in the hearse, grimacing to himself; he looked like a caged beast being transported to the zoo.

The procession crawled along the side of the highway.

Two trams rushed past in opposite directions on what appeared to be collision courses. The drivers' bells rang out tinnily. Air from the two cars buffeted the limousine. Passengers disembarked further up the highway onto the tram's island stop in the centre of the road. There were stares.

'Too bad Ah Dairdee not here to see how big send-off you peoples were giving him, hah?'

The sisters began to weep, the first public display of emotion so far. Wallace extricated his pocket handkerchief and made May Ling pass it to Second Sister. 'You two could share it at one time, OK?'

The mourners' wailing reached them through sealed windows. In the chauffeur's mirror Wallace stole a glimpse of the coolies.

'Wah, you thought they were doing this for real even.'

Mabel turned from her place in the front passenger seat and Wallace subsided.

The band was playing with noticeably less enthusiasm by the time they were on the coast road leading to the cemetery. The procession arrived at the porcelain gates in silence, in surprise, having rounded a sharp corner.

Ah Lung was waiting for them by the coffin, which rested with the back on the lowered tailboard of the hearse and the foot in the dust. He was doubled-up, swearing. Mabel put the flat of her hand in the small of his back and with the other cupped under his chin exerted pressure in opposite directions. Ah Lung exclaimed angrily and moved off. He halted suddenly: 'But it gone away.' Mabel made a claw out of her jewelled talons and showed him her teeth. 'I knew all these sorts of thing.'

Fong and May Ling had helped Mrs Poon down the first of the long series of steps to the heart of the cemetery. Without the detours made on the occasion of the last family visit at Ching Ming, it was a surprisingly short distance.

The grave-diggers succeeded in lowering the coffin into the hole without the kind of incident feared earlier by Ah Lung. During the last instalment of hymn-singing, Wallace looked around the plot. The unsightly raw scabs of earth in the plaster and cement he had seen on his last visit had been neatly plugged and the chinks in the paving underfoot weeded. The family had eaten their meal of commemoration at the ancestor festival on a gravestone not far from Mr Poon's resting place. Wallace tried to recreate the occasion, in particular plotting Mr Poon's movements to remember whether he had actually walked over his future place of interment.

Ah Lung was staring hard at him. Wallace found his face already wearing a contemplative expression, if anything slightly more intense than any of the others, and repressed a guilty start. Ah Lung twisted the boys' ears savagely: 'Cry, you little bastard. Cry.' The sisters snuffled but had discharged the burden of their grief in the car.

Mrs Poon was offered a yellow plastic bucket half full of the dusty soil from the hole. One after the other, they threw fistfuls of earth down onto the coffin, Wallace and Fong last, then finally Mabel.

Mrs Poon rubbed Tiger Balm into her temples and blew her nose. Wallace nudged Mabel: 'Actually she was lucky. If she was Indian wife they made a big fire and . . .' He was hissed quiet.

The grave-diggers began to fill the grave. There were sizable stones hidden in the dust and as each shovelful was tossed in they smashed against the wood. Only patches of the varnished wood were visible now, some areas dimmed with dust, others mysteriously unsullied until the moment they were engulfed. Then there was earth, a rising roof appearing to swell out of the ground, like a cake from a baking-tin. The headstone, with a tiny photograph of Mr Poon inset behind a perspex window, was rooted into the loose soil. Wallace saw that Mr Poon had been born in 1885. He had supposed him much older.

They took a different route to the cars, which had driven down to meet them at the bottom of the cemetery. They went through an avenue of trees with a dried up fountain at the end. The boys took Wallace's hands from behind. 'Green Spots, Uncle?'

'Not now, boys.'

The chauffeurs were smoking cigarettes against their open doors but the band and hired mourners had gone. As they were getting in, two more cars drew up. There was a moment's barely perceptible ripple of embarrassment. It was the Kowloon concubine with her family. Mrs Poon wavered, then ducked swiftly into the limousine.

The passengers in the other vehicle stared straight ahead in the opposite direction. They did not open their doors until the Poons had bumped some way down the track to the main road. Wallace turned to look through the rear window but the family and Mabel neither moved nor spoke.

3

Now there was the cold weather. The stream of milky, evil-smelling water in the nullah dried up for another season; the bed cracked like a giant slab of chocolate and sweet-smelling wild grasses thickened along the sides before colonising the centre. Children no longer came to the playground but by Wallace's special dispensation Clarence and Hogan were allowed to roam there in the hour before the completion of the 'homework' he had devised for them and their bedtime. Fong and May Ling would sit up to the table with the boys while they were at their studies. Although May Ling would have no part of the curriculum devised by Wallace – nutrition cunningly disguised to the best of his abilities at titillation – Fong proved an unexpectedly apt student. Her head for figures was remarkable and after dealing with Wallace's posers she would invariably beat her sons to the solutions from their own text-books.

The boys were currently on 'problems'. These were any form of arithmetic concerned with trade: the selling or complex apportioning of apples, bananas, marbles, and, on one memorable occasion, of *dhotis*, between three quarrelling families.

'Must of left this one on the boat at Bombay, hah?'

Fong grinned at Wallace's joke but her sons worked on, underlining the results of their sums with wooden rulers. The little competition with their mother, shocking at first to the boys, had ended by providing them with an abiding source of interest and incentive.

They were a cosy little group. The fire drew well. It was built up every evening by the amahs. Before giving a demonstration to the servants Wallace had peered up the chimney, feeling around in the flue for any specie that might have been overlooked by Mr Poon. The search for treasure had been unsuccessful but the fire had not; it purified the air, cast interesting shadows on the walls and provided a focal point for the household in the winter evenings. Wallace joined the gatherings after doing accounts, bringing for offering a brown bag of raw chestnuts. He carefully supervised the roasting, instructing the boys when to knock them off the grate.

Mabel was an increasingly frequent visitor to the house. At first she seemed to be in the process of adopting May Ling as a substitute for the absent Pippy. Himself flattered by Mabel's indirect attentions, Wallace tried to coax May Ling into some kind of response. But while she entertained the older woman's approaches respectfully enough, it was soon apparent that she was not about to become anybody's protégé. To May Ling participation in Mabel's social projects would have been tantamount to secession from her husband. Wallace came to realise this and stopped pressing her.

Regretfully, Mabel abandoned the idea of mixed-race launch picnics or tea-dancing but continued to attend and enjoy Mrs Poon's frequent mah jong parties.

Her choice now fell on the boys. She bought them their uniforms and books for the second term of the year. It also came to be understood – though no explicit undertaking was ever actually given – that she would sponsor them through such post-school educations as they wished to embark on. It was decided that Clarence was to be a brain-surgeon.

Whilst condemning Western medicine in general and those of its practitioners with whom she had come into professional contact still more vehemently in particular, Mabel was known to book into a private room at the Queen Mary Hospital whenever she herself was in need of serious medical attention. For instance, the hysterectomy her social enemies rumoured her to have undergone. Wallace, who had several times heard her comparing Occidental science violently to its disadvantage with traditional Chinese herbal medicines and acupuncture, was nevertheless mildly surprised.

'You didn't want him to be a ... a ... what you were calling it?'

'Apothecary,' Hogan supplied.

'No, no. Low-class profession. You could do better than that Ah Kei.'

Clarence grinned uneasily, hopping from one foot to the other, while his future hung in the balance.

'I was alway wanting to be engineer when I would have grow up,' Hogan suggested sycophantically.

Wallace regarded him with favour. 'I could see you were a real boy straightaway, Hogan.' Clarence's grin became more fixed under the implied slight.

Mabel pulled him protectively towards her. 'You was the clever one,

Ah Kei.' She opened her black patent leather handbag with typical preciseness and produced three crisp red and gold envelopes. After hesitating, she handed one to Hogan as well as his brother.

'Wah, *dojeh*, Auntie Mabel.'

She placed another envelope under the lacquered tea-tray. 'For your mudder, hah?'

Fong spent the money on an abacus, thereby irritating May Ling who had been hoping they might spend it together on, say, an evening at the Roxy with grilled Malay satay to eat afterwards.

Ah Lung laid no claims on Fong. He was now rarely in the house. Soon after the death of his father he had resumed the nocturnal habits of Wallace's early days at Robinson Path. Often he would not return for several days at a time. Unknown to the others, he would frequently spend the early hours of the morning on a bench by the waterfront.

Wallace's erroneous surmise, loudly made in Fong's presence and severely tut-tutted by May Ling, to the effect that Ah Lung 'got himself girl-friend' could not have been further from the truth. It was generally known that the disease contracted by Ah Lung some years ago, and now in its final stage, prohibited him from such courses, or at least their logical conclusion.

Strange stories came back to Wallace.

As of Ah Lung's visit to the floating brothels at Lye Mun.

This was a chain of linked sampans moored in the circle of darkness just behind the gaudy illuminations of a large barge that served as a marine restaurant. Not content with the impression he had produced on a previous visit, when he had handed hundred dollar notes to the occupant of each sampan's cabin, Ah Lung had himself rowed across the shadows to the restaurant where he bought several tankfuls of large groupers. In all there were several hundred catties of expensive fish. He had ordered spot-lights trained on both himself and the startled sampan-girls and their customers and, in full view of cheering diners, thrown the fish into the harbour, screeching: 'I gave you your freedoms.'

Despite the fact that it had not actually been Ah Lung's own money but Mrs Poon's which funded this and similar escapades, Wallace had to admit there was a studied magnanimity about the gesture. Even Mabel, who related the episode to Wallace, could not help a note of approval infiltrating her nasal accents.

It was not a surprise when Ah Lung left. The intention was never announced. Indeed his absence was never officially remarked. It was as if he were on a foray which had become indefinitely extended. Only Wallace was worried. Mrs Poon, who continued to indulge her son, never gave herself a moment's concern about his welfare when he was out of sight. A fortnight after he was last seen in the house, a card came from Ah Lung – it was surmised – bearing a Macau postmark. The sender had correctly addressed, stamped and posted it but forgotten to inscribe it with a message. A month afterwards another card, this time with a conventional greeting on the back, arrived from the Philippines. A third card came, again from Macau, a few weeks later. This was the last of the messages.

Wallace suspected Mrs Poon of supplying Ah Lung with funds to support him in his new existence – he had written something about working as a croupier in the casino – but reckoned it a cheap price for ridding the family of its black sheep (Mabel's expression).

He was, above all, glad that the boys should have that last grandiloquent gesture by which to recall their father, until they should meet again.

After the provisions of Mr Poon's will had been made public Wallace was glad Ah Lung had been able to leave with some dignity. He even had the notion that his brother-in-law might have had prior knowledge of the contents of the testament. Self-imposed exile. It would not have been an abnormally complicated way of preserving face.

Mr Poon had not cut his prodigal son altogether out of an inheritance but it might have been less wounding had he done so. The whole document was densely bound up with qualifications, riders and provisos; it was still possible, however, to discern the original architecture of his malintentions in the undergrowth.

Limited control of the estate passed into Mrs Poon's hands during her lifetime, although trustees would carry out a large part of the administration. Neither Ah Lung nor the sisters were left lump sums. They received annuities as pensioners of the dead man. The sums would ensure a comfortable enough existence, even independently; communally, they permitted a degree of luxury.

For the sisters the mode of transmission was hardly significant. To have conferred a capital sum upon them would not have been in their best interests. Mr Poon had always been wary of fortune-hunters.

For Ah Lung, however, the terms of the settlement meant he was to be kept in perpetual tutelage: not a ritualistic veneration of the dead man but a concrete, persistent reminder of his unevolved condition. It amounted to a subtle but nevertheless total obliteration of identity; a deed reminiscent of Mr Poon the domestic tyrant, at the height of his powers. Which, of course, it was. The will showed signs of having been composed as a unity before the war, with accretions and deletions made pragmatically as the need required.

May Ling would have received a stipend of two thousand dollars a year had she remained a spinster; married, she was to have three thousand of her own while her husband would receive two thousand, on condition he used the family surname in his business dealings. Should there be children from the marriage, they would be educated by the estate.

One third of the estate went to the Kowloon concubine and her family. The Poons accepted this as equitable, as did the concubine and her family.

Mabel was remembered: she and Yip were given a large lump sum and shares: ten thousand dollars in all.

The amahs were given a hundred dollars each: they had found the will in the teak desk on Mr Poon's bed. There was nothing else in it.

Otherwise, Mrs Poon was titular beneficiary of the rest of the estate.

One thing intrigued Wallace: the number of Mr Poon's business aliases. He must have had over twenty European names: Henry, Harold, Alfred, Guy, Kenneth, Jeremy amongst them.

'Who would have thought he was a Alfred?' Wallace enquired outside the solicitor's office. For the rest, May Ling's tentative formulation: 'Eiyah! We all rich peoples now,' summed up the general consensus of opinion fairly well.

4

The individual members of the family were ill-prepared to cope with the relative wealth they had inherited; a little frightened. Even permitting themselves such extravagances as two main meals a day, with duck and barbecued pork (bought cold from the cook-shop) as routine items, there was still substantial cash in hand at the end of the month.

Mrs Poon had delegated the early wranglings with the trustees to her son-in-law. Now she handed over her surplus moneys to him. Wallace opened a deposit share account for her at the Dao Heng Bank. Then he bought some shares.

The rest of the household was quick to follow in pressing their claims upon him. 'You knew this kind of thing, Ah Wallace,' they would say, approaching him at his desk. Finally, the amahs came to him. He accepted their brief graciously.

The savings grew.

Then came the request from the village to act as the settlement's town agent. Wallace declined. The elders insisted. Wallace accepted.

'It look like they heard about our moneys,' he remarked to May Ling. But his cynicism was assumed. He was deeply flattered.

The boys were commissioned to compose his letter of acceptance: classical apprenticeship turned to use. The family stood behind as they moistened their ink bricks and pinched their brushes to a fine point.

It was a considerable responsibility Wallace had undertaken.

The takings from the lake and the subsidiary enterprises around it had accumulated into an impressive capital stake. And the income was rising all the time. Together with the rent from the allotments cultivated by the vegetable farmers, it was a five figure monthly sum.

Shortly after May Ling and Wallace had left, the vegetable farmers had taken over a sizeable portion of the paddy, including some of the oldest clan segments. The paddy had been turning brackish after its inundation; unless farmed it would soon have become desert. On the other hand, most of the villagers were now lucratively employed around the lake. The rents paid by the immigrants for these new plots, prime pieces of ancestral land, were actually lower than those charged for their original sandy allotments. These had appreciated in value, following further extension of coolie-built link road, which now ran past the outermost plots.

The perishable nature of the vegetable produce and the ease with which the new market could now be reached from the most distant plots had transformed land values. Fertility was no longer the consideration. All the same the rent from the paddy was still sizeable.

Naturally the village wished to see these funds invested in the most productive way.

These new arrangements suited the headman. The new lakeside occupations left no time for irritating meetings in the ancestral hall, held at odd times of the day; the tea shop proprietor was happy with his profits and had lost his political ambitions, for the time being; and the vegetable farmers were out on the land. He had even been able to lay aside cash sums for distribution after his death – they would be in the nature of consolation prizes.

At first, a fine sense of discrimination led Wallace to keep the village and family investments separate. Then, realising that this not only created extra work but also lowered the potential dividend, he started to pool the Poon pensions and village earnings in joint schemes. He found himself courted on the stockmarket, a figure of minor consequence. Every month the holdings would be regularly augmented. Dividends he ploughed back or diversified into other areas of enterprise on the principle of not putting all one's eggs in the same basket.

He was scrupulous to keep track of profits and the periodic in-puts, so that he could at any given moment produce an accurate rendering of his dual stewardship. It was never required. But from his books he could work out how much less the investments would have been had they been kept separate. He kept a portion of this extra margin of profit for himself. He informed the family and the village of his intention. There were no queries. When he raised his commission again, he did not trouble to raise the issue.

The family drew pocket-money: new cheongsams and quilted jackets for the women, Raleigh bicycles for the boys.

Apart from his financial brief for the village, Wallace was also entrusted with odd-jobs of a more miscellaneous kind: purchase of varnish, lily seeds, insecticide. He hired a lorry to take these purchases to the village. On the trip back it freighted vegetables. The idea caught: he bought a second-hand vehicle of its own for the settlement.

It was not possible to conduct operations of this scale from Robinson Path. Soon after becoming the village's town agent Wallace found himself chambers in Victoria. He was on the ninth floor of a modern building. There was an elevator with stainless steel doors that pinged as it opened. Downstairs, his name appeared in white on a black board, giving his floor and room number. There was enough space for two desks, a filing cabinet, and a tall fan. Next door was a dentist.

Soon he was comfortably installed. Gifts of fruit arrived from those who desired his commercial goodwill or its continuance. There was a big basket from the Indian who supplied him with varnish and proper, seasoned planks for repairs to the boats. He was the only one of his kind. Wallace preferred to do business with Americans and Chinese. 'Damn crook with all their curry,' he said. He also found the British somewhat devious and avoided all but necessary contact with them.

Wicker cornucopias of fruit decorated the room: spiky pineapples, peaches, oranges, slim, fragrant bananas, sour Chinese pears, tight clusters of grapes. In his turn he chose to reciprocate with bottles of cognac and boxes of cigars: *yang* to *yin*.

At last he could no longer restrain himself.

'You mean you not too busy, Wallace? You were just starting after all?'

'No, no you took taxi down. I would pay.'

May Ling arrived a little earlier than he expected the next afternoon. He was unsnagging the venetian blinds which had caught after running five times cleanly in a row.

There was a small knock on the door.

'Come in.' And what power of magic lay in those words!

May Ling poked her head around the door. 'You didn't mind I brought Fong? Eiyah! So little!' She clapped her hands, clasping them across her chest.

'Well, we all had to start from somewhere. Even your father, hah?' Wallace was acerbic.

'No, no. I meaning it *nice* and small. Like toy house.'

'You was real stupid sometime, May. You want some ice coffee and curry puff?'

He phoned the order down to the *foki* in the café below and tipped him extravagantly when he came up.

The *foki* stared curiously round the room. 'OK, you could go now, you had seen everything,' Wallace snapped. After the *foki* had left the room he added for May Ling's benefit: 'All nosey-parker these Cantonese fellow.' She nodded, impressed.

Daylight poured into the office.

'Thank, Fong, you got clever finger, hah?'

While Fong had been busy May Ling had eaten the other curry puff as well as her own.

'You getting quite fat, May, you knew that?' He pinched her upper arm affectionately.

He had the boys down during their holidays, as well. They were meant to be running errands for him: getting quotations at the stockmarket, buying evening editions of the newspapers, going to the money-changers. Wallace felt sure their grandfather would have approved of such a precocious commercial baptism. Mostly, though, they drank Green Spots and read comics. He paid them fifty cents a day pocket-money. If privacy were required for an interview, or if he just felt like giving them a treat, he would send them to the cinema.

'Of course we wouldn't go to Sheraton,' Hogan would assure him in apparently shocked tones.

Wallace was not deceived. 'You fellow were a real pair of rascal. Here, buy yourself some dry beef sweetie to eat, too.'

They would press all the buttons in the lift, stopping on each floor, on their way down.

He was quite sorry when the 'Easter' vacation was over. Business had grown to the point where he needed help. Apart from this, the boys had been company. It could be lonely in the little office. But though the boys had been useful in their way as messengers, he really needed someone with a head for figures to help with conversions and calculations of interest.

At the same time, he was unwilling to employ a stranger. The family savings and village investments were intensely personal to him. He was not looking for an employee, an outsider. Slowly, he realised Fong was the person for the post; it came to him as a deepening sense of reassurance rather than a sudden illumination. It was obvious.

Fong sat directly opposite him, their desks jammed together. They hardly spoke but in the following weeks she was to prove her discretion and competence many times over. Her speed on the abacus was extraordinary. She reeled off complex calculations of compound interest in a moment, the beads of the abacus whirring along the rails.

'It came from her father,' Wallace explained to May Ling. Within two months Fong had also mastered book-keeping and was producing trial balances for him. He wondered how he had functioned before.

5

One of the first things Wallace did with the interest on the family capital was to have the exterior of the house re-painted. He had to overcome resistance from Mrs Poon. She was upset by the idea. To her it smacked of a slight on the dead man. There was opposition from the amahs as well, the most uncompromising reactionaries in the household, who feared an extension of reform into the kitchen. But the sisters were unlooked for allies on this issue.

'What about *fung shui*, though?' Mrs Poon asked as a half-hearted last resort, only to be argued down by her daughters. The vote was therefore carried democratically.

Colour was the next issue. What the old paint had been originally it was now impossible to determine. Dingy was no longer the word for it. Since Wallace had been absent there had been accelerated deterioration in the façade, so that the tatters and plumes of filth, now symbiotically indistinguishable from the paint itself, could be mistaken at dusk for a hanging garden.

They could all agree on a coat of white paint, bright white, not cream.

Wallace contracted the job to a firm of marine painters, who had offered him a substantial discount in return for work on the village boats. It was not unlike de-barnacling a hull. First of all, every window in the house was battened down. Then the façade was scrubbed with a jet from a high-pressure hose. Great clumps of matter were dislodged and fell to earth like wounded fowl. The boys went into the street with Wallace to watch. They were allowed to wield the hose; they played it along the ledges and runnels, moulding sodden balls of dirt, blasting the windows which clattered under the force of the water. Faces appeared at the streaming glass. They clarified as the sisters. The boys redirected the jet at the window again, causing the faces to disappear – the sisters had leapt back involuntarily.

The workmen ate while Wallace and the boys took turns with the hose. They moved over to play it on the side of the wall.

'You wanted go, Uncle Wallace?'

He was about to surrender the hose again when the rod of water issuing from the nozzle slowed to a trickle and then finally ceased.

'Very clever, Hogan. Now you could jump off the pipe.'

'Look, Uncle.'

Fong and May Ling were retiring from the water-main by the nullah with exaggerated stealth. They giggled, hands over their mouths.

'OK, boys, you run and switch it on again.'

Wallace was careful to miss.

'Really do it, Uncle.'

Wallace wheeled on the boys.

'Eiyah!'

They remained at a safe distance, occasionally darting in and out of range.

Between them they completed most of the preliminary stage for the workmen. After the wall had dried, the workmen began to apply the first layer of paint.

During the painting May Ling had complained that fumes were making her bilious. And indeed her face lost the remnants of her healthy summer tan and took on some of the pastiness of earlier days. She became less active, preferring to stay in bed longer, rising at the same time as her sisters, and taking her first tea of the day with them. They braided her hair for her, which she had left uncut to grow straight from the original bob. Wallace found the style quite fetching.

One morning, after the painters had left and Wallace had hoped the trouble over, she threw her covers off, dashed from bed where she had been lying on her stomach, and slammed the bathroom door after her.

Wallace listened with concern.

She crept into bed with a face as white as the demon's in a Chinese opera.

He put his blanket over her. 'Wait, May. I gave you my pillow, too.' He was unable to distinguish between the temperature of her forehead and the heat of his own palm.

'Mmm, you like a Horlick, May?' Notwithstanding her vehement refusal, he instructed the amahs to bring her the hot drink on his way out.

He telephoned from Victoria at noon to be answered by Mrs Poon. The old lady had an irritating habit of holding the receiver at some distance from her as a dual precaution against possible accidental electrocution and infection from the germs of other users lurking in the

206

mouthpiece. Her mania for hygiene in this respect was not evident in other aspects of the domestic economy.

Her *'Wai? Wai?'* came faintly over the line.

'May Ling,' Wallace requested.

'Wai? Wai?'

'May!' Immediately there were angry knocks from the adjoining offices, the loudest from the dentist's waiting room.

Wallace heard the scrape of the receiver being put on his desk in the corridor at Robinson Path and then Mrs Poon's retreating footsteps. He amused himself by arranging his pencils according to height in their papier-mâché receptacle. Fong worked on without looking up.

At length May Ling shuffled to the telephone.

'Wai?'

'It was me. You OK now, hah?'

'Wai?'

'Me. Wallace. You OK now, hah?'

'Everything OK now, Ah Wallace. My sick feelings go away.'

There were gigglings in the background.

'Who did those laughings?'

'It was only the sister.'

'What you were doing with them?'

'Did hairs together, then played mah jong.'

'So you well enough to do that kind of stuff, huh?'

'Well again. Wallace, you would bring me some bread and sticky milk.'

'May, you are definitely crazy.'

'Bye-bye, Wallace.'

It was Mabel who broke the news to him. It had been common knowledge in the house among the women for some weeeks. She arrived without notice at his chambers one afternoon, rapping imperiously on the frosted glass. Wallace recognised her silhouette, thrown in relief against the fluorescent lighting in the corridor; he fancied he could already detect a whiff of her scent.

'Come in, Mabel.'

She came to the point straightaway, after refusing his offer of refreshments.

'Of course, I would be godmother.'

'Of course, Mabel.'

'I wouldn't expect you to call it after me but you wanted to, I didn't mind.' She laughed coquettishly. 'It would be girl, of course.'

'Of course, Mabel.'

'What you were "of coursing" me for? You only knew how to talk like parrot.'

'Ah.'

Mabel relented. 'I already put one hundred dollar in Hong Kong and Shanghai Bank for twenty-first birthday. And I would give Christening egg-cup. Thank you, Wallace, I found my own way in, I could find my own way out.'

Fong had been working throughout. After Mabel had made her exit Wallace looked down at the top of her bent head. He opened his mouth, then said nothing. He grimaced.

Now that he knew, Wallace imagined May Ling bigger with every day. She slept uncomfortably on the joined camp beds and he had a wooden bed brought up for them, with difficulty. When it grew warm enough to swim, May Ling was no longer able to go to the beach, even had Mrs Poon allowed her to do so. She had been looking forward to showing her new strokes off and even improving them. But the steps to South Bay were too dangerous for her.

Wallace went with the boys, leaving his office in the late afternoon and getting to the beach in the early evening. He had an hour before the sun went down. They went almost every day. It was a clear, dry summer, without typhoons – which meant there would be water-rationing in the autumn.

Office work in these months was lucrative but undemanding. Wallace could leave feeling he had neglected nothing. The money almost looked after itself. Although the boating lake had never been busier, the large earnings made it easier for him to invest. Wallace moved into the 'big-time', buying blocks of shares in property and land companies. Fong coped with the rent on the office and other items of routine expenditure.

Wallace had tried to lure her to the beach with her sons but she never came. The boys looked on their mother with something akin to embarrassment.

By the autumn it was plain that the springing of a new life had divided the family into two camps. The two groups split along the line of sex, superseding earlier alliances and divisions. On one side, a citadel of besieged masculinity, were Wallace and the boys. On the other, Mrs Poon, the sisters, the amahs, and Fong, with May Ling as their figure-head.

Now that it was too cold to swim, Wallace took the boys up to the Peak Café on the dark mountain-top or down to the light and clamour of the cook-stalls that sprouted at night in the car-park of the Macau ferry. Wallace would always keep a wary eye out for Ah Lung but they never saw him.

'You boys want to watch out. One day you got marry too and then you would have to put up with all this stuff like you saw me now,' Wallace warned them, waving a large shelled prawn as he delivered his homily between bites.

But he enjoyed his new role with its hint of a raffish irresponsibility (having achieved the matter, as it were, behind everybody's backs, without warning) coupled with the eminently serious part of general breadwinner.

Mrs Poon had long give up hope. Now she was overjoyed. May Ling become her captive, treated like an honoured hostage: her smallest whims anticipated, depriving her of the least excuse for move-ment. In the last months of the pregnancy the radius of her daily move-ments contracted to a matter of yards. The staircase was naturally too unstable for a person in May Ling's unwieldy condition. Wallace agreed. There were other precautions he found excessive, such as the double locking of the inner door. This was meticulously fastened by the servants and inspected by Mrs Poon after every opening, as if the household contained a member of severely diminished responsibilities. Beyond the obvious areas of physical danger Mrs Poon considered certain rooms unlucky. These included the kitchen and washroom. While she could not prevent May Ling from using the washroom, the kitchen was made out of bounds to her. Mrs Poon only relaxed when she had her foster daughter under her eye in a chair in the reception room, perspiring gently beneath layers of blankets. The windows were kept fast. Mrs Poon pooh-poohed Wallace's tactful suggestion that the resulting airlessness might be detrimental to health.

'Air come down chimney, you didn't have to worry,' May Ling assured him. Secretly, she was pandering to Mrs Poon. She would catch Wallace's eye and smile weakly as he hovered on the outskirts of the little pallisade formed by the women's chairs, and he would shrug his shoulders.

'You want boy baby or girl?' she asked him one night, near the end of the pregnancy, alone in their room.

Wallace considered.

'Boy baby better,' she prompted.

'Any type baby OK, May.'

'Boy better,' she confirmed.

As May Ling had hoped it was indeed a boy. Almost a year after their return, somewhat prematurely, shortly before closing time on the small stock-exchanges, she gave birth.

Wallace returned to the office to find a note from Fong on his desk. Although he took a taxi, he arrived after Mabel and met the midwife on the stairs.

The child was in May Ling's arms. As she raised the bundle to her husband a limb, it looked like a leg to Wallace, fell out.

'Wah, it so thin.'

Mabel cracked Hogan on the head with a bony knuckle.

'Wah, that sure hurt.'

'You got some more five-finger fruit coming your way, you didn't watch your tongue. You were not suppose to be here anyway breathing all your germ around.'

Wallace took the baby from May Ling, holding it nervously at arm's length. It was crying.

'Watch out, Uncle, it going to bite you.' Hogan neatly evaded Mabel. Her irascibility, as the boys knew, was only apparent. Her eyes were bright and moist. She quickly lowered her head to insert one of her bright cigarettes into the ivory holder.

'No, no, Auntie.'

Mabel patted Clarence on the head. 'Good boy, Ah Kei, you were a little doctor already.'

Wallace had been rocking the warm, small, palpitating weight. Now it began to gurgle and choke alarmingly as the wails diminished.

'I give it back now, May?'

His trepidation began to be replaced by the warm glow of achievement. He parted the hood of blanket folds around his son's head. Wrinkled, simian features, in which he could detect no trace of his own or May Ling's, stared back at him. If anything, it looked like Mr Poon, reincarnated. A hand like a miniature bunch of pink bananas coiled around his thick forefinger. His eyes met May Ling's; circles of fatigue gave her the appearance of a panda. He retracted his forefinger and his son began to suck his perfect thumb.

Mabel took Wallace and the boys out for celebratory ice-cream sodas at the parlour after May Ling had gone to sleep. In the taxi she inhaled deeply and blew the smoke through her nostrils. 'Like I said all along, it was boy. You could be proud, Wallace.'

He smirked, pinioned between the boys in the back seat.

They called the child Cheung Ching, 'Runner through the Universe'. There was to be a constant theme running through the names of the generation, with the repetition of the prefix 'Cheung'.

'Like you would be calling his brother Cheung Tsin,' Mabel explained when she came to visit during the Christmas business holiday.

After she had gone, leaving chemistry sets for the boys, Wallace had to give May Ling a formal undertaking that there should be no family additions in the foreseeable future.

Otherwise, May Ling had regained her high spirits with great rapidity. Mabel's physician, Doctor Adelstein, was giving her a course of iron injections. With her rosy cheeks, she looked even healthier than during the long summer in the countryside. She had retained a little of the plumpness of the pregnancy, and this was pleasing. She suckled the child modestly in their own room. Wallace watched in fascination. He found it difficult to recognise the child as anything other than May Ling's exclusive property but was not jealous of his son.

He was now able to consort quite freely with his wife, although in the first month Mrs Poon was still vigilant.

Wallace looked forward to Sunday mornings when they would take the boys and push Cheung Ching's perambulator along Bowen Path, a pleasant hillside walk leading to the massive phallic outcropping visited by the amahs.

The boys would push the perambulator ahead, while Wallace and May Ling strolled leisurely behind. 'You took it nice and easy, May,' he told her. 'No one expecting you to run one mile in four minute just now.'

There was a pedigree to the perambulator, which had been presented by Mabel. It was a majestic, over-sprung vehicle in royal blue, with a gold water-line three-quarters of the way up the thick hull. It bounced and heaved, backwards and forwards rather than laterally, in a generally nautical manner.

Mabel claimed it was the same make and model as the one ordered by the Queen for the British Royal Family.

'What you mean she didn't buy new one for the girl?' Wallace had queried.

'No, same one.' Mabel was adamant.

'How you thought you knew?'

'Easy to see from photograph. It had small dent on side. I tell you: the peoples with the big moneys, they didn't have to do all this swanking stuffs, not like Hong Kong peoples. Of course it was all time same pram.'

'Mmm, maybe you were right.' Continuity was, after all, at the heart of the monarchical principle. Another thought struck Wallace. 'Just like old Mr Poon, hah? We never would have guess he was so rich in a million year.'

Mabel waved her hand dismissively but was unable to discourage Wallace from moving on to a parallel tack. 'Mabel, you were remembering when we first go to beach with Pippy, Mr Poon was knowing whole time, hah? So he hope you could be getting me job?'

Mabel found the subject boring, not to say irritating and irrelevant. She abruptly changed the topic of conversation. 'I was quite worry about Ah Chung.'

Wallace stuck up for his nephew. 'Hogan was good boy. Just do a little mischiefs like all boy, that was all.'

Mabel seemed easily reassured.

6

At the lunar New Year Wallace entertained lavishly, breaking tradition by personally pounding the flour for the seasonal puddings. A fire-cracker display had been arranged in the children's playground. The grand finale was to be the ordered demolition of a relief model of the village at the time when the valley had been flooded. It was a larger, less detailed version of the demonstration Wallace had originally rigged for the sceptical villagers. The boys had been nagging him for a re-enactment ever since his return.

Wallace had sent invitations to anyone in the village who might be on the island during the festival but he knew that the villagers would be too busy with customers to observe the day fully even in their own homes.

He got the business of the charities over with early in the day. He made it a brief, clinical ceremony but the red envelopes he distributed were considerably thicker than the ones Mr Poon had been in the habit of making up.

In the afternoon he took the family to a Lion Dance in Western District. May Ling carried Cheung Ching in a sling on her back. They had ice-creams in the crowded parlour and took three taxis home, proceeding in convoy up the hill.

While Wallace sat on the throne and drank tea the adults in the family respectfully left him with his thoughts. But the boys were becoming increasingly impatient.

'Uncle Wallace, when we did the fire-cracker?'

'Later, boys, later. You want it nice and dark to enjoy best.'

At length he surrendered. The family trooped out. The model, constructed in the children's sand-pit a few days before, had created considerable local interest. Amahs and children from the lower floors followed them across the nullah.

It was pitch dark under the tall trees.

'You gone and leave it too late, Uncle Wallace.' Clarence was on the brink of tears.

'Don't worry, you would see, Ah Kei.'

Wallace stuck sparklers in the sand. They began to fizz, throwing an angry glare across the deep puddle of nullah water in the centre of the sand-pit. Wallace lit the combination fuses. There were a series of sharp cracks. The sparklers went out, leaving orange trails burnt across the darkness, but not before Wallace had seen his congregation of up-ended match-boxes engulfed by a wall of water.

The boys seemed satisfied, as did the other spectators. May Ling engaged Eldest Sister in explanatory conversation. There was a spattering of polite applause.

At home there was more food. Mrs Poon invited the neighbours and tenants inside. Festivities continued. Wallace had an ache at the top of his neck; he made his excuses for the night, leaving May Ling to represent him. In bed he was unable to get the stink of gunpowder out of his nostrils.

The New Year celebrations could be seen to end an era. It was as if an interregnum had expired, with its rough-hewn expedients and hesitant initiatives. There was a new rhythm to the life in the household with a set of evolving and rapidly established precedents. Seemingly more confident, crisper about their daily duties, almost autonomous, the members of the family were on the surface less heedful of Wallace. But his authority, diffidently worn, went unchallenged. Their assurance was that of subordinates certain of what was expected of them. There was no longer any need for them to keep consulting him, and he welcomed this. Their deference had been a burden, the weight of which he had not appreciated until it had been removed.

In April there were freak rains in a false spring. The corrupting rubbish that had been accumulating in the nullah – detritus so sodden it was unrecognisable – was swept away in a foaming, iridescent wash of water. The trees dripped mournfully, a constant subtle pattering, audible above the growl and gurgle of the flood.

One night during the rains, Wallace had a dream. He was at a banquet. The other diners were in shadows, their faces familiar but not quite recognisable. He sat in the place of honour. Ivory chopsticks and a long, curved spoon with sharp edges, such as might be used to excavate marrow-bones, lay before him, unsullied, on a silver cruet. This was odd because the hardened scabs of white grease on the table-cloth and nests of small bones suggested a meal that was half-concluded. There was an atmosphere of anticipation. From behind the wings of his chair a square box, covered by a black drape, was placed on the table. Although he had not noticed it before, there was an exquisite silver hammer in the centre of the banqueting board. It had a slim, flexible-looking horn handle. A pair of long, female hands, the nails enamelled, appeared out of the shadows and placed a tiny spirit lamp by the hammer. A miniature cauldron, slightly bigger than a thimble, hung above the flame from a glittering toy tripod. Wisps of almost colourless smoke rose from the drop of clear amber oil it contained.

The drape was pulled off the box to reveal it as a cage. Inside the cage, immobilised with manacles around its feet and hands, an iron band clamped around the top of its head, the dome of which protruded through a hole in the top, was a young monkey. It wrinkled bloodless lips back, baring its teeth in rage and terror. Its head had been shaved, leaving a tonsure in the centre of the skull. A knotted blue vein throbbed beneath the rubbery membrane of scalp. Seen from above, the part of the monkey's cranium poking through the cage looked like a brown egg in its cup.

There was an expectant rattle as the diners reached for chopsticks. The woman's hand took up the hammer; another, a man's, the pot of now seething oil. The hammer-head glittered as it hovered a fraction at the top of the swing. It came down in a silver blur.

Bone peeled away easily on skin, like shell attached to a tissue of crinkling albumen. The oil hissed, popping as it encountered a slimy surface.

Wallace awoke. Outside, the rain was falling fiercely, suddenly redoubled in intensity as he listened, crackling on the sparse leaves of the trees, thrumming a deeper note on the roof, scratching on his window-panes.

The deluge ended as sharply as he knew it would. Stray drops plopped into the deep flooding in the road. Beside him May Ling swallowed in her sleep. He pulled a blanket over her and waited for the dawn.

Short-listed for the
Booker Prize

SOUR SWEET
Timothy Mo

An intriguing and finely written novel of the enclosed Chinese community living at the centre of 60s London.
'Brilliant . . . classic comic scenes . . . an excellent book.'
Sunday Times
'Uncovers a vivid, densely populated city within the city, whose inhabitants have an individuality and energy that makes the surrounding English look very grey. More than a touch of early Dickens . . . has a flavour all of its own.' *Observer*
'In SOUR SWEET Timothy Mo has brilliantly combined the comic with the frightening.' *Daily Telegraph*
'The characters and atmosphere in SOUR SWEET are enthralling, and Mo has a deliciously gingery sense of humour.
The Listener

FICTION   0 349 12392 6   £3.95

MADISON SMARTT BELL

Consider the pitfalls of a would-be streetwise vigilante, a love-sick shrimp fisherman, an officer of conscience at the battle of Little Big Horn. Tune into Manhattan through a hidden mike in a sleazy downtown bar or observe an old widower negotiate the hostile zones of his living room and prepare to do battle.

From the dining halls of Princeton to the hog farms of Tennessee, Bell's vision sets humour against raw and dramatic realities, private ambitions against uncertain futures. The result is one of compelling artistry.

'Considered separately, the stories in this collection are astonishing; considered together, they are even more astonishing, for they indicate a dazzling range of voice'
New York Times Book Review

0 349 10082 9   FICTION   £3.99

Abacus now offers an exciting range of quality fiction and non-fiction by both established and new authors. All of the books in this series are available from good bookshops, or can be ordered from the following address:

Sphere Books
Cash Sales Department
P.O. Box 11
Falmouth
Cornwall TR10 9EN.

Please send cheque or postal order (no currency), and allow 60p for postage and packing for the first book plus 25p for the second book and 15p for each additional book ordered up to a maximum charge of £1.50 in U.K.

B.F.P.O. customers please allow 60p for the first book, 25p for the second book plus 15p per copy for the next 7 books, thereafter 9p per book.

Overseas customers including Eire please allow £1.25 for postage and packing for the first book, 75p for the second book and 28p for each subsequent title ordered.